HOT
REBEL

A HOSTILE OPERATIONS TEAM Novel

USA TODAY BESTSELLING AUTHOR

LYNN RAYE
HARRIS

Copyright © 2014 by Lynn Raye Harris
Cover Design © 2014 Croco Designs
Interior Design by JT Formatting

www.**lynnrayeharris**.com

Printed in the United States of America

First Edition: September 2014
Library of Congress Cataloging-in-Publication Data

Harris, Lynn Raye
    Hot Rebel / Lynn Raye Harris. – 1st ed

    ISBN-13: 978-1-941002-04-9

    1. Hot Rebel—Fiction. 2. Fiction—Romance
    3. Fiction—Contemporary Romance

OTHER BOOKS IN
THE *HOSTILE OPERATIONS TEAM* SERIES

ONE

"REPORT."

"Nothing happening." Nick Brandon squeezed one eye shut and sighted down the scope of his sniper rifle. "No sign of the target."

"Jesus H. Christ," came the frustrated reply over the comm. "Where the fuck is this bastard?"

A bead of sweat trickled down Nick's neck. He ignored it since it was only one of many that had soaked the cotton of his T-shirt and made him damp beneath the desert ghillie suit. Discomfort was part of the job. Ignoring it was a necessary survival skill.

"Wish I knew."

Hell, yeah, he wished he knew. He'd been in position for days now, in a bombed-out building in one of Qu'rim's distant towns. The fighting still raged in this war-torn land, in spite of the fact they'd neutralized Al Ahmad months ago. It had eased up for a while, buoyed on the reforming spirit of the new king and his promises to the people, and then it fell apart again as other factions took advantage of the Freedom Force's confused and fractured leadership to fill the void and continue the civil war.

Perhaps it wouldn't matter so much to the rest of the world if there weren't a giant fucking uranium mine in the middle of the conflict. At least it was heavily guarded by an international peacekeeping force, but that was small comfort when it was still technically in a war zone.

Now that the Freedom Force was regaining strength, the whole fucking thing was a fresh nightmare. But this mission, if it went well, would help to stifle their regrowth, at least for a little while.

"Checking with HQ. Hold tight, man."

"Copy."

Nick sighed as he put down the sat phone and rotated his neck to pop out the kinks. His spotter looked up from the floor where he'd taken a few minutes to catch some sleep. It was odd to think of doing this job without Jack Hunter, but Jack was on assignment elsewhere these days. Being married to a pop star changed a guy's life, apparently.

Though if Jack were still here, Nick would be the spotter instead of the sniper. He liked being the sniper.

Dexter "Double Dee" Davidson rubbed his hand over his head. "Man, what a dream."

"Did it involve naked girls and swimming pools?"

Dex grinned. "Not quite, but that would've been a good one too."

Nick scanned the area once more. A donkey meandered down the street on one end while a woman in full burka shuffled along on the other. He focused on the woman, watching her sharply for a minute before deciding she was exactly what she appeared to be. Her face was hidden behind the burka, but she didn't move like a man.

She had a basket slung over her shoulder that seemed to contain a few meager dates and some rice so far as he could see. She was clearly hurrying to get out of the street before anyone noticed her.

This town was about half-inhabited anymore, but the ones holding on were determined to stay and make as normal a life as possible in the midst of a war. It would be far more convenient if no one were here at all, but war wasn't about convenience.

Nick watched the woman until she disappeared down the street, and then he sank down against the wall and pulled water out of his pack. He took a sip and then capped it and put it back.

"Why don't you take a nap? I'll watch for our tangos for a while."

Nick yawned. "Yeah, I'd like that."

Dex lifted his scope and crawled into position in the opening in the wall. Nick had just closed his eyes, looking forward to twenty minutes or so of uninterrupted shut-eye, when something rumbled deep in his chest.

He opened his eyes again, certain he was imagining things. But Dex was peering intently at something.

"Trucks," he muttered. "Mile away, coming toward us."

Nick scrambled back up. "Could be our guy," he said, sighting down his own scope. It was the first interesting thing to happen in days now, and his adrenaline spiked as he imagined completing this mission and bugging the fuck out.

"Can't tell yet."

They waited, watching the trucks that bristled with armed men—and then the column turned and drove north.

3

Far in the distance, Nick could see a dust cloud making its way south. More trucks, no doubt.

His heart thumped with excitement. "I think this is our meeting. But they aren't coming to the town."

Dex was busy with calculations. "Almost twenty-eight hundred yards when they converge. Damn," he breathed.

"We'll make it."

"Dial seven mils to the right," Dex said. "Fucking wind."

"On it."

The two columns moved closer together.

"Long shot," Dex said.

"I got it, Dex."

"I know."

The two columns converged after what seemed like hours but in reality was only minutes. Sand swirled, obscuring the men for a long moment before finally settling. Men got out of the vehicles and ranged into the open. Nick searched for the target. The man was a new lieutenant in the Freedom Force and rumored to be pulling the strings in this quadrant of Qu'rim. Not to mention, he'd been rebuilding the shattered network of terrorists and giving them a cause to unite behind.

"Found him," Nick said, satisfaction rolling through him with the sharp sweetness of an orgasm. Not quite the same sensation, but damn close. The second-best feeling in the world, he decided.

Dex double-checked the deck of cards they carried that had the names and faces of the men they were hunting. This one was young—and American-educated, which left a bad taste in Nick's mouth.

"Yep, that's him."

Nick's finger hovered over the trigger. He had to sight this one carefully, had to take the shot when he was fully ready. The man had no idea he was being targeted, so there was no need to rush. When the wind was right, Nick would squeeze the trigger. The shot would fall long and fast before it finally arced into the head of the target. It was critical he get this right.

Once it happened, they had to break down and get the hell out fast. Nick let out his breath, ready to squeeze on the exhale. Another split second and this bastard was going down—

The man beside the target dropped just as Nick's finger tensed. He jerked, but it wasn't his bullet that had hit the other man. He hadn't even fired—but someone had. He sighted the target again, but the men in the group had realized something was happening. They went berserk, shouting and running and throwing the terrorist leader into an armored vehicle before Nick could get a clear shot.

"Goddammit!"

Dex echoed him at the same moment the report of a rifle rang back to them over the distance. Of course someone else had taken a shot. They both knew it before they heard it.

The mission was a bust. Nick scanned the area around their hideout, looking for signs of another team. Who else could have come after these bastards if not another government with competing interests?

But if there was another team, they were damn good, because he and Dex had been in position for days and they'd never gotten wind of anyone else in the area other than a few locals.

Damn, that had been a beauty of a shot. It was almost impossible, in fact—and yet another sniper had made it in the split second before Nick could make his. He could admire the skill even if the bastard had fucked up the mission.

Half the column of men had slammed back into their trucks and sped away. But another group, a small group, was heading toward the town with assault rifles and antiaircraft missiles.

"Copy," Dex said into the sat phone before ending the call he'd just made to their team. His eyes were filled with determination when he looked up at Nick. "Extraction point moved due to enemy fire. We gotta bust our asses if we're gonna make it."

They broke down the equipment double-quick, stowing the weapons and shouldering the gear. They had a head start, but not a long one. They'd have to move from this building and keep moving while the enemy combatants searched for them. And they needed air support if they were going to make it out.

Nick's comm link crackled for the first time since this mission had gone to hell. "Need that firebird, Flash," he grated before Ryan Gordon could speak. Jesus, this mission had been plagued with bad luck from the start. In the past few hours, a dust storm had interfered with their primary comm and sent them to backup. And now this.

"Called it in. HQ says it's coming. What the fuck happened?"

Flash and the team were a couple of miles away, waiting for Nick and Dex.

"We got company, that's what. They took out the opposition commander. Our guy got away."

6

"Shit."

"Yeah. No sign of our shooter or his team."

"Don't worry about them, Brandy." It was Kev "Big Mac" MacDonald. "Get the fuck out and we'll let HQ sort it out."

Like Nick would do anything differently. But, yeah, if he got a glimpse of this asshole, he'd take the chance.

"Birdie's ETA is fifteen minutes. You guys all right?"

"Yeah," Nick said as he and Dex busted out the back door of the building they'd been haunting like ghosts and made for the next zone they'd set up.

The sun was setting, and long shadows lay across the desert landscape. The heat of the day still shimmered on the horizon, and the sounds in the town were subdued. A goat bleated somewhere. Nick's head jerked up as something moved to his left. But there was nothing and he kept running.

Dex made it first and burst into the building they'd scouted days ago. There was always the chance someone had taken shelter in the past few days, but the building was abandoned and the chances were slim.

Dex headed for the long bank of windows at the rear and hunkered down inside the wall. Nick could hear shouting coming from outside now. It was still a few streets over but moving closer.

The door they'd come through just a few seconds ago shot open, and both men raised their weapons automatically.

A woman in a burka stood there, silhouetted against the setting sun. Nick wondered if it was the same woman he'd seen earlier, but then he realized this one didn't have a basket like the last one had.

"Fuck me," Dex breathed softly at the sight of a rifle cradled in her arms.

The woman ripped away the face covering and tipped her chin up, and Nick shook his head as if to clear a mirage.

"Not just now, boys," she said in perfect English. Or as perfect as a Southern accent could come to it, anyhow. "We've got a company of tangos on our heels, or hadn't you noticed?"

Victoria wished it weren't two against one, but she'd lost her spotter three days ago when the dumb bastard had tried to suggest she was only good for one thing—and that thing hadn't been shooting.

She hadn't shot Jonah, but she'd wanted to. Turned out it hadn't been necessary since he'd gotten himself killed by a Russian mercenary on the way here during a dispute over God knows what.

Whatever. It wasn't her problem. She'd called it in. If the boss wasn't happy, that's what he got for hiring military rejects and Rambo wannabes in the first place.

She didn't bother to wonder where that put her in the catalog of hires. She already knew what she was and why.

The two men were staring at her as if she'd materialized out of thin air. Which, for their purposes, she nearly had. She'd shadowed them for days now, and she knew they were Army Special Ops. She hadn't seen their faces, but now the setting sun arrowed into the room and picked them out where they had their backs to the wall and guns drawn.

Both were dark-haired, muscled, and sported several days' beard growth. One had his jaw hanging open. But the other...

Recognition hit Victoria like an unexpected encounter with a bat. She knew that face. Knew that mouth, the hard curl of those lips as he'd hurled insults at her during the few weeks they'd spent as competitors at the Army Sniper School. He'd been the only one there who'd had the ability to get to her, to rattle the smooth surface of her calm. And he'd done it again and again. Where the other guys tried to cozy up to her, he'd done nothing but push.

In a way, she supposed she should be grateful. He'd made her remember what she was there for, that she'd been determined to graduate and earn her right to be an Army sniper.

She would have done it too, had things not changed.

Victoria pushed the door shut and rushed over to the tattered rug that lay on the floor between her and the men.

"Don't just sit there looking stupid," she snapped. "Help me get this trapdoor open."

The one she didn't know stood as if to obey. The other one—Nick Brandon—shot a hand out and stopped the guy from moving.

Victoria shoved a stray lock of hair from her face and sputtered. "You're going to let them find us just because you're pissed, is that it?"

"You took the shot."

"Damn right I did."

Nick unfolded himself and got to his feet, his hands flexing on the case slung over his shoulder. "You took the goddamn shot, Victoria. But you shot the wrong mother-fucker."

She jerked at the trapdoor, levering it up with a grunt. Sweat rolled down her face. She wanted to rip the burka off entirely, but she still needed the damn thing. If this shit went south, it would provide a measure of protection that her assault suit wouldn't.

If they looked under the burka, however...

"So you do remember my name. And for the record, I didn't shoot the wrong guy. I shot the one I was hired to shoot."

Nick's face twisted darkly. "You still shot the wrong guy. And for the wrong fucking reasons."

She shoved the trapdoor until it fell with a thud. "How do you know what my reasons are?" She slapped her forehead. "Oh wait, I forgot. It's easy for you to be self-righteous, isn't it? Preacher's son who shoots people for a living. How's that working out for you, hot stuff?"

The other guy's gaze had been swinging back and forth between the two of them. But now he put his hand on Nick's arm. "Dude, I don't know how you know this chick, but I think she's right. We need to get inside there and wait this one out."

The sound of machine-gun fire rolled through the streets, closer than before. Typically, the Qu'rimi opposition wasn't that organized, but this group was taking orders from someone new. And that person had a plan.

"Yeah," Nick said, tilting his head to listen.

Victoria huffed a breath as she swept her hand toward the darkened stairs into the cellar below. "Be my guest, boys."

"You first," Nick said, his hazel eyes lasering in on

her, gleaming hot.

Victoria shrugged as she tossed her gear into the hole. "Fine. Just be sure to hook the rug on the door on the way down."

Nick's eyes narrowed. She knew he didn't have clue what to do with the rug at this point—and they didn't have time for him to figure it out when she already knew.

"Dex can go first then."

The other man shrugged and came over with his gear, tossing it into the opening. When he was down in the hole, Nick passed the rest of the gear to him. And then he climbed halfway into the opening before he stopped and glared at her as if he didn't trust her.

Victoria sniffed. "Make room, asshole, or I can't follow."

"How do I know you intend to?"

She blinked. "What do you think I mean to do? Wave the scumbags in and show them where you are? How do you think that'll go for me once they discover I'm not a Qu'rimi woman?"

He grunted before lowering himself farther into the opening. He was almost at the bottom when she spoke.

"Stop right there," she said as she grabbed the trapdoor and folded it over so he could prop it up. Then she snagged the rug and went about fixing it over the door. Once she was certain it was in place, she had to lower herself onto the floor and slide into the opening.

Nick was still there, still holding the door up so she could shimmy beneath it. The opening was tight and she found herself wedged against him suddenly, the hard press of his muscles making her jump and tingle in all the wrong places.

Or right places, depending on who you asked.

"Jesus," he muttered as she dropped, her body sliding against his.

"Let the door go," she urged. "Slowly."

He went the rest of the way down the ladder, letting the trapdoor sink behind him. The rug, though tattered, had a heavy weft and would lie flat.

The cellar was surprisingly cool for a dirt hole carved out of the desert floor. They were near an oasis here or it wouldn't have been possible, but the bedrock was solid and allowed the villagers to dig cellars in order to store vegetables and water.

The room wasn't big, and the only thing preventing it from being completely dark at the moment was the glow stick the man named Dex had broken.

The ground rumbled and dirt showered from the ceiling. Victoria clenched her hands into fists. God, she hated this part. Being buried alive was bad enough, but buried alive with this man...

Nick's head was back, his eyes on the ceiling as the dirt stopped falling. His skin glistened in the dull glow of the light. She let her gaze slide over him, cataloging the chiseled planes of his cheekbones and nose. And those lips.

Dear God, she could never forget those lips. She'd hated them and adored them all at once—and hated them even more because she'd been weak enough to want to feel them against her own.

At least she hadn't allowed that indignity before the end.

"How did you know this was here?" he asked, not looking at her, his voice a low rumble in the dark.

"Part of the job. I'm surprised you didn't know it. Or maybe you're not as good as you like to think."

His gaze snapped to hers and she found herself swallowing, which wasn't easy considering her mouth was as dry as the sand covering the desert over their heads.

"At least I'm here for the right reasons."

He sounded cool and judgmental, and it pissed her off even though she knew she shouldn't let him get to her. He couldn't know what her reasons were or how right they were to her.

"Of course you are. I'm just here for the fun. What girl wouldn't want to be trapped in a cellar with you two jerks while a bunch of jihadists tromp the ground over her head?"

"Hey," Dex said, "I didn't say a damn thing. Leave me out of your pissing contest."

"The one you let get away," Nick growled, "will prolong this conflict and cost American lives. How does that make you feel?"

Victoria tilted her chin up as fresh heat flooded her. She knew precisely who she'd let get away. And it still made her sick inside.

"And I say the one I shot would have done the same thing. There are no easy choices out here, and you know it."

"I work for an organization that knows what they're talking about. Who do you work for?" He took a step toward her, though they were already close due to the tight proximity of the cellar.

She wanted to back away, but she wouldn't show that much weakness. And she wasn't telling him anything, either.

"Whoever it is," he continued, "they don't give a fuck about what's right or just, do they? Guns for hire never do. It's all about the money and who can pay to get what they want. You shot an opposition commander of no consequence. You let the terrorist get away. And that's the fucking truth of it, Victoria, so save the rationalizing for some other dumb ass who might believe it."

His words hurt, but she wasn't going to let him know it. She reminded herself that she was here for Emily, and she was going to do whatever it took to get her sister back. Besides, Victoria's name was already sullied in the eyes of the United States Army. What was one more transgression?

She was hot on Emily's trail, thanks to Ian Black and his business. She started to tell Nick to fuck off, but there was a burst of gunfire overhead and the words died in her throat. The three of them cast their eyes to the ceiling and gripped their weapons.

There was a sudden thump on the trapdoor and Victoria's heart lodged in her throat. Any second, the door would lift—and they'd be caught in this hole like rats.

TWO

NICK PULLED HIS SIG AND prepared to shoot. Behind him, Dex did the same. Victoria yanked an HK submachine gun from her bag and rocked back into a fighting stance. Above them, booted feet thumped and scraped, and men called to each other in Arabic.

Someone was going to realize the floor was hollow in that one spot, and when they did, all hell was going to break loose. Nick forced his heartbeat to slow, his breathing to deepen. Calm sank over him like a soft blanket. This was what he did, what he'd trained for. If those bastards came down here, he'd fight until he couldn't fight anymore.

He glanced at Victoria, wondering how she was going to handle this. It still stunned him that she was here at all. A fucking mercenary. A gun for hire. How had that happened? Why?

She'd been incredible at the sniper school, one of the best shots in the whole damn class. They'd gone head-to-head more than once in competition, and it was often a draw as to who was better.

She'd been so fucking good, but then she'd disappeared one day. The instructors never remarked on her absence. Plenty of people washed out, but he'd have never guessed she'd be one of them. Not many women were allowed in, so the fact she'd been there at all had already made her special. Which was why he'd had a hard time believing she'd failed.

The trapdoor began to lift, a slice of daylight shining inside. Dex stowed the glow stick, and the light inside the cellar winked out. The door moved another inch—and then Nick heard the distant whine of a jet engine.

Air support.

The jet rocketed toward them, the engines screaming as it approached. The trapdoor closed with a thud, and booted feet pounded across it and faded into the distance. Who knows where the tangos were going or why, but they'd clearly decided this hole wasn't worth exploring. Nick let out a long breath and lowered the Sig. He couldn't see his companions, but he knew they must have done the same. Another moment and the glow stick reappeared.

No one spoke. They made eye contact and nodded at each other. And then Nick went over to join Dex against the wall. They sat on the floor and pulled water and food from their packs. It was no use trying to use the comm just yet.

Victoria was still standing and watching them, her eyes wide and innocent-looking in a way that was incongruous with the submachine gun resting against her leg. Nick motioned her over and gestured at the food.

She cast one last glance at the trapdoor over her head and then came over and sank onto the dirt floor.

"That was close," she said softly.

"Yeah." Nick handed her an energy bar.

Her fingers touched his when she took it, and his skin tingled with the contact. Her eyelids dropped to shutter her gaze from his view.

She opened the bar and took a bite, lifting her gaze to his once more. "Thanks."

He shrugged. "If you hadn't showed us this cellar, we'd have had a shoot-out up there, I think."

In the distance, they could hear explosions and gunfire. Victoria turned her head as if she could see the fighter jets above them.

"Now that's a nice touch," she said.

Nick calmly took a bite of his own energy bar. "Yeah, guess you don't have air support on tap with your outfit."

"No, we definitely don't."

"What happened to you?" he blurted, unable to hold it in any longer. "You had a promising career, and you threw it all away to do what? Become a mercenary? What the fuck, Victoria?"

Her lips thinned and her rain-gray eyes flashed. She still had the head covering on, but he knew that her hair beneath the cloth was a deep, rich red. Or so he hoped anyway. What if she'd changed it?

"Maybe I didn't have a choice, Preacher Boy. Did you ever think of that?"

He tried to let the jibe roll off him, though surprisingly it irritated him when she said it. Yeah, his dad was a preacher, and yeah, he'd had a pretty strict upbringing because of it. Nick had been accustomed to being teased growing up because of his father's holier-than-thou lifestyle. But he'd stopped defending himself on that score since the only people who jabbed him about it were simply trying to get under his skin.

It didn't usually work. Until now.

Still, he focused on what she'd said—that maybe she didn't have a choice—and ignored the rest. "You failed the course."

Her eyes widened. Color blazed in her cheeks. "I did *not* fail." She waved a hand. "I'm not discussing this with you. As soon as it's clear out there, we can go our separate ways and you can believe whatever you want to believe."

"Go our separate ways? No fucking way. You're coming with us."

Dex merely grunted. Nick was perfectly aware that the other man had been watching them with the kind of fascination most people reserved for reality shows.

Victoria blinked. "Why would I do that? I have my own people, you know."

"I don't think so. Where's your spotter? Where's your backup?"

"Where's yours? All I see is two of you."

"Our team is out there. About two miles away, and if they have to come blast us out of here, they will."

She lowered her gaze. "My spotter got shot a few days back. I'm on my own until I return to HQ."

Somehow, he didn't let his jaw fall open. "You took that shot without a spotter?"

She shrugged. "Obviously."

Of course it wasn't impossible to do—but it was more helpful with a spotter than without. He didn't know five people who could have made that shot, but she'd done it—and she'd done it alone.

He was more intrigued than he cared to admit. She'd disappeared a little over three years ago, and now she was here in the middle of a war zone, fucking up his mission.

"Unless you've got a team out there, you're coming with us."

"I don't think so," she snapped. "I did my job and I'm done. Soon as it's safe to leave, I'm going my own way."

He should let her go. What did he care? But then she'd just fucked up his mission, and he wasn't inclined to be nice about it.

"There're a whole lot of tangos out there, and we've got help. Do you?"

The flash of her eyes gave him the answer. That and the fact she'd come here alone and made this shot without a teammate to take shifts or watch the scope while she rested. God knew this job was dangerous at the best of times, but what she was doing was practically suicidal.

"I'm just a poor Qu'rimi woman, trudging between villages. No one's going to bother me."

"But if they do, you've already pointed out that it's obvious you aren't Qu'rimi. What then?"

She ripped a piece of the energy bar off. "I've been working this way for two years, Preacher Boy. Where were you then, huh? I made it this far without your help."

"Yeah, well, now you got it. So stop bitching and let's work together to get out of here."

Of course he had an ulterior motive, but she didn't need to know it. He wanted her in HOT's control because then they could question her more closely, find out who she was working for. Mendez wasn't going to be happy about this mission, and Nick would really like to have the person responsible when the colonel blew his top.

Victoria chewed. He thought she might be on the verge of agreeing, but then another explosion rattled the ground and dirt showered down from the ceiling. Instinctively, Nick lunged for her and rolled her beneath him while Dex dived flat as well.

The ground shook again, and debris fell over them. Beneath him, Victoria was small and solid and warm. She'd tucked her head into his shoulder, and her breath tickled his neck. His heart thumped with adrenaline, but then there was another sensation rolling through him.

The electric hum of attraction buzzed in his veins. He'd always felt that hum when he'd been near Victoria, though he'd never acted on it. She'd always had her hackles up around him, and he'd never quite known why. They'd had some intense competitions on the range, but off it, he'd been perfectly willing to let the hostility subside.

She hadn't.

Her hands were wedged between her body and his, her palms flat on his chest. Her fingers curled—once, briefly—and then straightened again. Her breathing was shallow and quick, and she made a whimpering noise—again once and briefly. The shaking stopped a few moments later, and Nick lifted himself slightly.

He could only see the top of her head. The head covering had gone askew, and red hair peeked out. He didn't know why it made him glad to see she hadn't changed the color, but it did.

"You okay?"

She nodded. And then she lifted her head and those eyes slammed into his. His heart sort of stuttered.

"I'm fine. A little bruised, maybe. But fine."

His gaze dropped to her mouth. Such a pretty, pink mouth. If he lowered his head just a little bit, he could kiss her. What would she taste like if he did? What would she do?

Her hands curled into fists. And then she pushed. "You can get off me now."

He was strangely disappointed by that statement, but he rolled away and pushed himself upright again. Victoria sat up and tried to right her head covering. The black burka was shapeless and no doubt hot, but he understood why she wore it. She probably fooled a lot of people dressed as she was.

Hell, she'd fooled him—and that pissed him off. He now realized that the woman he'd seen in the alley with the basket had been Victoria. He'd confirmed she was a woman, but he'd never thought she was a military operative. It wasn't within the Qu'rimi psyche to allow women in their military, and he damn sure hadn't expected a mercenary.

Lesson learned.

His lips pressed together. It wasn't a mistake he would make again. Another mistake he wouldn't make was letting her go when they left this cellar. Like it or not, she was going with them.

Victoria dragged in a shaky breath as she smoothed the fabric over her body. She didn't want to look at Nick. She could feel his presence like a promise—or a threat—and she didn't like how he affected her. When he'd rolled her beneath him, it hadn't exactly been sexy. For one thing, there'd been the prospect of the ceiling crashing down and burying them alive. For another, he'd launched himself at her with the intent to protect her, so he hadn't exactly taken her down to the floor gently.

And yet her body insisted on shuddering beneath his, and not because she'd been scared. Once the shock of the situation passed, she'd become aware of all his hard angles pressing into her. He was big and strong, and her body was so deprived of contact it had decided to wake up and say howdy. She could still feel the thrum of excitement bubbling in her veins—and it pissed her off.

Why him? Why now? She didn't have time for this shit.

She gave the head covering one last tug and raised her gaze to Nick's. Her heart flipped and she ground her teeth together.

"We'll move out in an hour," he said. "As long as it stays quiet."

She could only nod, though it annoyed her to appear to be agreeing with him. Because there was no way she was going with these men. It might be nice to have someone at her back, but it was a risk she couldn't take. If the Army got hold of her, who knew when or if they'd let her go again? She hadn't exactly endeared herself to the United States government over the past few years.

But when you were desperate, you did desperate things.

She was only glad her grandfather wasn't alive any longer to see what she'd become. He would've died of shame to know that both his granddaughters were considered security risks at best and traitors at worst. Gramps, who'd fought in Korea and earned a Purple Heart—and then gone on to Vietnam in the early days and earned another one.

He'd been so proud of her ability with a rifle—but he'd never envisioned this, she was quite certain.

There were so many things he hadn't envisioned. His death from cancer. Her and Emily being sent into foster care. Emily's descent into drugs and drinking and her fascination with a man who led her down the wrong path.

Victoria rubbed her hands over her arms as if to warm herself. God, she'd been searching for so long, but she was finally getting closer. Ian had told her just a few days ago that a white woman had been seen in one of the terrorist camps. That didn't mean it was Emily, but how many white women could there be in the Freedom Force training camps?

Victoria bit the inside of her lip and turned away from the two men. She was so furious with Emily, even now, and so scared at the same time. Ian had promised he'd help find her sister, but it'd been nearly two years since she'd started working for him, and she had yet to get a glimpse of her wayward younger sibling.

There'd been calls, but those had ceased six months ago. Emily's phone rang, but no one answered. It had been nothing but hints and possible sightings for months. This mission to shoot the opposition commander had been the closest she'd ever come to the man who'd poisoned Emily's mind against her family and her country.

Zaran bin Yusuf. She'd stared at him through her scope today, her blood boiling with helpless fury—and then she'd shot the man who'd come to betray him when what she'd really wanted to do was kill Zaran herself.

But if he was dead, what would happen to Emily? It

wasn't a chance Victoria was willing to take. Besides, the money had been on shooting the other guy, and if she'd fucked it up, Ian wouldn't have been very understanding about losing the bounty.

No one spoke much in the next hour. Victoria went and huddled against the wall, sipping water from her pack and watching the two men as they checked their gear and made plans. Dex was tall and muscled, like Nick, but he didn't make her heart thump the way Nick did.

She thought back to sniper school and her first glimpse of him. He'd been cool and arrogant, so certain of his superiority. He'd been there when she'd arrived, and he'd been the one tasked with showing her to her room. He'd walked in front of her, silent and hulking, and she'd followed along with her heart in her throat and her brain chattering in fear that she was going to fail.

Not many women were admitted, but she'd been determined to be one of the few who made it through. And then Nick had reached her door. He'd turned and looked down at her with that superior glare that made her feel so small inside. He hadn't said anything rude or inappropriate, but she'd decided then and there that she was going to beat him before it was all over. She was going to beat them all. And she would have if Emily hadn't run away with a man bent on war against the United States.

"Time to go, Victoria," Nick said, and she shook herself from her memories to find him standing over her and holding out a hand.

She put her palm against his and let him pull her up. Her skin tingled, and she jerked her hand from his as soon as she was standing. Then she shouldered her gear and went over to the trapdoor. After extinguishing the light,

Dex went up first, raising the door carefully, his weapon at the ready. It was dark out now and he disappeared above them, his booted feet scraping over the floor.

"Clear," he said a moment later.

"You go," Nick said from behind her.

Her skin prickled at the proximity of his body, but she went over and scrambled up the ladder and into the room above. Lights from the town shone in the distance, providing them with some ambient light. Her eyes picked out Dex, and she realized he'd donned night-vision goggles. Nick emerged from the hole in the ground with his goggles in place, and she let out a frustrated sigh. Those were something she didn't have at the moment. She'd lost them when she'd lost her spotter.

She still had her night-vision scope, but what good was it to her now? And how was she going to escape these two when they could clearly see her every move?

Nick touched the side of his head. "Flash, you copy? … Yeah, we're here. Been in a cellar. … Coming in and bringing company. … Over and out."

"They still in position?" Dex asked.

"Roger that. We've got to move quick though. There's a brigade of enemy fighters headed this way. They could cut off our escape route if we aren't fast enough."

The three of them pulled weapons and moved silently through the abandoned building. When they reached a door, Nick motioned to them to hang back while he scouted the perimeter.

Victoria's heart hammered as he disappeared, her breathing quickening. She strained to hear any sound—and then she had to bite back a squeak when he reappeared, his dark form looming suddenly in the door. She didn't realize she'd stumbled back until she felt a hand on her shoulder.

"Easy," Dex said from behind her. "It's okay."

"I know."

But it wasn't okay, because time was running out and she needed to disappear.

"Clear," Nick said. "Let's go. And Victoria...?" he added as she started to move.

She stopped and looked up at him. The NVGs and assault gear made him look like a high-tech killing machine. "What?"

"Don't make me shoot you."

THREE

THEY RAN THROUGH THE TOWN, keeping close to the buildings so they'd remain in shadow until they hit the open desert. The scent of jet fuel and exploded ordnance hung in the air, and the town was quiet. After the chaos of battle, most people would stay inside until morning. A good thing for Nick and his companions as they moved toward the rendezvous point.

They passed a burnt-out armored vehicle, its shell still smoking. Whoever had been in that thing hadn't made it out. A little farther along, there were bodies strewn across the road where the jet's bombs had hit and the scent of burning flesh still permeated the air. There was no movement, however, and the three of them passed silently and quickly.

Nick glanced at Victoria. She forged ahead with a hard look of determination on her face, her rifle slung across her chest and ready to fire.

He'd told her he would shoot her back there, but he wasn't so sure he would have. Still, he didn't trust her. No matter that she'd shown them the cellar, she'd still shot the wrong dude earlier and fucked up the mission. She had an agenda that didn't match HOT's, and he wasn't about to forget it.

They crested a dune and hurried over the other side before stopping to get their bearings. He could hear Victoria and Dex breathing a little harder, and he knew the pace had been punishing. But they had no choice.

Dex took out a scope and scanned the desert below. "Shit," he breathed.

Nick's gut clenched. He knew what Dex would say before he said it.

"Enemy on the road. No indication they've spotted us."

"Fuck."

This was what he'd been hoping to avoid when they'd left the safety of their hideout. "We've got about twenty minutes to cross the valley before they're in a position to cut us off."

The valley was long and narrow, and there was only one way out at this end. If their adversaries reached the mouth first, Nick, Dex, and Victoria would be trapped.

"Then let's rock 'n' roll," Dex said.

Victoria merely nodded her agreement.

They started down the slope, angling away from the enemy as much as possible without losing sight of the objective. The opposition soldiers were moving relentlessly toward the mouth of the valley, but there was no indication the enemy had any idea the three of them were racing toward it as well.

Sweat rolled down Nick's face and neck. He could feel it inside the ghillie suit, dripping down his torso and soaking his T-shirt. A glance at Dex and Victoria told him they were equally as miserable. In the quiet of the night, the steady hum of dozens of engines drifted to him. These opposition fighters were tough and angry, determined to wrest control of the government from the king and his officials.

But it was more than that. So many of the militants were also radicals, and more than one terrorist group had seen a grand opportunity to get involved in Qu'rimi politics. The Freedom Force had been severely weakened with the capture of Al Ahmad—but it'd had a surprising resurgence in strength over the past year. It was once more becoming a threat to the stability and security of the region.

And the woman running beside him had only aided their cause today. That pissed him off and made him even more determined to find out her secrets.

The three of them ran hard for twenty minutes before reaching the mouth of the valley. He calculated that the enemy forces were about five minutes behind them as they ran onto the trail and burst through the gap. Nick wouldn't feel any relief until they connected with the rest of the team, but this was a major obstacle down.

A few minutes later, Victoria cried out and came to a stop. Nick pulled up and turned back. Dex followed.

"What's wrong?" Nick demanded.

Victoria limped toward him, waving a hand. "Twisted my knee. And I'm spent. I can't run another second."

"We're almost there. Half a mile to the extraction point. You can make it that far."

She found a rock beside the trail and perched on it. "No, I really can't. It hurts too much."

Nick shifted his pack and took a step toward her. "Then we'll carry you. I'll start—"

"Take another step and I'll shoot you." Her rifle was still slung over her shoulder, but she was holding a Sig pointed right between his eyes.

Fury exploded in his gut. "What the fuck, Victoria?"

"Two can play this game, babe," she said very coolly.

Her eyes glowed through his NVGs, making her look demonic. The determined look on her face said she meant the words she'd spoken. He didn't doubt she'd shoot him if he ignored her instructions.

"We just helped you escape a bad situation, and this is how you repay us?"

She shrugged. "I helped you too, don't forget. And I told you I wasn't going with you. You're the one who insisted. But I'm not in the Army anymore, and I make my own decisions." She flicked the gun. "So this is where we part company. You can be on your merry way, and I'll be on mine."

"Fuck you."

She stood and put both hands on the gun as she faced him. "Don't test me, Nick."

He wanted to. Not more than a few hours ago, they'd lain on a floor together, her body pressed tightly to his, her breath hot against his neck. She'd made him think of things he'd never had with her. Things he wanted.

Clearly, she didn't feel the same.

"You're a traitor, you know that?"

Her chin lifted a notch. "So I've been told."

"You could have done so much for our side. But you chose this life instead."

"Yeah, yeah, I hear you," she said. "I'm unmoved. Now go, and be glad I don't disarm you both and leave you here for the Qu'rimis to find."

He snorted. "You realize if you shoot me that Dex is going to drop you, right?"

He didn't have to look to know the other man had a weapon on her.

"I think you like yourself too much to make me shoot you. You'd rather live to fight another day."

He clenched his fists at his side. Rage rolled through him in hot waves. He'd let down his guard with her, and he shouldn't have. Just because she was soft and vulnerable beneath him back in that cellar.

"No, I'd rather live so I can find you again. Because I *will* find you—and I'll make you pay. You can count on that."

"You can try."

He took a step back and then another. He'd wanted to bring her in to HOT, but they didn't have time for this shit right now.

"Come on, Dex. Let's find our ride."

The two of them backed away from her and then turned and started running down the road.

"You have no intention of leaving her there," Dex said as they jogged along.

"Nope."

But when they doubled back and tried to sneak up on her, Victoria was gone. Nick cursed a blue streak.

"Man, we gotta go," Dex said. "If we aren't to the rendezvous point in fifteen minutes, it'll fuck everything up."

"Yeah." Nick cast one last look over the area where they'd left Victoria not more than two minutes ago, amazed that she was gone. The NVGs didn't pick up a heat signature anywhere.

31

She'd disappeared, just like three years ago.

Ian was waiting for her in Baq. Victoria was bone-tired as she entered the house where her boss was head-quartered. The guard watching the door was someone new, but she'd given her information and waited while he called it in. A few seconds later, she was walking into the cool interior of the nondescript house and yanking the burka off. She dropped it on a chair along with her gear and continued through the room.

Ian came out into the hallway and let his gaze slide over her as she approached. He was a good-looking guy, big and dark and intense, but there were no sparks between them. At least not for her. She'd never been sure about him, but then he'd never attempted anything so maybe he didn't feel a thing for her either.

"You made the shot without Jonah. Good job."

She stopped when she reached him. "If that Russian hadn't killed him, I would have," she said coolly. "He was an asshole."

Ian shrugged and turned back toward the room he'd emerged from. "Sometimes we can't be picky in this business. But nature has a way, right?"

"I guess so."

Victoria followed him into the room and flopped onto a chair. She knew she looked like hell. A week in the desert with no shower—and the last day spent on the run—had done a number on her hair. Not to mention the lingering odor of sweat that clung to her. If Ian noticed, he didn't let it show. He simply sat at his desk and continued to flip through the maps and papers there.

Victoria tried not to let her impatience show, but she couldn't help the burst of air that rushed from her when Ian continued to sit there so calmly. He looked up, his blue eyes piercing hers.

"You wish to say something?"

Victoria leaned forward, her elbows on her knees. "I wanted to kill that bastard, but I didn't because of my sister."

He eased back in the chair, the leather creaking. "We're not talking about Jonah anymore, I take it."

"You know we're not. You promised me if I did this job, we'd find Emily. That Zaran bin Yusuf would lead us to her. So where is she? When can I see her?"

Ian's expression didn't soften one bit. "It's complicated."

"Bullshit!" She shot to her feet and stalked toward the desk, slapping both her hands down on it as she faced him. "You promised, Ian! You swore if I protected that asshole, if I made sure the opposition didn't kill him, we'd find her."

Ian's mouth was a grim line. "It's not up to me. I told you that from the beginning."

Victoria swore. Tears of frustration knotted in her throat. "How do you do this? How do you justify working for those bastards when you know what they want to do?"

It was the first time she'd voiced her fears. That Ian was actually taking money from terrorists—which meant she'd been working for them too.

Maybe Nick was right when he called her a traitor.

She was trying to save her sister, but that didn't stop the sick feelings swirling in the pit of her stomach.

"I'm nonpartisan, Victoria. So long as the money comes in, I don't care who pays me to do the job. And I don't ask questions when it does."

She sank onto the chair again and rubbed her hands over her face. She was tired and heartsick and worried.

"I just want my sister back. I'd take money from the devil himself if that's what it took to find her."

"Go take a shower. Get some rest. I'll see what I can find out."

She stood to go, but then she turned back to him. Her stomach was still churning over the idea that maybe it was a terror organization pulling his strings. She'd never wanted to know before. And maybe she didn't now, either.

Ian was looking at her with an expression of sympathy on his face. It was the first time she'd seen that emotion coming from him.

"Go, Victoria. Don't come back for at least eight hours—or I won't tell you a damn thing."

"The outfit she works for is called Black Security."

Mendez dropped a folder on the metal table at the head of the room and stood there looking about as pissed as Nick had ever seen him. Which was never a good thing for anyone.

The rest of the guys shifted in their seats. It'd been a long few days, and no one was very happy at the moment.

The mission had been a total bust, and apparently they had Black Security to thank for it.

Nick suppressed a yawn. He hadn't slept eight hours straight in days now. They were at a forward base in Qu'rim, near Baq, where the Qu'rimi army trained under the tutelage of US troops. The base was a temporary facility run and maintained by the US, and HOT had their own bunker where a few of the individual teams came and went. They'd gotten the message this morning that Mendez was flying in. Not a good sign. Nick had known instinctively that it had everything to do with the mission in the desert and Victoria.

He hadn't been wrong.

"Victoria Royal has been working for Black for two years, and in that time she's had sixty-eight confirmed kills. We've known about Black for some time, but he's mostly gone after targets unimportant to us. Now he seems to be working for someone who wants to protect the Freedom Force."

Nick's gut knotted.

"Someone is feeding Black—or the Freedom Force—intelligence," Mendez finished.

Around the room, the guys all sat up a little straighter. And Lucky MacDonald, their lone female operator, looked utterly furious. Considering what she'd been through to put a stop to the Freedom Force, he didn't blame her. They'd all thought it was a done deal with the capture of Al Ahmad, but the organization was like a hydra. Cut off one head and more sprang up. None as powerful as Al Ahmad had been, but still nothing to dismiss lightly.

"A mole?" Garrett "Iceman" Spencer asked.

Mendez's lips flattened. "Probably. Someone in the

CIA is giving information to whoever pays Black. Or maybe to Black himself. We don't know."

No one said anything at first. They all knew that when Gina Domenico had been in danger, someone in the government had suppressed the information that the man who'd kidnapped her baby and lured her to the Caribbean was still alive. Metaxas had come to DC and abducted her before they'd known—and he'd almost killed Jack Hunter in the process.

But HOT had never learned the traitor's name, a fact that hung over their heads like a guillotine blade on a fraying rope.

"Someone told Black we were targeting Zaran bin Yusuf," Nick said. "And he sent Victoria to stop us."

Mendez turned dark eyes on Nick. "Almost, but not quite. They had intel that the opposition commander intended to have bin Yusuf killed. He was Royal's target instead."

Nick blinked. "Why didn't *we* know that information?"

Mendez's gaze was steady. "We did, son. But we couldn't take the chance that he'd screw up and bin Yusuf would walk away, now could we? The mission was still critical."

Mendez turned away without waiting for an answer. "As it is, he escaped anyway."

Nick didn't bother to protest that it wasn't his fault. It *was*. Victoria had been there, right beneath his nose, and he hadn't known it. She'd been setting up for a shot as difficult as his—but she'd fired first… and changed everything.

Dex looked over at him and frowned. Nick gave his

head a small shake. He didn't think Dex planned to tell the colonel it wasn't their fault, but the guy was still new enough that maybe he did. Dex leaned back in his chair and folded his arms over his chest, looking as pissed as anyone in the room.

"Good job identifying our mystery sniper, soldier," Mendez said, spinning around and pinning Nick with another look. "Without that, we'd still be in the dark about what was going on."

Nick blinked. Was the colonel screwing with him?

But no, everyone was looking at him and nodding their approval. And he felt like shit inside because he'd let her get away. *Jesus.*

He should have rushed her when he had the chance and to hell with the pistol in her hand. She might have hesitated. He might have surprised her enough to get the gun from her before she shot him. But he'd been so pissed he'd walked away, giving her the chance to escape before he could double back and take her by surprise.

"Yes, sir. Thank you, sir."

But the words stuck in his throat like barbs.

Mendez sat at the table and flipped open the folder. "Victoria Faith Royal. Twenty-five years old. Single. Red hair. Gray eyes. Her sister is Emily Hope Royal, twenty-three years old, blond hair, brown eyes. Emily has a history with substance and alcohol abuse. But then she began seeing a man a few years ago who helped her get clean. This man came to the US from Qu'rim to learn engineering but dropped out of school after a couple of years and started hanging around a mosque. He became radicalized."

Mendez paused and looked up. Nick felt himself leaning forward, hanging on the colonel's every word.

"Emily converted to Islam and went to Qu'rim with this man. We think she may have married him, but we don't know for certain. Once here, he became active in the Freedom Force. He was a minor player, but with the collapse of the organizational structure and the subsequent resurgence, he's become someone to watch. In short, he was our target."

Nick felt as if someone had sucker punched him. This was the reason Victoria had left the Army? She'd said that she hadn't failed. But her sister associating with known terrorists must have been too much for the Army to take.

"Jesus," Ryan "Flash" Gordon said, echoing what they all had to be thinking.

It was a tangled web of relationships worthy of a soap opera. But far more dangerous.

"Is that why Victoria left the Army?" Nick asked.

Mendez glanced down at his papers. "Though there was never any evidence she sympathized with her sister or bin Yusuf, she was thought to be a security risk. She was offered a desk job with no access to classified information, but she refused. Subsequently, she was discharged."

Nick shoved a hand through his hair and frowned. Victoria's sister ran away with a terrorist, and now Victoria was in Qu'rim, working for an outfit that seemed to be protecting the very organization her sister's lover—or husband—was part of.

Nick thought of how she'd threatened to shoot him, and fresh anger swelled. He'd let her get the jump on him because he'd believed her to be on his and Dex's side, however temporarily. She'd needed them to escape the opposition fighters, but what if she'd run right into the arms of the Freedom Force once she'd disappeared? It made Nick's blood run cold and his stomach tighten.

Mendez slapped the folder closed and Nick jumped. All eyes went to the colonel.

"I have an assignment for you, but I'm going to warn you this doesn't come from the top. If anyone wants out, he or she can get up right now and walk out the door, no questions asked."

The colonel paused for a long moment, but no one made a move. He cleared his throat. "Good to know." Mendez leaned forward, hands folded one on top of the other, and let his gaze rove across the room. "We're going after Black and his team. I want to know who's paying the bills over there, and I want to know what their end goal is. Most importantly, I want Victoria Royal. She's the key to whatever's going on—and I want to know what that is."

FOUR

AFTER TWO WEEKS OF BACK-and-forth, Ian had news for her—and she was finally going to see Emily after more than three long years of not seeing her sister at all.

Victoria smoothed her hair and pressed a hand to her belly. She was wearing a cotton dress and sandals, trying to look nice for her sister, and sitting at a cafe like a tourist. Now she was wondering if it had been a mistake not to wear her usual clothing and cover it with a burka. She'd have felt less conspicuous, that's certain, but she'd hoped to put Emily at ease by not appearing to be the hardened soldier that two years in Qu'rim had made her into.

It was almost laughable, but Victoria was trying to be ladylike, though she'd never had any training in how to be a lady. Not when she'd been raised by a crusty old man who'd died and left her and Emily to foster care—and to people who had no idea what to do with two teenage girls.

The Andersons had been good people, but they hadn't known the first thing about how to stop Emily from spiraling into drugs and alcohol. They'd finally given up and called Child Protective Services to come and take Victoria and her sister back to the group home.

Her fingers drummed the tabletop nervously. She picked up the cup of sweet Arab coffee and took a sip, telling herself she had to act normal and be patient.

The seaside resort town where she'd been instructed to meet Emily was largely untouched by the civil war, but there were signs it wasn't the idyllic paradise it was purported to be. There were security barriers on the way into town as well as random checkpoints manned by tanks and Qu'rimi Army personnel in full battle gear.

It was odd to be meeting Emily here, considering how this town was still firmly held by the Qu'rimi government. Emily wasn't precisely associating with law-abiding citizens who wished the king's government well, after all.

Still, Victoria had been told to come to Akhira and to wait at this cafe on this day at this time. She checked the time on her phone and blew out a breath. Emily was fifteen minutes late.

Victoria had no idea what she might say to her sister, or how she would get Emily away from the man who'd poisoned her mind. She'd only ever wanted Emily to be safe and well, but she hadn't known for the past several years if her sister truly was either of those things.

When she'd called in the past, Emily had said everything was fine. But she'd also said that Zaran wasn't a terrorist, either. He was a patriot, a man who cared deeply about his nation, his people, and his religion. He wouldn't hurt a fly.

Blah, blah, blah.

It made Victoria sick to think of everything she knew about Zaran bin Yusuf that was completely contrary to Emily's picture of him. Still, there'd been hesitation in

Emily's voice the last time they'd spoken, and that had worried her.

"Miss Royal?"

Victoria's head snapped up even as her heart pounded. A man in a white thobe and dark headdress stood beside the table, his dark eyes gleaming as he looked her over.

"Yes?"

He bowed slightly. "You are to come with me."

Alarm prickled Victoria's skin. "I don't know you."

"I am to take you to see Noor bin Zaran."

Victoria's heart tumbled. "I... I don't know who that is."

"She is the Light of Zaran, miss. She is your sister."

The Light of Zaran. Dear God, Emily, what have you gotten yourself into?

Victoria was desperate to see her sister—but she wasn't stupid. "How do I know you intend to take me to her?"

His smile wasn't precisely comforting. "You do not. But you must choose. Come with me now and see your sister—or stay here because you are fearful."

Victoria's mind raced. "Describe her to me."

The man's eyes narrowed. But he painted a verbal picture of Emily that was accurate. It was the best she could do under the circumstances, so Victoria rose and took some money from her purse to leave on the table. Then she began to walk with the man, her stomach churning the farther they got from the cafe.

The streets were so normal, but the white sands of the beach were mostly empty. A few women watched children playing, and a man walked out of the sea wearing scuba gear. Here and there, towels dotted the beach and foreign tourists lay in the sun. Europeans, mostly, since Americans wouldn't come to Qu'rim these days.

Victoria kept an eye on her surroundings, looking for anything out of the ordinary. When they rounded a corner, a car sat at the curb. A door opened and a man stepped out. She didn't recognize him. Her stomach tightened with fear, and she ground to a halt.

The man who'd been walking with her stopped and turned to look at her. "You must get in the car, miss."

She clutched her purse in front of her like a shield. She had a pistol in it because she was incapable of going anywhere unarmed these days.

"Not until you let me speak with my sister."

He frowned. "This is not permitted. We will drive you to her. Then you may speak as much as you wish."

A bad feeling swirled in Victoria's gut. "What's the difference? Call her now and let me verify this is what she wants me to do. If so, I'll go with you without complaint."

The man's face grew dark with anger. "You do not give orders to me, woman. I say what *you* will do, and you *will* do it. That is the plan."

Victoria took a step backward. She wanted to see Emily very badly, but this didn't feel right. And she'd spent too much time working for Ian Black not to follow her instincts.

"Then I won't see her today. I've changed my mind."

The man took a step toward her, but the sound of a pistol cocking drew her attention to the one who'd stepped out of the car. The black barrel of a Russian Makarov PM pointed at her heart.

"Get in the car, Miss Royal," the man said. "But first,

throw your purse on the ground."

Victoria was wedged between the two men in the back of the car. After she'd dropped her purse, they'd shoved her into the car and taken off. She was still trying to figure out how to disarm the one with the pistol pressed to her ribs when the car screeched to a stop.

The man who'd collected her from the cafe let out a stream of angry Arabic. Victoria didn't speak the language, but she'd picked up a few words here and there after being in the country for the past few months.

Her captors seemed to want to know why they'd stopped. Definitely not a good sign. But then they took off again, and the tension in the car dropped. No one spoke, and then the man she thought of as Cafe Man got a phone call.

He answered in clipped tones. A few seconds later, he tucked the phone into a pocket and said something to the driver. The car veered left and then sped along a highway with very little traffic. After a few more minutes, they whipped off the highway and down a road, toward the sea. Victoria's heart pounded, but she told herself to remain alert. If there was a chance to get the gun—or get away— she would take it.

The car drove beneath a bridge and halted. The men got out and dragged her with them. The big man with the gun shoved her and she stumbled forward. When she turned, he was pointing the gun at her.

"I'm sorry, Miss Royal, but you will not see your sister this day," Cafe Man told her.

"Why?" she said, her stomach churning with acid. "Why kill me when all I want is to talk to Emily?"

"You are a… distraction."

She curled her hands into fists and breathed deeply, though she was beginning to feel light-headed. After all she'd been through, all she'd done, this was how it ended? Here, under a bridge in the sand, when she'd been in combat situations repeatedly over the past two years?

"I saved Zaran's life two weeks ago."

"And he is grateful. If he were not, this would be far more painful."

"Emily will never forgive him if she finds out—"

"She will not know."

The man was infuriatingly calm. He spoke to her like she was a child, and she wished she could strangle him.

"Good-bye, Miss Royal." He made a motion to the man with the gun and started to turn away—

But the man holding the gun dropped to his knees and then fell into the sand with a thud. Cafe Man barely had time to exclaim before he collapsed too. The car's tires spun as the driver realized what was happening and put the pedal to the floor.

But then the car careened out of control as glass shattered, and Victoria knew he'd been hit as well. She threw herself onto the sand and grabbed the gun from the man who'd been about to shoot her. Then she started to belly crawl toward a pylon. She might be next, she might not be, but she wasn't going to make herself into an easy target.

An engine revved, and she looked up to see a van barreling down on her. Victoria scrambled upright and started to run. The sand sucked at her feet as her shoes slipped and slid, the tiny straps useless to keep them on. But she didn't have time to stop and unbuckle them.

Victoria ran, cursing her vanity and swearing she'd never give in to girlish tendencies again if God would just let her get out of this alive. It was a surprisingly unimportant thing to focus on at a time like this, but whatever.

Yet the van caught up to her in spite of her prayers and vows. Clearly, God wasn't amused.

Victoria whirled and took aim, ready to shoot the tires, the driver, anything. But the vehicle slid to a stop, and the doors opened before she could fire. Men in black clothing boiled out of the door, assault rifles drawn and trained on her, surrounding her.

Victoria kept her pistol aimed at one man, the one directly in front of her. They might kill her, but she was taking one of them with her. The air crackled with danger and electricity.

And then the man lowered the rifle just enough that she could see his face. It wasn't a face she'd expected, but relief flooded her at the sight.

Nick Brandon looked as handsome as always, but he also looked angry, his dark brows drawn low in two slashes over his face. Still, she knew he wouldn't kill her. She knew it in her bones. She dropped the pistol to her side, but the men still didn't relax their stances, and she knew they wouldn't until she was unarmed. She had to make her fingers uncurl from the grip, but she did it, and the gun slid to the sand where it hit with a soft plunk.

The team of special ops warriors lowered their weapons, but Victoria only had eyes for Nick. The last time she'd seen him, she'd also had a pistol aimed at him. He wasn't likely to forgive her for that, but right now she almost didn't care. She was safe, even if she wasn't entirely certain she would remain that way.

"Well, hey there, Preacher Boy," she made herself say, though her teeth wanted to chatter. "Didn't know I was quite so dangerous you had to bring the entire Delta Force with you. But I'm flattered, I have to say."

Nick couldn't believe that he was looking at Victoria Royal in a dress. It was white with yellow flowers, and her long red hair hung in a hot, thick mess down her back. It had been sleek earlier when he'd watched her at the cafe. Her gray eyes were wide and fringed with long auburn lashes that she'd darkened with mascara. Her full lower lip quivered for half a second before she bit down on it.

She looked like a somewhat frightened and helpless woman, and yet he knew she was a deadly assassin. The same as he was. She was like one of those startlingly beautiful creatures in the wild—colorful and attractive, but deadly when touched.

"We aren't Delta," Nick said. "And the weaponry wasn't for you."

He didn't bother looking at the two men lying on the ground, blood pooling beneath their heads and turning the sand black. They'd arrived just in time, and his heart was still thumping over how close they'd cut it.

Victoria pulled in a breath. "Well, thanks for rescuing me, whoever y'all are. Guess I'll be on my way."

Nick snorted. "Guess you won't." He stepped back and thrust his chin at the van. "Get in, Victoria."

She let her gaze slide over the men surrounding her, and then she lifted her chin and walked over to Nick. She had to tilt her head back to look up at him, but she met his gaze evenly.

"Another mystery ride? Sounds fun… especially if you're there, Preacher Boy."

He wanted to slap a hand over her mouth—or better yet, his mouth over hers—to stop her from calling him that. He didn't know why it rankled when she said it, but it did. Like a tiny splinter that ached whenever you accidentally pressed your finger against where it wedged beneath your skin.

No one called him that but Victoria. He couldn't even remember how she'd learned his father was a minister. It wasn't the kind of thing he talked about often, but he must have said something when they were in school together. It wasn't a secret… it just wasn't something he was especially keen on people knowing, either.

"Get in, Victoria."

She sighed and walked over to the van. Big Mac was closest and he offered his hand. She took it and climbed up. Nick's heart nearly stopped as her skirt lifted higher, revealing long, shapely legs. Her skin was the color of fresh cream, pale and delicate, but she was lean and muscled in a way that proclaimed her an athlete.

Iceman lifted an eyebrow as he walked by Nick. Then he winked and made a clicking sound with his tongue. Nick wanted to smack him. Flash also grinned and waggled both brows.

Jesus.

Nick was last in the van—and those bastards had left him a seat beside Victoria. He flopped down into it as the door slammed shut and the van lurched into gear. He knew what they were up to. Ever since Billy "the Kid" Blake had been the third to fall prey to Cupid's arrow, the guys had started to take the whole "who's next" thing far too seriously, making bets and throwing each other under the bus in an effort not to be the one.

First, Matt "Richie Rich" Girard went home on leave and returned with a fiancée. Then Sam "Knight Rider" McKnight fell for his best friend's little sister. Two was a coincidence, but three—which happened when Billy reunited with an old flame, helped her expose a dirty defense contractor, and fell in love—was a trend.

Right after Billy, Kev fell hard for Lucky. Then Jack "Hawk" Hunter got himself hitched to a pop star. Someone was next, but damned if it was going to be Nick. Victoria Royal was hot, and he was definitely interested in a little horizontal action with her—but she didn't like him and he didn't like her. So in spite of a sizzling attraction—at least on his part—horizontal was out.

Not to mention the fact she'd threatened to shoot him at least twice now. That kind of thing ought to dampen a man's enthusiasm, though he had to admit his dick hadn't quite gotten the message where she was concerned. Even now, the sight of her encased in a sweet little dress was wreaking havoc on his imagination.

Victoria let her gaze wander over the guys, finally turning to him. "Where are we going, Preacher Boy?"

Nick ground his teeth. "If you don't stop calling me that, I'm opening this door and throwing you out."

She laughed. "Sounds good to me. I doubt I'm going

to like where we're going, anyway."

Nick let his gaze slam into hers. She was putting on a brave face, but she looked troubled. Those bastards had nearly killed her, after all, and she hadn't been expecting rescue. He'd expect anyone to be shaken after that kind of close call.

Instinctively, he put an arm around her and squeezed her shoulder. She didn't try to pull away. If anything, the tension in her body seemed to melt for just a moment.

But then it was back again, and he dropped his arm away. She brought her hands up and rubbed her bare forearms, scrubbing him off her skin. His gut burned.

"We aren't going to hurt you, Vic. We're the good guys, in case you were wondering."

"I wasn't."

Iceman held out a bottle of water to her. Victoria hesitated, but then she took it, twisting off the cap and taking a long drink.

"Thanks," she said.

"You bet," Ice replied.

Nick tried not to let the smile she gave Iceman bother him, but there was no doubt the other man was a whiz with the ladies. In fact, Nick wasn't sure there was a smoother operator on the whole team when it came to women. Hawk and Big Mac used to be the ones to beat when it came to charming the women—but none of them had realized the full potential lurking in Iceman's six-foot-four frame until he'd suddenly turned it on a few months ago.

Up until then, Nick would have sworn the dude was celibate. Nick didn't know what had happened to the guy, but the rest of them could probably learn a thing or two from him these days.

"How did you know they were going to kill me?" Victoria asked of no one in particular.

The guys shifted, but no one spoke. Dammit, they were leaving it to him.

"Chatter," Nick said, and she swung her head around to look at him.

She knew as well as he did that the intelligence services listened to the chatter of known and suspected terror organizations as well as myriad other targets.

Including Black Security.

"Ian Black sent you to your execution, sweetheart," Nick said mercilessly. "Tied you up and handed you over with a pretty bow."

Okay, so they didn't know that for certain, but Black had sent her to Akhira alone, with no backup and no protection. So far as Nick was concerned, that made him a bastard.

Pain flickered in her eyes, and something very like jealousy stabbed into him. She cared about Black—and the asshole hadn't protected her the way he should have.

"I don't believe that," she said. "You're lying."

"Believe what you like. But you're here because we stopped it, so remember that when the colonel talks to you."

"The colonel?"

The van slowed to pass through a checkpoint, and then they were rolling down the highway at high speed as they headed toward Baq. Nick glanced out the window at the flat sand and shimmering heat of the desert.

"You'll meet him soon enough."

"I'm not sure I want to," she grumbled.

"Too bad, sweetheart. You landed in it when you let

bin Yusuf get away. Time to face the consequences."

FIVE

VICTORIA WAS STILL REELING FROM the accusation that Ian had set her up when the van slowed and then stopped. A man in full battle gear peeked into the interior. The driver chatted for a few seconds, and then they were moving again, much slower this time.

Victoria realized they'd entered a military base. The American base near the Baq airport, no doubt. She scrubbed her hands up and down her arms, a shiver moving through her despite the heat.

Zaran bin Yusuf wanted her dead. Had Ian really known that, or was Nick fucking with her? She didn't like to think Ian could be so cold and unfeeling after the past couple of years, but she didn't really know him all that well, did she? He was strangely enigmatic about everything. And he'd shown no emotion whatsoever about Jonah.

But Jonah had been an asshole. Ian knew it as well as she did, so why would he show any regret over Jonah's loss? The dumb bastard had gotten himself killed, and she'd been relieved more than anything.

She lowered her head and sucked back the uncertainty rolling through her. She'd nearly been killed today, she had no idea if her boss had known what would happen when he gave her the information on the meeting place, and she was no closer to finding Emily.

Victoria was used to being alone, used to feeling alone and having to take care of herself, but this time she just wanted to lean into the big body of the man beside her and have him put his arm around her again.

It had felt so nice when he'd done that. But the heat prickling her skin had surprised her. Worried her. Since when did any man make her feel like she was missing something in her life? Sex was not something she'd ever cared about in the past. She firmed her jaw. It wasn't something she cared about *now*.

Nick Brandon might be sexy and prickly in a way that made her want to get under his skin, but that didn't mean a thing. She felt drawn to him because he was from the past, and she had precious little contact with anyone from her life before she'd lost Emily and gone to work for Ian.

Ian, who'd betrayed her.

You don't know that.

It was true she didn't know that for a fact. Nick could be making it up. This colonel of his could be making it up. Anything to separate her from Black Security and make her willing to talk.

Well, she wouldn't talk. She wasn't gullible, and they didn't own her. She'd broken no laws—and she wasn't breaking any trust, either.

When they finally stopped in front of a building, Victoria sucked in a breath and smoothed her skirt self-consciously. God, why had she worn this silly dress?

The men poured from the van one by one, and then Nick held out a hand for her and helped her step down. She stood straight and tall—or as tall as someone five foot four could stand—and let her gaze slide over the men.

They were an impressive sight, these nine big bad warriors bristling with high-tech military gear and a whole lot of muscle. They turned and walked ahead of her toward a bunker surrounded by razor wire. Nick held out a hand, indicating she should follow.

She started to walk and he fell in beside her. He made her jumpy, and she wished he'd go away so she could stop feeling like her skin was on fire.

But the thought of him leaving her side made her frantic in an odd way. She kept her head down and walked the narrow path toward the building. Nick didn't speak. She filed into the building behind the last man and in front of Nick. No one held a weapon on her, but she felt like she was being marched in as a prisoner anyway.

Finally the men went into a room off to her left. Nick stopped her from following and pointed down the hall. She kept going, stopping when he indicated. He knocked on a door, and a gruff "Enter" was the reply.

Nick grabbed the handle and swung the door inward.

"After you."

Victoria went into a makeshift office. A man in civvies sat at a desk. He stood when she entered, his dark eyes raking over her. He was tall and handsome, but older than the men who'd brought her here. His salt-and-pepper hair was a bit more salt than pepper, and it made him look older than he probably was. Late forties, she guessed, and clearly in charge.

"Miss Royal, we're pleased you could join us."

"I didn't think I had a choice."

One corner of his mouth lifted in a smirk. "No, not really. Though I think this is preferable to the alternative, isn't it?"

The alternative being her lying in the sand with a bullet in her head? Yeah, no doubt.

"I guess I should say thanks for the rescue."

He nodded as he walked around to lean on the desk. Oh, so casual, when she was certain he was anything but.

He stuck out a hand. "John Mendez."

She lifted her hand and put it in his. It was warm and firm, but it didn't make her skin sizzle.

"The colonel, I take it?"

"That's right." He looked over at Nick and something passed between them. What, she didn't know. "Have a seat, Miss Royal. Brandy, you too."

Brandy. It made sense, of course, but it was rather dull compared to Preacher Boy.

Nick folded himself into a chair while she sank down in as ladylike a manner as she could muster.

"Zaran bin Yusuf isn't very appreciative of your help, Miss Royal."

"I didn't help him. I simply did the job I was sent to do."

"And yet he's your brother-in-law."

Victoria didn't react fast enough to hide the shock she knew had to be on her face. "That's not true," she said when she'd recovered sufficiently.

But her heart thumped and her brain hurt as it whirled with thoughts. *Had* Emily married him? She'd never said she had, but anything was possible with her sister. Emily had seemed hell-bent on self-destruction these past few years, and Victoria had never quite known why. The last time they'd spoken, Emily had said something cryptic. Something that chilled Victoria's blood and made her more determined than ever to get her sister out of Qu'rim. She'd said, "I miss Mom."

Emily hadn't known their mother. Both their parents had died when Emily was a year old in the kind of accident that shouldn't have happened. They'd been boating with friends when the boat got caught in rapids. They weren't especially big or terrible rapids, but the river was swollen from rain and the undercurrents were stronger than usual. When the boat capsized, only one person made it to shore alive. The rest were dragged under and drowned.

Gramps had been the only relative they had after that.

"And why not? Your sister gave up everything she's ever known, all the comforts of home, to come to Qu'rim with this man."

Victoria wanted to snort. Comforts? What comforts? Twenty-four-hour television, liquor stores, shopping malls, cell phones? Those things didn't make a person happy. If they did, then Emily would have been ecstatic.

She hadn't been. Far from it.

"He's a very dynamic sort of man," she said carefully. "He convinces people to do what he wants. She came with him, but that doesn't make her happy here."

Colonel Mendez tilted his head, studying her. "What makes you think she hasn't married him by now? It's been, what, a little over three years since she ran away? Six months since you've spoken with her?"

Victoria felt his words like a blow. How the fuck did he know these things? She glanced at Nick, but his eyes

57

were blank. His expression, however, was stony.

"You seem to know quite a lot. Do you know for a fact they're married?"

"Does it matter? She's here with him—and you're here protecting him. These things are pretty damning, Miss Royal."

"I'm not protecting him," she said through clenched teeth. "I'd have preferred to shoot him, truth be known. But that's not what the client wanted."

And not how she would get Emily back either. She had to play it cool and safe, and shooting bin Yusuf before she had Emily was neither of those things.

"And who was the client?"

"I don't know."

"Ian Black knows."

"Then you should ask him."

"I'd like to." Mendez reached for a folder and spun it toward him on the desk. "The intel on Ian Black is surprisingly bare," he said, making a show of perusing the information in front of him. "Thirties, six-three, dark hair, green eyes—or brown, the report isn't certain—former CIA. Disavowed, apparently. A rebel, Miss Royal."

His gaze met hers again, and she couldn't stop herself from swallowing.

"Like you," he said evenly.

"I'm just doing a job, Colonel. For a paycheck." She didn't like that she sounded hoarse. Squeaky, as if she couldn't get the words out. She swallowed and waited for his next words.

He gave her a look that said he knew there was a healthy sense of guilt writhing around on the floor of her soul. Well, dammit, when he ran out of options the way she had, maybe he'd understand.

"Then do a job for us. For a paycheck, of course."

Victoria blinked. "Ian pays me more than the Army ever did. No, thanks."

She'd spent the past two years saving everything she had for the day when she could get Emily out of Qu'rim and back home to New Orleans. Even if she needed money, which she didn't, working for the Army didn't appeal. They'd thrown her out without a second thought, and all because Emily had the poor sense to fall for a man like Zaran bin Yusuf.

A terrorist bent on destroying the United States, you mean.

Mendez's mouth curled in a smile. "Then do it for yourself."

Victoria stared at him for a long moment. And then she scoffed. "Unless you plan to help me extract my sister from bin Yusuf and clear my name—*both* our names—you don't have a damn thing I want."

Mendez straightened, and she bent her neck back to look up at him. Her heart thumped against her chest wall at the serious expression on his face. He couldn't possibly... no way...

"Maybe that's exactly what I'm offering. Does that change your answer?"

Nick watched Victoria's reaction. Mendez was still standing there, still looking intently at her, and her head was tilted back to gaze up at him. There was something unbearably elegant about her profile. And lonely, he thought. There was definitely something lonely about her.

He'd read the brief on her that Mendez had gotten from Intel. She'd been working for Black for two years now. Before that, she'd held down odd jobs after being booted from the Army. She'd never formed any relationships with anyone, though the report said nothing about casual hookups. On the subject of her and Ian Black, it was silent.

"I… What do you want me to do?"

That was Mendez's cue. He slipped backward onto the desk, hands on his knees, and focused the full power of his attention on Victoria.

"I want to know who Ian Black is. Who he works for. Who pays him to do these jobs, and where he gets his information."

Victoria stiffened. "I don't know any of that. I already told you."

"But you could find out."

She lifted her chin defiantly. "What makes you think that? I've worked for him for two years and know nothing more than he lets me know."

"Are you sleeping with him?"

Nick felt as if someone had jabbed him with a sharp knife. He didn't like the burning sensation creeping through his gut at the thought of Victoria and Ian Black. The man was a disavowed spy, working for the highest bidder and selling his loyalty like a convenience-store clerk sold cigarettes. He was no good, and if Victoria was working for him—and sleeping with him—then she was probably no good either.

But she had something they wanted, and Mendez was willing to barter to get it.

Victoria got to her feet, the picture of offended innocence. And fury. Holy hell, she was pissed. Crimson slashed her cheekbones as she tossed her hair. Another feeling knifed into Nick at that moment. A feeling that had a lot more to do with the way her breasts thrust forward and her waist dipped neatly in. And then there was the flare of that skirt. Like something a girl back home would wear to church.

Jesus.

"You wouldn't be asking me that if I were a man," she said. "And frankly, it's none of your fucking business."

Mendez nodded, once and firmly. "If you work for me, it is my business. And yeah, I *would* ask a man. You'd be surprised how many of these guys can't keep it in their pants." He shook his head as if pained, and Nick nearly laughed.

"Half my damn team's shacked up with someone they met on the job, so don't bet any money on me not asking every motherfucker that comes through this door who he, or *she,* is sleeping with."

Victoria folded her arms over her breasts. She hadn't forgotten he was there, Nick was positive. But she wasn't slanting a look his way at all. As if she could forget all about him if she didn't look.

Fine with him. It just meant he could study her curves and angles to his heart's content. Until Mendez sliced a look his way.

Nick straightened and dropped his gaze, but the colonel snorted as if he was in on a secret.

Fuck.

"What's the job?" Victoria asked. "Not that I'm saying yes."

"Answer the question."

She blew out a breath. He thought she might tell the colonel to fuck off.

"No, I'm not sleeping with him. I'm not sleeping with anyone. I take my job seriously, and I take getting Emily out of this shit hole even more seriously."

And that was the crux of the matter. By all accounts, her sister was her Achilles' heel—and Mendez knew precisely how to dig in the blade.

"I want you to tell us everything you know about Black. Then I want you to go back to work for him. And take Brandy with you."

Victoria's mouth dropped open. Then she shook her head, her long hair brushing her back. It was almost to her waist, and Nick wanted to wrap his hands in it. Preferably while buried deep inside her. Pounding into her while she gasped and moaned and screamed his name.

Nick shifted in the chair as his dick began to sit up and take notice of what was going on in his brain.

"I can't take him to Ian. That's not how it works. Besides, I thought you wanted me to believe Ian set me up. Why would I go back to work for him when the job wasn't finished? If bin Yusuf wants me dead, he won't stop until I am."

Mendez cut a look to Nick, and Victoria followed his gaze, looking at Nick for the first time since she'd sat in that chair. But it was Mendez's stare that had him sitting up straighter. If Nick had a collar to pull, he'd have pulled it.

Thankfully, Mendez's iron gaze cut back to Victoria.

"We don't know that he had any idea what was about to happen. We also don't know he didn't."

Victoria glared at Nick before whipping her gaze back to Mendez. *Busted.*

"You're talking in circles. You've made promises, but no specifics, and you want me to walk back into the line of fire—and to take Preacher Boy with me? You're crazy, Colonel. And since I've committed no crime, I demand you let me go."

Mendez folded his arms over his chest. Then he scratched his head casually while Victoria waited.

"I can have you driven to the gate. But you'll be on your own then. A target for bin Yusuf, for Black, for whomever. No support, no rescue. And your sister stays with bin Yusuf."

Victoria swallowed. "I can't just take him to Ian. He'll be suspicious. New recruits are ex-military, ex-cops, whatever. And they usually arrive after Ian checks them out with his contacts. He has operations elsewhere, so there's no guarantee he'd assign Nick to Qu'rim."

"Trust me, Sergeant Brandon will have a very long and checkered history when we're done. He'll be a very dirty operator and precisely what Black wants. Besides, you need a spotter, don't you?"

Nick gritted his teeth. This was the part he didn't like. He didn't mind being kicked out of HOT or having a record as a dirty soldier. All of that was temporary anyway. But acting as Victoria's spotter was going to drive him to drink.

She glanced at him and he gave her a bland smile. Inside, he was seething. But no one else was right for the job. It had to be him. Dex was still too new to HOT—and Jack Hunter was flying in to take Nick's place in the squad. They'd be shadowing him and Victoria as much as possible. But mostly he'd be flying without his backup.

Victoria was pissed enough at him to turn him over to Black. But her sister was the key here. So long as Mendez held out the promise of something she'd been unable to get from Black, her loyalties would swing toward them.

"You'll get Emily away from the terrorist camp? You'll send her back to the States with a clean record?"

"You do realize that your sister may not want to leave bin Yusuf?"

"I know that." She hesitated. "But I don't believe it. If she was happy, he'd have no reason to keep us apart."

Mendez studied her. "I can't promise a clean record. She's been living in a terrorist organization for years now. She'll be on no-fly lists, and she'll be watched. But she'll be free to come and go, and she'll be able to find work."

Victoria nibbled her lip. "Ian isn't stupid. If he didn't know bin Yusuf wanted me dead before, he probably will now. He'll want to know how I escaped—and how I managed to kill three men after they'd disarmed me."

"Was he there? Does he know they took your weapon?"

She didn't answer, but Nick could tell she was thinking about it.

Mendez kept his gaze on her. "I've sent a cleanup team. There won't be any bodies left. You can say whatever you want about how you got away. Are you a good liar, Miss Royal?"

"I can be."

"Then tell a damn good lie and stick with it."

She blew out a breath and shook her head. "This is a bad idea. Ian will be suspicious—of me, of Nick, of the whole damn thing. He's not going to suddenly tell me anything about his operations."

"He doesn't need to. Just get Sergeant Brandon into the outfit and leave the rest to him."

SIX

WAS SHE REALLY GOING THROUGH with this? Victoria stood near the car waiting to take her into Baq and stared off into the desert. The sun was setting, turning the sky blood red and the dunes orange. It was beautiful, but not the sort of place to take for granted. Forgetting for even an instant that the desert was a constant struggle between life and death could be fatal.

Victoria shuddered. She'd nearly been killed earlier today when she'd stood under a bridge and stared down a man with a gun. She would have died if not for Nick Brandon and his team.

She still didn't know who they were or what this outfit was, but they were definitely special operators. She suspected they were Delta Force, no matter what Nick said. It was either that or Green Berets. What else was there?

And she was about to walk back into Ian's headquarters and tell him she'd found a spotter. Someone she used to know and had met again today when he'd come to her aid in Akhira.

God, it was risky as hell, but apparently this Colonel Mendez had access to things that normal colonels didn't. Like CIA reports. She'd had no idea Ian was former CIA. He'd always styled himself as ex-military, and he worked unconventionally. He had the trust of the locals in a way that surprised her, but that hadn't worried her until the mission two weeks ago. Now she wondered just whose side he was on.

Nick came out of the building and swaggered toward her. He'd taken off the gear, but he was still dressed in desert camouflage. He was tall, his shoulders stretching the uniform impressively, and there was a day's worth of stubble on his face. Soldiers had strict rules for grooming, but not out here. Just another indication he wasn't regular Army.

Her belly did a flip the closer he got. She pressed a hand to her middle and told herself to breathe. He came to a stop and stared down at her, his kiss-worthy lips forming a hard frown. She could see the ball chain from his dog tags glinting against his neck where he hadn't tucked it into his T-shirt. Why, oh why, did he have to be so damn appealing?

"I know you don't like me," he said, "but you *can* trust me to protect you out there."

Her heart thumped and she swallowed. "First of all, I can protect myself—been doing it for two years without you. And second, I never said I didn't like you."

He snorted softly. "Have it your way then. And you haven't liked me since the moment we met, so no use pretending otherwise."

"I didn't like your superior *attitude*, Preacher Boy. Big difference."

He blinked. "What attitude? I showed you to your room. I was polite."

She was surprised he remembered that. "Ha! You looked at me like I was something you'd scraped off the bottom of your shoe. I thought it was because I was a woman invading sacred territory. And you weren't polite when we were in the field."

"No, I was trying to win. But I never took you for anything less than an equal. I thought you knew that."

"You insulted me. I'm sure I'm not remembering *that* wrong."

He actually grinned, his teeth flashing white in his tanned face. He had lines at the corners of his eyes that hadn't been there before. He'd been almost too pretty three and a half years ago. Now that he had some hard edges? Geez. *Sexy, sexy man.*

"I insulted your ability. Not your gender. Typical trash talk."

Victoria frowned. Was that right? He'd pushed her buttons, but as she searched her memory, she couldn't remember him ever calling her weak or implying she wasn't good enough because she was a woman.

Why had it felt so damn personal at the time? And, dammit, why did he have to be so agreeable now when she really needed to keep distance between them?

"You didn't insult anyone else like that. Just me."

"You were the closest competition I had." He shrugged. "I won't apologize for rattling your cage. I'd have done the same to anyone."

She was still looking up at him and trying to figure out where this unsettled feeling in her belly was coming from when he reached out and smoothed the pad of his thumb over her forehead. Shock ricocheted through her, and she took a hasty step backward, breaking the contact. Her body tingled, a surge of moisture dampening her panties.

Nick dropped his hand to his side and stood there like a mountain. He looked... safe. She wanted to do what she'd never done before, which was wrap her arms around him and press her cheek to his chest. It was disconcerting as all hell.

"Sorry," he said. "That was out of line."

"What were you doing?"

"You had a frown line. I didn't like that I'd caused it, so I thought I'd smooth it out."

She frowned. "Well, don't touch me. I don't like it."

She liked it too much.

"See, I was right." One corner of his mouth twitched up.

"About what?" Why couldn't she think when he looked at her like that?

"You don't like me."

She backed up another step. She did like him. More than she should. She was out of her depth with him—and she couldn't let him know it. She'd been taking care of herself for too long to let one sexy man screw with her goals.

"I like you just fine. But don't touch me, and we'll get along a whole lot better."

He shook his head slowly. "Ah, Vicky, you are a challenge."

"And don't call me Vicky," she said automatically.

He perked up at that. Then he laughed. "So that's it, huh? Vicky." He narrowed his eyes at her. "Don't call me

Preacher Boy and I won't call you Vicky. Got it?"

Dammit. "You drive a hard bargain. So what do I call you? Shithead?"

"Brandy works. Nick works. Pick one."

"Not as interesting as Preacher Boy, but whatever."

The driver of her car came outside in civvies. He was supposed to drop her in a market in Baq. She'd make her way back to Ian's from there. And then she had to talk Ian into bringing Nick into the outfit. Her pulse skipped. What if Ian simply handed her over to bin Yusuf and washed his hands of her?

Nick lifted his gaze to the car for a moment before dropping it back to her. "Don't worry, Victoria. I'll be nearby, waiting to hear from you. If anything feels off, call me and I'll come for you."

"I'll shoot my way out and call after."

He'd given her back her purse after she'd agreed to Mendez's proposal. She hadn't even known he had it. But everything was there, and she'd taken out her phone and programmed in the numbers they gave her.

He laughed. "Fine, whatever. But calling first might make getting away easier."

Nick shoved his hands in his pockets as they faced each other. The driver started the car, and she knew it was time to go. But she didn't want to turn away from Nick, didn't want to get in the car and watch him fade into the distance.

It wasn't like her to feel this way at all, and that was just the cue she needed to force herself to turn and walk away. Ridiculous to feel any sort of attachment simply because they'd known each other a lifetime ago in a simpler world.

She pulled open the car door and started to duck inside. But her gut churned.

Driven by some emotion she couldn't name, Victoria turned and walked back over to Nick. He was frowning at her when she reached up and pulled his head down. She pressed her lips to his cheek, felt the roughness of his stubble and breathed the smell of him—sand, spice, and cool water—deep into her lungs.

"Thanks for saving me," she said, her lips close to his ear.

She started to step away, but he caught her close and turned his head, his lips meeting hers. The contact was shocking—and delicious in a way she hadn't anticipated. She'd been kissed before, but this... this was better than any of those kisses had been.

His mouth was soft and hard against hers, his hands firm on her hips as he held her against him. The kiss was hot and tame all at once. Simultaneously the most arousing and most chaste kiss she'd ever had. He didn't force her mouth open, didn't thrust his tongue between her lips—he just kissed her hard and thoroughly before setting her away from him and taking a step backward.

And, God, she wanted his tongue so badly now. Wanted to feel it sliding against her own, stroking her senses higher.

But the kiss was over and he was looking at her, his jaw firm and a hard look in his eyes.

"You're welcome," he said, and it took her a moment to remember that she'd thanked him for saving her.

"I... I have to go." Her cheeks flamed as she said it because he knew she had to leave as well as she did. The car was running, and she'd left the door open. She took a step backward, and then another.

Then she turned and got inside the car, determined not to look at him again. But she failed because she looked up, her gaze clashing with his right as she closed the door. And she didn't look away as they drove off. Nick didn't move from the spot she'd left him standing in.

It was only when the car turned and he was out of sight that she remembered how to breathe.

She'd imagined the whole thing. It was the only explanation. Victoria lay in her bed and pushed her hair off her face. The air conditioner wasn't working right, and the room was hot. She lay on top of the covers in a pair of tiny panties and a tank top and stared up at the ceiling fan whipping overhead.

There was no way she'd kissed Nick Brandon. No way she'd felt the hard muscles of his body, the solid pressure of his thighs against hers, the mildly disturbing hardness between them. No way in hell.

She closed her eyes and bit back a moan. She always slept alone, but for once she wished she had company. And not just any company. Victoria pressed her eyes tight and tried to rid herself of the vision of Nick Brandon watching her drive away.

The house was silent, which meant that Ian was asleep or working alone. Only a few operators stayed here at a time when they weren't on assignment. Others were quartered in different hotels or rentals nearby.

She'd been nervous when she'd walked into the house today, but Ian hadn't seemed in the least surprised to see her.

"You don't look like someone who's seen her long-lost sister," he'd remarked.

Victoria kept her purse close, her fingers itching to wrap around the butt of her pistol. "I didn't," she said. "It seems as if Zaran bin Yusuf had something else in mind."

"Oh?"

She'd faced Ian then, dropping the purse and lifting the gun. "He wants me dead."

Ian's brows drew down. It took him a second to speak. "You think I knew."

"Did you?"

He lifted both his hands and held them beside his head. "No. I was told you would be allowed to see your sister for an hour. That's all."

She'd chewed her lip, her heart hurting over the fact she'd not seen Emily at all. "What's the loss of another operator to you? We're all replaceable, right?"

Something flickered in his gaze. But then his eyes went flat. "Yes. But I don't have another sniper of your caliber. You're the best, Victoria."

The praise didn't feel as nice as it should. She was tired and confused—and just a little bit heartsick at the idea this man could have betrayed her. She *liked* Ian. Or had, anyway.

"I need a spotter. A good one."

"I'm working on it."

Her heart had pounded. "I found one."

One eyebrow arched. "Really? While thwarting an attempt on your life?"

"Someone I went to sniper training with. He's left the Army—not voluntarily, I take it—and he's here in Qu'rim. And yeah, he was at the cafe where bin Yusuf's men tried to grab me."

"Convenient." He'd leaned back in his chair then, his hands folded on top of his head. Not provoking her. "If all they tried to do was grab you, how do you know bin Yusuf wants you dead?"

"I didn't get a warm fuzzy feeling from them. Why else would he try to grab me?"

"To reunite you with your sister? To keep you in his camp for himself? How the fuck would I know?"

She still didn't lower the gun, though he sounded thoroughly baffled. "You'd know if he told you."

"I don't take orders from bin Yusuf. I do what I want, for whom I want, so long as I get paid."

"If he paid you to kill me, would you?"

His eyes flashed. "I might. But he'd have to pay me a whole fucking lot to replace you, and I don't think that's his priority right now."

"Geez, I'm beginning to think you care."

"Sweetheart, I care as much as I can. It's all dollars and *sense* to me. And it makes no sense unless he's got the dollars."

"So romantic. I feel positively safe now."

He'd snorted. "Shoot me if you have to, but otherwise put the fucking gun down and tell me about this spotter."

She'd stood there for a solid minute, debating. And then she'd lowered the gun and gone to sit in the chair in front of his desk, like always.

"You know, I should be insulted you'd think I'd set you up. Why the fuck would I send you to Akhira just to

74

get you killed? I could do it myself—or let bin Yusuf grab you in the market down the street if he wanted to do it personally."

She hadn't mentioned that bin Yusuf didn't seem to want to do it himself since he'd instructed his men to shoot her on a remote stretch of beach.

"His name's Nick Brandon. He was some kind of Special Forces or something, but he's been involuntarily separated. He wouldn't tell me why. But he says he's looking for work. And I know he's good. The best, besides me."

"You have a contact number?"

"Yes."

"Then give it to me. No promises, but if he checks out, we'll see."

And that had been the end of that. She'd given Ian Nick's phone number and she'd gone to bed. She wasn't worried about Nick's story not agreeing with hers. They'd gone over it again and again with the colonel before she'd been allowed to leave.

She couldn't sleep as her mind churned with too many thoughts. She thought of her fear when she'd been standing under that bridge, and then she thought of the moment when the men around her dropped to the ground, their lives ended by a sniper's bullet. She'd never been that close before. She was the one shooting from a safe distance, not the one standing beside somebody when he went down.

Then she thought of the moment those men had poured from the van and she'd thought she'd gone from one hell to the next. But it was Nick. She'd been so relieved because she knew that whatever else was going on, he wasn't there to kill her.

And now she was supposed to bring Nick into Ian's private security firm and let him spy for his colonel. And the United States Army. Ian, who'd given her a job and given her the promise of finding Emily. Ian, who'd seemed thoroughly unaware of bin Yusuf's attempt on her life and angry that she'd think he had anything to do with it.

But, dammit, Ian wasn't her brother. He wasn't her lover. He was a man with an agenda of his own, and for all she knew he was a pretty terrific liar. He could be on the phone with Zaran bin Yusuf right now, arranging for her death.

Not that this Colonel Mendez was any better. Just because he had the backing of the Army didn't mean he wasn't dirty. He'd targeted Ian, and she'd agreed to help because he'd promised to get Emily for her and transport her back to the States.

Emily might not have a clean record once it was done, but she'd at least be safe and out of an evil man's control. Victoria would spend every moment she had making sure that Emily got the life she deserved.

Victoria balled her fist and thumped it on her thigh. If only Emily was still alive. That was the thing that worried her in the middle of the night. She'd gone over and over that last conversation, Emily's statement that she missed their mom, and she wondered. Why had Emily said it? What did it mean? Was she ready to leave this place? Was she afraid of Zaran?

Why hadn't she called in six months? She hadn't been *allowed* to call, obviously. But what if it was something worse? What if she was unable to call?

Victoria closed her eyes and sucked in a breath. And

then she reached for her phone on the nightstand. She'd tried calling Emily before, but there was nothing except endless ringing. Even the voice mail didn't work anymore. She got the same result this time.

She ended the call and scrolled through her contacts until she found Nick's name. He'd said he'd be nearby if she needed him. She'd wondered what that meant, but she'd decided it was best if she didn't know. Now she clicked on his name and called up text messaging. She hesitated for a moment before typing.

You there?

She pressed Send before she could change her mind. It took only seconds before she had an answer.

Yes. You okay?

Fine. Just checking.

Thinking about me, weren't you?

She could feel his smirk through the phone. Her cheeks heated. Two could play this game.

Oh yeah. Touching myself too.

Jesus, don't say that.

Why not?

There was no reply for the longest time. Her heart sank a little as her phone remained silent. And then it buzzed.

Because I want to touch you, V. Everywhere. Until you scream my name.

Her breath shortened. And her pussy tingled with heat. She knew how to take care of herself—hell, it was how she got off when she needed to—but she found herself wishing he could touch her.

We barely know each other, PB.

We know each other enough.

Her skin was so hot. The fan didn't help, and she wanted to go kick the AC unit. But it wouldn't do a damn bit of good.

Best we don't go there. Work and play don't mix.

Maybe not, but we won't always be working.

She sucked in a breath. Her nipples tightened against her tank top, the fabric almost torture against her sensitive flesh. She pushed that thought away and typed.

What were you doing when I texted?

Sleeping.

Sorry I woke you.

I told you to let me know if you needed me.

She stared at the screen, her heart thumping, wondering what to say in reply. She'd needed someone just now, someone to answer her in the middle of the night when she was lonely and scared for her sister. But she couldn't say any of that to him. She couldn't let him know she was anything less than tough. Because he wasn't her friend. He was just a guy she knew who'd helped her out of a tight spot.

Good night, V. See you soon.

She texted him back, then slipped the phone on the nightstand and flopped onto her side. She'd left him in the desert two weeks ago, desperate to escape him. Now she couldn't wait to see him again.

SEVEN

NICK MET IAN BLACK AT an out-of-the-way cafe. The other man was sitting at a table, chatting to the server in Arabic, when Nick walked in. Black stood, his eyes moving over Nick, assessing him. There was nothing but suspicion and hostility in those eyes, but that's pretty much what Nick had expected to find.

Black held out his hand and Nick took it. They gripped each other hard, that age-old contest between men to prove they had a firm handshake. Nick could remember his dad yelling at him when he was about eight years old for not squeezing harder. The old man had been worried he'd turn into a "sissy," as he put it. Nick hadn't quite known what that meant then, but he did now.

It meant, among other things, that his father was a hypocrite who preached about forgiveness and loving one another and yet still had hatred in his heart for those he didn't approve of. Even when that person was his own daughter.

"Have a seat," Black said, motioning to a chair and taking the one opposite. When they were settled, he fixed

Nick with a level stare. "So you managed to be in the right place at the right time yesterday. Happy coincidence."

Nick shrugged. "Not quite a coincidence, but whatever."

Black's eyes gleamed with interest. "Really? What's that mean?"

"It means I've been watching Vicky. Saw her in the market once and followed her home. Then I followed her to Akhira."

Black's brows drew down. "Why would you do that?"

Nick shrugged. "You've seen her, man. She's hot." He paused for a second, gauging the other man's response. Black's jaw tightened a fraction, and Nick's gut clenched. Victoria had said she wasn't sleeping with him, but that didn't mean Black didn't want to. Or that she'd been telling the truth. That was possible too.

"But that's not the real reason," he continued. "I've been looking for work since I left the Army, and when I saw Vicky that day, I didn't think she was here as a tourist, considering her special skill." He leaned back in his chair. "Wanted to check you out, see what the lay of the land was."

"And what did you decide?"

Nick could tell that Ian Black was angry. The implication that he'd followed Victoria, found out where Black was holed up, and then kept tabs on them for days wasn't sitting well with the man's inflated sense of self-importance. Fucking mercenaries.

Fucking *traitors*. Or at least Black was, anyway.

Nick leaned forward, elbows on the table. "I'm good at what I do. Hell, I'm as good as your girl—probably better, quite honestly—and I'm willing to do whatever needs doing."

"And if what needs doing involves things that might be considered counter to the best interests of your country?"

This was the part Nick hated. Fucking bastard. He wanted to reach across the table and wrap his hands around the man's neck. The Hostile Operations Team was solid red, white, and blue, and the operators worked hard days and long hours in the most dangerous situations. They worked to protect America and all it stood for, and Nick had taken a vow to die in the line of duty if required. They all had.

But this asshole didn't care about any of that. For the purposes of this assignment, Nick couldn't either.

"*My* best interests come first," Nick said. "But I'm not helping some terrorist shit smuggle a nuke into Baltimore Harbor or anything, so that's out. The rest is up for discussion… for the right price."

That hadn't been part of the script, but he was fucking pissed and he wanted Black to know he had limits.

Black leaned back in his seat and tapped his phone where it lay on the table. He wasn't punching in buttons, just tapping the back of the case.

"You have quite a checkered history in the Army," he said.

Nick knew not to show any surprise, but it still astounded him how quickly the man had gotten the information on him. Definitely a leak somewhere.

"Yeah, well, me and the Army don't quite fit. Better if I go out on my own."

"You disobeyed a direct order from a commanding

officer."

"It happens. And the stupid shit was wrong. If we'd done what he wanted, the whole unit would've bought it when we drove through that town."

"How do I know you'll do what you're told out in the field if you're working for me?"

"I've heard about you. You don't send men on suicide missions or fail to listen when they tell you something doesn't feel right. You don't have West Point up your ass and think because you have a couple of bars on your shoulders that you know more than the men who've been on the ground since your worst problem was who to ask to prom and how to get rid of a fucking zit."

Black's mouth twisted in what might have been a smile or a grimace. And then he stretched his hand over the table. "Operations are getting busier these days, and I need people willing to work. Your background checks out, and I'm willing to give you a chance to prove your worth."

Nick clasped Black's hand and they shook.

"Fuck up, though, and you'll be on the next transport back to the States." Black's smile faded then. "And I promise you, fuck with me at all, and I'll make sure you don't work for anyone in this business ever again. You'll be back home bagging groceries and wondering what the fuck happened, you got it?"

Nick forced himself to smile. "Fuck yeah, I got it."

Black motioned to the waiter and the man hurried over with two glasses and set them down. Black lifted one and sniffed it. "Black-market whiskey."

Nick picked up a glass. Alcohol wasn't precisely allowed in Qu'rim, but of course there was always a black market in just about anything you might want. And a whole lot of people wanted alcohol, even if it was against the law.

Black held out his glass and clinked it with Nick's. "To a profitable future."

"Amen," Nick said. He didn't drink, however, and Black finally laughed.

"Don't trust me?"

"Don't trust anyone."

Black tossed the whiskey back and stood. "Your call. Drink it or leave it, but we've got work to do."

Nick slammed back the whiskey and got to his feet. "Lead the way."

Victoria was inspecting her gear in one of the common rooms when Ian walked into the compound with Nick Brandon. Her stomach did a flip and her heart kicked up a notch. She pushed herself upright and faced the two men. Nick's gaze slid over her, leaving her feeling jittery in its wake. She dropped the cloth she'd been using to polish her rifle and waited.

She hadn't known whether Nick would be successful or not, but Ian needed new men and Nick had all the right qualifications. Apparently, Ian agreed. Still, it made her stomach churn since she knew why Nick was really here.

"Brought you something, Victoria," Ian said.

"I see that."

Something tall and dark and handsome, with bulging muscles and a scowl that said he wasn't all that amused.

Nick had a pack over his shoulder and a duffel hanging off one arm. If he'd brought all his gear, he was here to stay.

"You doing all right after yesterday?" he asked, his expression as serious as ever.

She swallowed before nodding. "I was shaken up a bit, but I'm over it now."

If only that were true. She was over the physical fear of the situation, but she was more worried than ever about Emily. And if Zaran bin Yusuf wanted *her* dead, that definitely wasn't a good thing for her health.

"Good."

Ian motioned to her. "Take him to see Rascal."

Nick frowned and Victoria hurried to fill the silence before he popped off. She already knew he wasn't predisposed to like Ian, and she damn sure didn't want him saying something that could compromise her ability to get Emily out of Qu'rim.

"Rascal's our quartermaster, so to speak. He'll get you a place to sleep and explain how we operate."

"All right." He shouldered his gear and followed her through the compound. They walked into an open area where the sun beat down with blistering intensity and the only shade was provided by a couple of date palms. The compound wasn't huge, but it was big enough for their small army. Still, you wouldn't quite know what was going on here by the open space. There was no military-grade equipment out in the open and nothing that seemed out of place.

"You look pissed off," she said as they walked. A fountain tinkled in the center of the courtyard, nothing but a tease in this heat.

"I've been better."

"If you say or do anything that means I can't get Emily back home, I'll shoot you myself."

He snorted. "Hell, you've already threatened to do that twice before. Hasn't worked out so far, has it?"

"You haven't pushed me far enough."

"And you all friendly last night. Texting me, saying naughty things... did you touch yourself, Victoria?"

She sucked in a breath laced with searing heat. "I wasn't serious about that, and you know it."

"How do I know it? Just because you say so?"

They walked into the shade of a building, and she hurried to the door and opened it. Behind her, Nick laughed softly. She didn't care; she wasn't taking the bait.

"Hey, Rascal, got a new recruit."

Rascal was a big man with a bald head and arms that looked like he'd bench-pressed a Humvee repeatedly. He was bald on purpose, not because he had no hair. He hulked over from where he'd been counting boxes of something and gave Nick a once-over.

He looked meaner than hell, but Victoria knew he was actually one of the nicest guys Ian had, unlike some of the assholes Ian hired who had Rambo complexes. Those guys were typically much smaller than Rascal, so maybe they felt like they had something to prove. He didn't.

"Welcome aboard," he said, holding out his hand.

Nick took it and the two men shook.

"So what's your story, man?" Rascal asked.

"Couldn't take the Army bullshit anymore. They asked me to leave, so I did."

Rascal snorted. "And a job back home didn't appeal, right?"

"Nope."

Rascal cocked his head. "Got any special skills?"

Nick shrugged. "Almost four years as a Ranger. My specialty was sniper."

Rascal's eyes twinkled. "I see. Come to give our girl here some competition?"

Victoria snorted. "As if. He's my spotter."

Nick's gaze burned into her, and she wondered if Rascal could sense the heat coming from her skin. It wasn't all irritation, either. In fact, most of it wasn't. Damn sexy jerk.

"For now," Nick said. "Until I prove I'm the better shot."

"Anytime, asshole," she snapped.

Rascal laughed. "Well, don't kill each other yet. Boss Man has too much work needs doing, and we all benefit when the jobs get done."

Victoria turned pointedly away from Nick. "Don't worry. I'd rather have the money anyway."

"Amen, sister. Amen."

"I'll leave you to it," she said. "I've got gear that needs cleaning."

She could feel Nick's eyes on her back as she left. A burst of male laughter came from inside the building when she walked outside. She had no idea if they'd been talking about her or not, but since she'd spent her life feeling like the odd one out, she always assumed it.

She went back to where she'd been inspecting her gear, collected everything, and carried it up to her room. It was a small room with a small bed, but at least she was alone. There were no other women in Ian's outfit—at least not here in Qu'rim, anyway.

There was a window that looked out onto the courtyard, and she went over and watched for Nick. Eventually he came out of the building where she'd left him. He stood there for a minute, letting his gaze slide across the court-yard, and she knew he was cataloging it for his guys. A pang of guilt sliced into her, but she pushed it firmly away.

She'd given Ian two years to find Emily for her, and he'd gotten nowhere. Besides, though he'd treated her well and paid her even better, she had no idea what he was real-ly up to or where his loyalties lay. That thought had both-ered her quite a bit since her chat with Colonel Mendez yesterday. Disavowed CIA. You had to do something pret-ty serious to piss off the CIA enough to do that to you.

Just proved she didn't really know Ian at all, and she had no real idea what he would do or how far he would go to protect his little empire. If giving her up to bin Yusuf was more profitable than not, she had no doubt he'd do it.

Nick began to walk toward the main building, his gear slung over his broad shoulders. He moved with the catlike stealth of a sniper, all fluid movement and tightly coiled attention. When he disappeared from sight, she breathed a sigh and picked up her phone. It was a habit to check for messages from Emily, but of course there was nothing.

She heard movement outside her room, and she turned toward the door, her breath stopping in her lungs. Whoever it was moved on again, and she waited before going over and putting an ear to the door. Her phone buzzed and she gasped.

It's just me. No need to panic.

Nick.

Who said I'm panicking?

You're standing with your ear against the door. Of

course you're panicking.

Victoria stepped backward, her heart thudding. Dammit. *What makes you think that?*

Shadow beneath your door. Didn't you learn a damn thing during training?

She shoved her hair behind her ears and stifled a groan. Basic Sniper Training 101, for fuck's sake. Be aware. She usually was, but having him here was throwing her off her game.

Fuck off, she typed.

More fun with a friend, he shot back.

Victoria started to text something else, but then she shoved her phone in her pocket and yanked open the door. Why was she trading insults with him on a phone when he was right there?

He was standing in the door to a room across the hall, leaning against the jamb like he had no cares. One eyebrow lifted when she appeared. Then he smirked.

"Why are you giving me a hard time?" she growled.

"Sweetheart, I'd love to give you a hard time. Anytime you want."

Victoria clenched her hands at her sides so she wouldn't strangle him. "You're a dick, you know that?"

"Not trying to be. Just telling the truth."

"You never looked at me twice when we were in training."

"I looked at you all the time, Victoria. You just never caught me."

Her blood hummed through her veins, and her body stirred in ways she'd prefer it didn't. She didn't have time for this kind of distraction. Not right now. And not with him.

"We're here for a job. Nothing else. So keep your eyes and your comments to yourself."

He straightened in the door. He was so tall, so intense, and she almost took a step back. But then she forced herself to stand her ground. It wasn't like her to avoid a challenge of any kind.

Footsteps sounded on the stairs. She turned toward them just as Ian's head appeared. He stopped when he saw her.

"Need the two of you to get down here. Got a mission for you."

EIGHT

NICK FOLLOWED VICTORIA DOWN THE stairs and into the room that Ian Black was using as his command center. Nick didn't let his surprise show, but the equipment was pretty high-tech—computers, flat screens, a secure satellite phone on the desk, and other gear. But the most interesting thing was a door at the rear of the room. He might not have paid much attention to it if not for a couple of factors. First, when he'd been outside in the courtyard, he'd noticed the heavy-duty generators. Naturally, a man like Black would want to power his own facility. Not unusual in itself.

The AC units were pretty standard, nothing exciting. Nothing that indicated a server room in the building.

But the door to the room had a combination lock and a cipher lock. Not only that, but Nick could hear the distinct hum of an AC unit behind the door.

Jackpot.

There was no need for an interior AC unit—or locks like those—unless Black had a server back there. Nick scanned the office, recalling what he'd seen on the outside, and realized the room behind the door had to be interior. There was a door near the window, but it was probably to a closet or a narrow hallway that Black had had built to shield the server.

You couldn't have a server on an exterior wall, and you had to keep it cool. Not only that, but you had to pressurize the air in the vault just enough that there was a whoosh of air whenever it was opened. This prevented dust from reaching the equipment, which would be critical in a desert environment.

Nick let his gaze slide over the walls. It crashed to a stop about a foot up the wall behind Black's desk. Goddamn, there was a cable coming out of the wall and passing beneath the desk. He'd bet anything that it went to the sat phone.

It meant that Black had secure comm going out of this place, and he was using his sat phone to do it.

Son of a bitch.

The dude was clearly high-tech. And well funded if he had this kind of setup.

According to Victoria, Black had been using this place as a headquarters in Qu'rim for the past eight months, and he'd clearly made some modifications. Serious modifications if what Nick was seeing was any indication. The walls were already thickened, but that was the style in the desert anyway. Kept the interior cool and helped the AC work.

But these modifications... Well, the man intended to stay for a while. Business for Ian Black must be damned good.

Victoria took a seat across the desk from Black. Nick took the other one. Black tapped on some keys at the computer and then looked up at them.

"The job's in Ras al-Dura. Two days' drive into the desert. There'll be an apartment waiting."

He pushed a key toward Victoria. She slipped it into her jeans pocket, and Nick pretended not to be irritated while he waited for the rest of the information.

"You need to leave right away," Black said.

Victoria shoved back and started to stand.

"Wait a minute," Nick said, and she stopped moving.

Black looked up, his dark eyes landing on Nick with a look of annoyance. "What is it?"

Nick blinked. "The target? The objective? Don't we need to discuss that?"

Black flicked a glance at Victoria before looking at Nick again. "Just get into place. You'll learn the rest when you need to know."

"Come on," Victoria said. "You'll get the hang of it soon enough."

Nick scraped his chair back and stood. He didn't like this. He didn't fucking like it at all. Black was still watching him, one eyebrow lifted as if to say, *"What of it, asshole?"*

Nick managed to shrug as if it was no big deal. "Yeah, whatever."

He followed Victoria from the room, seething the whole time. This wasn't what he'd expected. Mendez wanted him to learn what Black was up to, not take off into the desert after some unknown target immediately upon arrival. But what the fuck could he do about it? Nothing, because that would arouse Black's suspicion. Nick had expected to be sent on a mission—just not within literally an hour of arriving.

Either he had shitty luck or Black was one crafty motherfucker. Nothing to do about it now but get his gear and head into the desert.

There was a white Land Rover waiting inside the outer courtyard to the compound when Victoria came downstairs from retrieving her gear. She started for the driver's side but realized that someone was already in it.

Nick.

She thought about telling him to slide over and give her the wheel, but then she decided what the hell. Two days' drive, which meant they'd have to share the duty anyway.

And if he wanted to start the trip, then fine with her.

She yanked open a rear door and slung her gear inside. Then she climbed into the passenger seat and put on her seat belt. Nick was quiet, but she knew he was seething. He was wearing mirrored sunglasses, and she couldn't see his eyes as he looked over at her. But his hands flexed on the wheel as if he were using it like a stress ball.

She slammed her door and met his gaze. "You planning to drive or stare?"

He shifted into gear, and the gate to the street opened. They emerged into the bright sunlight of a hot desert day and turned left, heading toward the highway. They'd driven maybe ten miles when Nick slowed the car and pulled over onto an access road. Cars whizzed past as Nick stopped.

"What are you doing?"

He whipped the glasses off and gave her a hard look. "Gotta piss."

Except he didn't. He sorted through his gear until he found something small that looked like a fat pen. Then he walked around the Land Rover, sweeping the device back and forth. He bent down for a second, then popped back up. Last, he swept the interior.

"No bugs," he said as he stowed the device and got inside again. "We're free to talk."

"You found something outside."

"Tracking device. Rather expected that, though."

"Your guys?"

"Nope. Yours."

She blinked as Nick looked at her.

"What, you think Black doesn't keep tabs on you, sweetheart? Because he does."

She swallowed as a bead of sweat trickled between her breasts. No, she hadn't known Ian put a tracker on the vehicle. It wasn't necessarily a bad thing, considering how dangerous Qu'rim was, but it surprised her she hadn't known. That he hadn't told her.

She reached out and turned the AC up, though not quite enough. You had to be careful not to tax the cooling system on the engine too much out here or you could find yourself sitting on the side of the road with a blown radiator.

"What of it? It's his equipment. And I have nothing to hide."

She knew as soon as she said it that it wasn't true. Not anymore, anyway. She had plenty to hide since she'd walked into a bunker with this man yesterday and shifted her loyalties to a colonel who'd promised her the moon.

And if that colonel didn't deliver—if Nick didn't deliver—she'd kill them both if it was the last thing she did. She had no time for softness, no time for anything but finding Emily and getting her home again. But after two years, her ability to tolerate disappointment was eroding fast. Since she figured she was already an outlaw in the eyes of the US government, she didn't much care if she made things worse for herself if these guys didn't give her what she wanted.

"Maybe a couple of things to hide," Nick said as he eased back onto the highway. "I can't disable it because he'll know right away. After we've been on the road a while, I'll make sure it's damaged."

"So he'll think it happened while we were driving."

"Yep."

Ahead, the desert was flat and brown, but in the far distance, above the shimmering heat on the horizon, there were sandstone mountains. She knew it more than she could see it, but that's because she'd been out here before. The desert was strangely compelling in its own way, the kind of place that was harsh and beautiful all at once. She both loved it and hated it.

"This is a damn strange way to work. No idea who the target is or why."

Nick's voice cut into her thoughts, and she turned to look at his profile. Her belly did a little flip, like always. Annoying, but nothing she could do about it.

"You always know who you're sent to kill?"

"Hell yes, I know. And I know why." He shot her a look. "You just take your orders and go, never knowing who you're killing or why? Doesn't that bother you at

95

all?"

Her stomach started to burn. "Ian knows what he's doing. I trust him."

Or she used to trust him, anyway. Now she didn't know who to trust. Ian had an agenda. Nick had an agenda. She was unimportant in the scheme of things so long as they got what they wanted in the end. She wasn't naive enough to think she mattered to either one of them. Just because Nick had promised to help her find Emily didn't mean he cared one iota about her or her sister.

"He sent you into danger in Akhira. Alone."

"He said he didn't know that bin Yusuf wanted me dead. I believe him."

"And you think this job isn't a setup?"

Of course she'd considered the possibility. She had to. But she wasn't admitting it to him. "This mission? Why would it be? Ian doesn't need to send us two days into the desert to kill us, if that's what you're thinking."

Nick's fingers tightened on the wheel. "No, he doesn't. All he needs is for someone to intercept us on the way."

Sweat moistened her palms. Yeah, she'd thought of that too. And they both knew that since there was really only one main road from north to south, disabling the tracking device would only give them a margin of protection.

"Then you better hope your people are watching out for us. Did you get a message to them?"

"Direct communication is too risky, so no, I didn't."

Victoria licked her lips. "You mean they don't know where we are?"

She'd been counting on that to keep them safe. Picturing all those big men bristling with high-tech gear in a van somewhere on the road behind them.

"I didn't say that. But I wouldn't put all my hope on the cavalry riding in to save the day if we're ambushed."

"Then we'll just have to do it ourselves, won't we?" Victoria unbuckled her seat belt and started to crawl into the backseat.

"What the fuck are you doing?"

Her hips bumped against his shoulders but she kept going until she was in the back. Then she reached for her gun case and unzipped it. Her fingers brushed cool steel and her heart slowed a fraction. This was what she knew how to do.

"Getting prepared," she said, finally answering Nick's query.

He was watching her in the rearview, a hard frown on his handsome face. She lifted the barrel and stock and started assembling the weapon.

NINE

THERE WAS SOMETHING DAMNED AROUSING about a woman in a tank top and faded jeans assembling a rifle. Nick kept glancing into the rearview to watch Victoria work. Her fingers were small and slender, and they moved over the parts of the rifle with confidence. But that wasn't the best part.

No, the best part was the way her top stretched over her breasts and gave him a view of rounded swells as she leaned over and her flesh was exposed. His dick was hardening whether he wanted it to or not. He shifted in the seat, trying to ease the pressure on his swelling cock.

Jeez.

He knew he should just watch the road and stop looking, but hell, what man could resist tits on display? Especially when they belonged to the only woman who'd ever disliked him on sight. Hell, even if she hadn't disliked him as she'd insisted, she'd done a good job of acting like it.

But then she'd kissed him at the American base, and even though he'd known it was meant to be a sweet kiss on his cheek, he'd turned his head and taken what he really wanted from her.

And she hadn't resisted. She'd kissed him back, her body melting for an instant. She'd been soft and sweet and so intoxicating. He still didn't know how he'd let her go. How he'd stood there and watched her get into that car, her eyes fixed on his until the car turned out of sight.

She finished assembling the gun and looked up, her gaze colliding with his in the rearview. There were dark circles beneath her gray eyes, and the corners of her mouth were pinched. Victoria was under a lot of strain, but he wasn't sure what kind of strain it was.

What if she'd betrayed him to Black and this was all for show? What if she trusted her boss more than she trusted Mendez, and she'd lured them in like a spider on a web? For all he knew, he was barreling toward his own execution instead of a job they were meant to do together.

Maybe that's why Black hadn't given any information. And maybe that's why Victoria hadn't insisted. *He* could be the one being set up. He knew it, but that hadn't been enough of a reason to abort the mission. He was here, and he wasn't going down easily or quickly.

In spite of the fact the woman in the backseat held a loaded rifle and had access to an entire arsenal at her fingertips. He wasn't unarmed, but it wasn't enough against a woman of her skill. He took comfort in the fact she wasn't going to shoot him while he was driving since that would be suicide.

"Got what you need?" he asked.

She leaned her head back on the seat for a second. "Yes. No one's taking us without a fight."

He couldn't help but grin. "That's pretty much my philosophy too. You didn't think I planned to pull over and give up, did you?"

She shook her head. "Not precisely."

Maybe she was only putting on a show, but she looked determined as hell to repel any would-be attackers. She sighed and shifted the guns around so they were in easy reach, then she climbed back into the front seat and tucked a pistol into the door pocket at her side. She'd come over the seat face-first, her top dipping so low he could see her belly button, her hair sliding over her shoulder and onto his. He could feel her heat, smell her perfume—not actual perfume, but soap and shampoo and sweat—and he wanted to groan. Then he wanted to find a nice hotel and take her to a room where he could have his way with her for several hours.

Not a good time for this, dude.

Victoria glanced at him, her cheeks reddening slightly. "What?"

He cleared his throat and hoped she didn't look down at his crotch. He was wearing cammies and jump boots, but still. The pants weren't tight, but his problem would be rather obvious if she looked close enough.

"Just enjoying the view." Because he couldn't help teasing her, even if he probably shouldn't.

"You mean the desert, of course." She swiveled her head to look at the flat landscape before them. "Lovely."

He couldn't help but laugh. Or tell the truth. "I meant you, but all right."

"I knew you were looking down my shirt," she said, her voice sounding all prim and scandalized. God, it turned him on. Because she looked tough and dirty, not at all innocent. The voice of a virgin and the body of a sinner.

"You can look down mine if it makes you feel better," he said.

He didn't think she'd say anything, but she suddenly reached over and jerked his T-shirt from his pants, revealing his belly and chest as she shoved it upward. It was shocking. And arousing, goddammit. He wanted to groan.

"How about I look *up* your shirt instead?" she purred.

"Jesus, Victoria. If you want more, all you gotta do is fucking ask."

She let the shirt go and it fell. "You're not my type," she said, sitting back and adjusting her sunglasses. "Sorry."

He snorted. "What, male? That not your type, sweetheart?"

She made an indelicate noise. "I like men just fine. I don't like big, brawny men with more muscles than brains."

He gripped the wheel and stared at the road in front of them. Then he laughed as he remembered that kiss they'd shared. Not interested in him? Yeah, right. "You're so full of shit. Up to your pretty eyebrows."

She propped a foot on the dash and wrapped an arm around her knee. "I'm too focused on what I need to do. Sorry. Another place, another lifetime, maybe you'd be fun for a few hours." She shrugged. "But not now. Not when Emily's out there somewhere, counting on me."

Yeah, she was full of shit. Because he was beautiful, his skin golden and hot, and she'd nearly jerked her fingers away as they sizzled from that simple touch when she'd yanked his shirt up. God, what had she been thinking to touch him like that?

She'd just wanted to unnerve him a little bit, but she'd unnerved herself instead.

Victoria shoved her hair off her shoulder and concentrated on the flat desert sand in front of them. They'd been riding for less than two hours now, and already her body was keyed up, like a lightning rod that had taken a strike and had nowhere to discharge it. Her skin sizzled with energy, and her fingers tapped a relentless beat on her leg as she held her knee and focused her attention ahead of the car.

"Tell me about her," he said, and her head swiveled around to look at him. He glanced at her but then turned his attention back to the road. His big hands gripped the wheel steadily, and she found that she could almost relax with him. Almost, but not quite. She hadn't trusted Jonah as far as she could throw him, and he'd driven like shit. Her partner before him had left after a month, unable to handle the heat—in more ways than one—and eager to get back to Iowa, or somewhere equally normal and reasonably safe.

None of her partners had ever asked about her life. Oh, some of them had expressed an interest in getting horizontal with her, much as Nick had—but there was something about his suggestions that made her belly spark and her pussy clench and her breath shorten. The others had simply pissed her off.

She was so used to holding her past close that she almost told him to fuck off. And then she decided what the hell. What did it matter? He was risking his life by being here, the same as she was, and while he was doing it for his colonel and a cause, he was still doing it when he didn't have to. It could have been anyone else in his unit— but it was Nick Brandon, and at least she sort of knew him.

Besides, part of her wanted him to understand.

"She used to be a sweet kid. Open, trusting, desperately seeking love and belonging." Victoria sucked in a sharp breath. "We were orphaned, you see. My grandfather took us in—but then he died and we went into foster care. It didn't work out so well."

"I'm sorry."

"It was a long time ago. No one harmed us. But we were... unwanted, I think. Emily felt it worse than I did because she was younger. I still remember our parents. She doesn't. Gramps was all we had—and then he was gone."

"You think bin Yusuf made her feel as if she belonged somewhere?"

Victoria swallowed the sudden lump in her throat. Her hands clenched into fists, her nails digging into her palms. She wouldn't cry, wouldn't let him know how much she blamed herself. If she'd been there, instead of in the Army...

"He must have. He's very... charismatic. He's obsessed with Americans—or was, anyway. Completely gets the culture and psyche."

"You think he singled her out."

"I don't really know. I wasn't there." She ran her hands through her hair, scrubbed her scalp as if she could scrub away the bad memories and the guilt. "I joined the Army, looking for a way out, you know? I wanted the security and the college fund. I wanted to make her my dependent, help her get clean. But she took up with Zaran, and that was the end of everything. The Army didn't appreciate the connection to a radical terrorist, apparently."

He was silent for a long moment. "So you left the Army and ended up here."

"I have a skill that's useful. I'll never get to use the G.I. Bill now, but with the money Ian pays me, I'll be able to take care of Emily and maybe go to college someday too. It was the best option I had."

"I'm not judging you, Victoria."

"You already did that, Preacher Boy. A couple of weeks ago, unless my memory fails me."

He didn't even comment on her use of the nickname he hated. "Yeah, I did. But I was fucking pissed. You ruined my shot, and you let that asshole get away."

"I had to, don't you get that?" she snapped. And then she shook her head, wondering how she'd let the conversation get this far away from her. Why had she thought she could spill her guts, even a little bit? There was a price to be paid when you let it all out.

"He's the only link I have to Emily. If something happens to him, then what happens to her? I couldn't take that chance."

The silence stretched out between them like a wire pulled tight. "I have a sister," he finally said.

His voice was even, mild, and she blinked as if they'd entered a time warp. She'd expected him to say something about what she'd done out there when she'd shot the opposition commander instead of bin Yusuf. Or something about Ian and how dirty he had to be for ordering it done.

She hadn't expected him to say he had a sister. It confused her and made a feeling swell in her chest that she didn't quite know how to process. Her gut reaction was to lash out, to push him away.

"Congratulations."

The minute she snapped at him, she felt sorry for it. But he didn't snap back.

"Her name is Shelly and she's gay. Not that I fucking care, but my parents did. Still do. They disowned her—and I disowned them. So yeah, sweetheart, I get why you're doing this. I'd do anything to erase the pain of our parents' betrayal, to make them see that Shel is normal and beautiful just the way she is. But they don't fucking care. It's a sin, and Shel is evil in their eyes for not changing to suit them. They don't care how much they hurt her by refusing to acknowledge her existence." His fingers tightened on the wheel. "Well, *I* care. And I'd do anything to make her happy, so yeah, I get it."

Her vision was blurry now, damn him. Finally, someone who might really understand. Not just express sympathy and secretly wonder why she didn't simply let her sister self-destruct. Anyone who was so foolish as to get herself tangled up with a man who professed hatred of the United States and all Americans surely deserved what she got, right?

Well, not when you could still remember her hugging you tight at night because she was scared of a monster under the bed, or when she followed you on her bike even when you told her not to because you were meeting with your friends and then cried when you got angry and said you didn't want her around because she was still a baby and you weren't. Victoria had soothed fears, bandaged scrapes, and taught her sister what it meant when she got her period.

Gramps had been wonderful, but there were some

things he either didn't think of or didn't want to think of because he was uncomfortable with them. Ushering two girls into teenage-dom hadn't been easy, that's for sure.

Gramps had told them endless stories about his days in the Army. "We didn't leave no man behind, little missies. Not ever. You could count on your fellow soldier to take care of you. And you can count on us to take care of each other, am I right?"

Leave no man behind. That's what she was doing. Or no woman, in this case. Victoria rolled her fingers into a fist, digging her nails into her palm so she wouldn't cry at the thought of Emily and all that had gone wrong.

"Thanks for telling me that," she said, her voice tight. "Shelly is lucky to have you for a brother."

He shrugged, but a muscle in his jaw tensed as if he were suppressing strong emotion. "We'll find your sister, Victoria. I promise we will."

TEN

NICK DROVE WELL INTO THE night. When he finally got too tired to keep going, he found a place to pull off the road and park. There were other cars parked along the roadway as well, jammed up in little clusters for safety—or the illusion of safety. The road to the south was well patrolled by government forces, and they'd managed to keep it open for the past couple of months now. But there was always a risk that the opposition forces would cut the roadway off again.

Victoria sat up as he put the Land Rover in park. She'd been curled into her seat for the past two hours, sleeping. She blinked and pushed her hair out of her face. "Where are we?"

"Stopping for the night."

She peered through the window at the cars. "Is this safe?"

He let his gaze slide over the other cars. A couple of men had gathered together to smoke and talk, but mostly it was quiet.

"As safe as anything, I imagine. Better this than pulling off somewhere alone, wouldn't you say? At least we're part of a group."

"Hmm, maybe so." She didn't sound completely convinced.

He'd disabled the tracking device a few hours ago now, so even if Ian Black was targeting them for someone—feeding information to bin Yusuf—they weren't easily identifiable at the moment. He'd made Victoria shut off her phone earlier, though she'd argued, but there was really no way he could be certain Black hadn't tagged her phone. She'd agreed with the logic, though she'd been pissed.

His phone was fine because it had never been out of his possession, but he'd still turned it off after a quick message to his team leader. Matt Girard would know what to do with the information, and that was the best Nick could hope for.

"I could drive for a while," Victoria said. "Get us a bit farther."

Nick shook his head. "We'll stay here for a few hours, then leave again at daylight."

He could feel her bristling in the dark. And he just knew that one eyebrow was arched imperiously.

"Since when are you in charge?"

"Since you agreed to work for us in exchange for your sister and clearing your name."

She was silent, and he knew he had her.

"Fine," she said after a minute. But she didn't sound happy about it.

He opened his door and put a foot out. "I'll put the seats down in the back, and we can bed down there."

Her eyes flashed in the lights from oncoming traffic.

"Shouldn't someone stay in the driver's seat? Just in case?"

"We're armed, Victoria. If anyone fucks with us, I'd rather shoot them than drive over them."

"I meant in case we need to escape, dickhead."

"I know what you meant. And I don't think it's something we have to worry about tonight. We weren't followed, no one pulled off when we did, and the tracking device was disabled hours ago. I think we can sleep for a few hours—though we'll sleep with guns beneath our heads."

She didn't say anything else and he powered the windows down an inch or so before he got out and opened the passenger door. The desert was cool at night, thankfully, and all they needed was a little fresh air. Then he went about putting the seats down and shifting their gear until it lined the sides and they could sleep in the middle with their packs as pillows. After the bedding was ready, he shut and locked the driver's side and then climbed into the back. Victoria didn't move from her position in the passenger seat as he stretched out as much as was possible for a six-three male inside a vehicle with the seats down.

He arranged his weapons so he could reach the Sig first. His knife was strapped to one ankle, and he had a smaller pistol strapped to the other.

"You staying up there?"

"Maybe."

"Suit yourself. Just means I have more room back here."

She leaned the seat back a bit, though it didn't go as far as it might have if he hadn't put the back seats down.

"This is the part I hate," she said after a while. "Sitting and waiting."

Nick snorted. "That's what being a sniper is, honey. But you knew that already."

"I know. I like being inside my own head, thinking about things—but the longer I do this, the more I hate the prep. I'd rather just get the job done and go."

"Some jobs are that way."

"Some. Not enough."

Nick shifted to his back and bent his knees. "Where did you learn to shoot?"

She sighed. "My gramps. He was a Green Beret in Vietnam. He didn't much know what to do with two little girls, but when he thought we should know how to handle a weapon, I took to it like a fish to water."

He could hear the wistfulness in her voice. She'd had a tough life. He was beginning to realize that. His had been tough in a different way, but it hadn't been as lonely as hers. He'd been surrounded by good people, and he'd been encouraged in every way possible so long as he toed a straight and narrow line. Fishing and hunting had been a way of life where he was from, and he'd grown up with a rifle in his hands. He'd never thought back then, spending his days in the beautiful Ozarks of Missouri, that he'd one day target people with his rifle.

"That was a beautiful shot you made," he said. They both knew he was talking about that day two weeks ago in the desert. "I admired the skill even though I was pissed as hell you fucked up my mission."

She sighed. "I didn't know who the target was until I got out there. And I didn't know bin Yusuf would be there until the last minute. It wasn't easy to do the job and not accidentally on purpose hit him too."

He chuckled. "Yeah, I imagine so." He let out a sigh and put his hands behind his head. He didn't want to say the next part, but he had to know if she'd considered it. He had to know where her head was. "You know she may already be gone, right? That it could already be too late?"

"I know." Her voice was small, and he hated that he'd said anything at all.

He could hear her breathing and figured she was working hard to hold in her emotions.

"Victoria…" He wanted to drag her into his arms and hold her close, but he didn't think she'd welcome it. So he lay there, staring up at the ceiling, and did nothing.

"I can't think that way yet." She sounded almost breathless. "I can't give up until I have proof."

"I understand that. If she's out there, we'll find her."

"You're my last hope, Nick. That's the only reason I'm doing this. I don't like the way betrayal tastes in my mouth, but I'll do anything for Emily."

"You care about Black." He didn't like that she did. Not at all. It made something inside his belly twist and writhe.

"We've been together for two years. He's always treated me fairly."

"And if he set you up? Betrayed you to bin Yusuf?"

He saw her shake her head in the darkness. "There's no proof he did."

She had a strong sense of loyalty, and this situation had to be testing her to the limit.

Or maybe not. He had to remember that it was possible she was on Black's side and this whole thing was a setup for him and HOT. He couldn't discount anything just because she made him ache with need. In fact, that was

111

probably the best reason of all to be more vigilant than ever.

"Sometimes there is no proof. Sometimes there's only a gut feeling."

Victoria slept badly, slouched as she was. Finally, when she could take it no more, she crawled into the back of the Land Rover and lay down beside Nick. He was curled on his side, his knees drawn up, and she had to work her way carefully into the hole he'd left for her. The only light was from the stars and a very late-rising moon that was already sinking fast toward the horizon.

But it was enough to see the curve of his jaw. Her heart thumped, and her fingers ached to reach out and caress the stubbled skin. In spite of everything, in spite of the heartache and danger, she hadn't stopped thinking of the way his mouth had felt pressed to hers. Of the way her body had lit up like a gasoline-soaked rag, burning hot and fast, and how she'd wanted to cool the flame by merging into him and letting him ease the burn.

In spite of everything, that knowledge had sat at the bottom of her psyche, teasing her, testing her, making her miserable.

She turned on her side, away from him, determined to sleep and not look at him. No wonder. She'd just started to drift off when a hand settled on her hip, instantly waking her. Victoria swallowed, her pulse kicking up, and held herself very still. He was asleep and no doubt accustomed to sharing his bed with a woman. A woman he would touch while they lay together.

Torturous seconds passed, and then his hand slid over her hip, to her belly, and tugged her back against him, fitting her bottom snugly against his groin.

And oh, he was hard. Full and hard, and big enough that sweat popped out on her skin as she imagined what taking him inside her would feel like. His lips settled on her neck, nibbling softly, and she suppressed a whimper. She should move, she knew she should. She should shove him away, shove herself away, and wake him up with a choice curse or maybe a bite to the hand currently cupping her breast over the fabric of her tank top.

Her nipple hardened and she had to bite her lip to keep a moan from escaping as his fingers scraped across the surface again and again. She half wanted him to slip his fingers beneath her shirt and touch her bare skin, but if he did that she thought she might come unglued.

His mouth found her earlobe, his teeth nibbled gently, and liquid heat flooded her. She was wet and hot, and her heart beat hard. She'd been touched before, been kissed, and she'd felt the heat of attraction burning her from the inside out. But she'd never felt quite this way, quite this turned on and aching for a man no matter the consequences. Before, she'd always known what the consequences were, and she'd always managed to use them to stop herself from doing something she might regret.

Nick turned her in his arms then, his body pressing her down into the carpet, one leg going between hers and putting pressure right on the sweet bundle of nerves at the apex of her thighs.

His hands slid up her sides, shaping her as his mouth

came down on hers. Victoria was too stunned to protest. And too overwhelmed by heat and emotion to care. Her hands went up, presumably to push him away, but instead they wrapped around his neck. Her mouth slipped open as his tongue plunged inside, drawing her into a sensual stroking that made her grow wetter than before.

He kissed her long and hard before he broke away with a groan, his mouth on her throat, moving down toward her breasts.

"You're so fucking hot, Victoria," he said against her skin, and she stiffened at the sound of her name.

"You're awake?" she gasped.

His head lifted, his brows drawn low. "Of course I'm fucking awake. Would you prefer I did this asleep?"

She shoved at his mountain of shoulders until he took the hint and rolled away. Victoria scrambled out from under him, her body a mass of thwarted desire and anger.

"I thought you were asleep!"

He shoved a hand through his hair. "I kinda was at first, when you lay down. I thought I was… somewhere else. Don't usually have a woman lying beside me on a job, do I?"

"But then you realized who I was. And you didn't stop." She tried to sound as offended as possible, but even she realized it was pretty ridiculous. She'd had her tongue down his throat too.

"You didn't seem as if you wanted me to stop. You were kissing me back. Rubbing your body against mine. I thought you were as turned on as I was."

She was, damn him. But she wasn't going to admit it. She folded her arms over her chest and rubbed her forearms. "I… I didn't want to be rude."

"Rude?"

He started to laugh then and her face flamed. God, what a stupid answer. What a stupid, stupid answer.

"The right response if you don't want to fuck someone is either to say no or to knee him in the balls. But use the knee only if he won't take no for an answer. And I would have, believe me. I'm not some mindless asshole who's ruled by his dick. I kinda like the woman to want me too."

"I'll make note of that." She sounded prim and he laughed even harder. Really, was it too much to ask to disappear into the sand below the vehicle right about now? Why couldn't she just shrug it off and tell him no big deal? Or, even better, why couldn't she drag him back to her and tell him to have his wicked way because she was more than ready?

He popped open the door and stepped outside. "Go ahead and sleep, Victoria."

"Where are you going?"

"Gonna drive, sweetheart. Unless you'd rather do something else?"

She couldn't think of a single thing to say. He shut the door, climbed into the front seat, and started the car. She lay down again, fuming at herself, at him, at the whole situation. She kept trying to think of things to say, a way to redeem herself, but nothing would come. Eventually, the road noise and hum of the engine lulled her to sleep.

ELEVEN

THEY DROVE ALL THAT DAY, taking turns, and long into the night. When they pulled over this time, Nick told her to get in the back and he'd stay up front. When she protested that he'd be more comfortable in the back, he gave her a steady look with those gleaming hazel eyes of his.

"Think it's best one of us stays on watch," he said.

"I don't disagree. But why does it have to be you?"

"Why is everything an argument with you?"

For some reason, that made her smile. "You like it that way and you know it. What would you do with someone who obeyed every command you gave her?"

He snorted. "I'd give her a lot of filthy commands that she could fulfill."

"Pig."

"Really? You're the one who mentioned this theoretical woman obeying all my commands."

"Oh, for fuck's sake, I'll sleep first," she grumbled, crawling in the back just to shut him up. Next thing, he'd be telling her what those commands would be—and she didn't need to hear it.

They were much farther from Baq than they'd been last night, and the roads out here were less traveled and more dangerous. It didn't take two days to get to Ras al-Dura because it was so far. It took two days because of the crumbling infrastructure and the roving patrols. But Ian had contacts, and so far they'd sailed through every checkpoint.

Still, it didn't pay to forget they were far from help if something happened. Victoria went to sleep much quicker than she expected, only to be awakened by a rough hand what seemed like minutes later.

"Get up, honey. We gotta move on."

"But you didn't sleep."

"You drive. I'll nap in the passenger seat."

She got behind the wheel and headed out onto the road. The sun was still behind the horizon, and the sky was darker tonight because of cloud cover. Nick leaned back in his seat, eyes closed, hands folded over his belly. She didn't kid herself by thinking he was unaware, however. The handle of a Sig Sauer peeked out of his shoulder holster, and she knew he'd snap awake and draw it in a flash if they encountered trouble.

Fortunately, they didn't. They rolled into Ras al-Dura as the call to prayer rang from the minarets of the city's mosques. It took about fifteen minutes, but they found the apartment where they were supposed to stay. As soon as she saw it, she knew what the target was. She glanced at Nick. He was also studying the big compound across the street with interest. There was a crest on the gate, which indicated that it was an official building. There were two guards stationed on the street, holding machine guns and watching the traffic slide by.

Whoever they were here for, he was going to be in that building.

Nick looked grim as she turned into the parking garage attached to the apartment building. "I don't fucking like this at all."

"The job is the job, Nick. It'll be all right."

"Unless Black's setting us up."

She didn't like to think of that possibility, but she knew he was right. Anything was possible out here. Her gut told her Ian hadn't known that bin Yusuf had intended to kill her in Akhira, but that didn't mean he wasn't on board with the project now. Ian was all about the business and the money, and if selling her out kept the money flowing, then she wasn't so certain he wouldn't do it, no matter what he said about her being his best sniper.

"Do you have a better plan? Because so far as I see it, we've been sent to do a job. The job is here. If you and your people want to know what Ian's up to, you have to complete the job and return to Baq. If we bug out now, it's over."

"I know that. I still don't like it."

She parked the Land Rover and they got out. Nick's gaze roved the darkened garage, but nothing was out of place and no one came gunning for them out of the shadows.

"Give me the key to the apartment," he told her.

"Why?"

"Because I'll go up and check it out, see if it's safe."

"What makes you think I can't do it?"

He was a big hulking shape standing over her in the gloom. For a second, she thought he might take the key by

118

force, but then his mouth opened and his teeth flashed white. "Be my guest. I'll wait here."

She seriously thought of doing it, but then she had to acknowledge that if this was a setup, it probably wasn't the best idea to go strolling upstairs alone. Still, she wasn't letting him have his way about everything.

"We'll go together," she said, reaching into the Land Rover for her gear.

He jerked his own bags from the vehicle. "If that's what you want, honey."

They took the elevator up to the fifteenth floor. She glanced over at Nick before the doors opened. His jaw was set and he had his hand on his Sig. The doors slid open… and nothing happened. They exited the elevator into a long hallway. It was quiet as they moved down the corridor. They found the apartment, but before she could put the key in the lock, Nick stopped her.

"Just a minute," he said, pulling something from a pocket in his duffel. He took out a white swab and a small item that looked like a tube with a flashlight at one end. Then he proceeded to run the swab over the doorframe and handle before inserting it in the tube and looking at it under the light.

"Is that an ETD?"

She could tell he was testing for explosives residue, but she'd certainly never seen a device so small.

He nodded. Then he dropped the items into the duffel pocket and nodded. "It's clear. Go ahead and open it."

"That's amazing. Where'd you get it?"

If that was available on the open market, Ian would have had one. But he didn't.

Nick grinned. "We're well funded. And we get to

play with prototypes."

She blinked at him. She still didn't know who *we* was. She'd thought they were Delta Force, but Nick said they weren't. Didn't mean he was telling the truth, but then again, this part about him being here with her and undercover was a bit out of the ordinary. More like the CIA than anything.

But she didn't think he was that, either.

She slid the key into the lock and turned. The door swung open to reveal a long room with two chairs and a small table. The apartment was a corner unit with a sweeping view of the compound across the street. The windows were wide and tall—and they slid open on tracks, which was perfect for access.

They dropped the gear in the center of the room. Nick went into the adjoining rooms with his bug sweeper.

"We're clear," he said when he returned. "And there's a bed, so at least we have that."

Victoria pushed her hair over her shoulders. "I hope there are towels, though I'm going to shower regardless."

"There are."

She walked over to the refrigerator and opened it. There was food and water, and she took a bottle out and twisted off the cap. "I need to call Ian and let him know we're here."

Nick's expression said he wasn't thrilled about it, but he knew as well as she did that it had to be done. She'd turned her phone off two days ago, and Ian would be pretty pissed if he'd tried to call.

"Keep it as short as you can."

"This isn't my first rodeo, stud."

She went and fished the phone out of her bag and

turned it on, her heart hammering on the off chance that Emily had sent a message. She hadn't liked leaving the phone off, but it had been months, and she'd reasoned with herself that it was highly unlikely Emily would suddenly get in touch now.

Her phone started beeping with messages once it powered up. She scrolled through them with her heart in her throat, but they were all from Ian.

She dialed and walked over to the window. Ian picked up right away.

"Where the fuck have you been?"

Her already frayed temper spiked. "Driving, asshole, what do you think?"

"You dropped off the grid."

"Nothing unusual about that." She always went into radio silence on a job, though she usually checked in once a day. She hadn't done so this time, and he wasn't happy about it. Or maybe he wasn't happy for a different reason, such as bin Yusuf was breathing down his neck about being unable to find her.

Though now that they were here in this apartment, it was like turning on a homing beacon for anyone looking. The resigned expression on Nick's face said he knew it too. He was busy removing guns from his case, stowing them in easy reach. He also set something that looked like a speaker on the table—she knew it was actually a white-noise device—and then turned back to his gear and kept unpacking.

"Well, don't do it again. Jesus, Victoria, what if the target had changed locations? Or what if I had to get critical information to you?"

"I'll check in once a day, as always."

"Every four hours on this one. And keep the phone on. This one could change fast."

She gritted her teeth. "Fine, every four hours. Care to tell me what I'm here for?"

"I'll transmit the information when it's time. How's the pretty new recruit doing?"

Victoria swallowed. *Pretty?* She glanced over at Nick and her belly flipped. Yes, definitely pretty. Gorgeous, in fact. And, whoa, could the man kiss. Parts of her started to tingle. "Fine. Why?"

Ian chuckled. "Don't get distracted, Victoria."

"What makes you think I would?"

"You've been out here a long time. Gets lonely, doesn't it? Besides, I saw the way you looked at him."

She was pretty sure her ears were red. "A girl can look. Doesn't mean a damn thing."

"Let's keep it that way, all right?"

"Not that it's any of your business, but that's my intention."

She ended the call and looked up to find Nick watching her. Her mouth grew dry looking at him. Tall, dark, and brooding—just her type, it seemed. She hadn't known she had a type, but this one was pressing buttons she'd thought so rusty they wouldn't work.

"A girl can look at what?" he asked, his head tilted to one side as he leaned against the doorframe, oh so casually.

"At you." No sense lying about it. She'd stammer and turn red and he'd know anyway. "Ian seems to think there's interest and that maybe I can't keep my hands to myself."

One corner of that sensual mouth turned up in a grin.

What would it feel like if she let him put that mouth on her skin again? If he slid his tongue around her nipple and pulled it between his lips?

The answering throb in her pussy was not a good sign.

"I'd like to think Ian's right. And if he is, you just feel free, sweetheart. Anytime you want to put your hands on me, I'm yours."

Victoria tucked her phone into her pocket. "Sorry to disappoint you, but you aren't that irresistible. Hot, yes. Tempting, yes. But not irresistible."

He unsnapped his shoulder holster and shrugged it off. Then he lifted the black T-shirt he was wearing and tugged it over his head with a grin. Broad shoulders tapered down to a narrow waist and abs that she could count. He wore a set of dog tags that hung between his nipples, gleaming silver in the light shafting into the room. His body was untouched by a tattoo needle, which was rather unusual for a military guy these days—or at least the ones she'd known—and he had a single scar that ran diagonally from beneath his left pectoral muscle to midway down his side. It wasn't an ugly scar, but it was noticeable.

Hell, everything about this man was noticeable. Her head started to swim. Her feet stuck to the floor. Nick slid a hand down his chest and flicked open the button of his cammies. Oh dear God...

"Wh...what are you doing?" She managed to force the words from her stiff lips.

"Heading for the shower, sweetheart." He arched an eyebrow at her. "If you care to join me, you know where it is. I promise I'll take good care of you. Wash every inch of your beautiful body and then lick it all over while you pant my name and beg me to finish the job."

Her skin was on fire. Her nipples, traitors that they were, were tightening. She folded her arms over her breasts and fixed him with a glare. "The only thing I plan to beg you to do is hurry up and get out of the damn shower so I can use it."

He laughed as he turned away. "Your loss."

She heard the shower turn on a couple of seconds later. She resolutely went over and slid into the chair to wait. For good measure, she sat on her hands and forced herself to think about the mission instead of the man.

Nick finished his shower and put the cammies back on with a fresh T-shirt. He didn't usually go on jobs with showers or beds, but when they were there, you had to take advantage of them. He strapped his guns back into place—shoulder, ankle, small of back—and walked out into the hallway. Victoria was at the small stove, doing something with food that was beginning to smell heavenly.

He picked up an orange from the bowl on the counter and started to peel it. "Thought you wanted a shower."

"My stomach growled."

"Is there enough there for me?"

She flashed him a look that would flay the hide off a lesser man. "I'm not your maid, Preacher Boy."

He separated the orange segments and put one in his mouth, savoring the juice sliding over his taste buds. He imagined rubbing a segment around Victoria's nipple, licking the sweet juice off her body. His cock liked that idea too, throbbing to life in an instant.

"Didn't we discuss this name business, Vicky?"

"Sorry. I'm not your maid, *dickhead*. That better?"

He couldn't help but laugh. Victoria Royal was one of the crankiest women he'd ever known. Hell, one of the crankiest *people* he'd ever known. And even if she didn't like him, she did want him. That he was certain of after their little misunderstanding in the car.

"You need to get laid, Vic. Ease up some of that tension you got going."

"And you know just the guy, right?"

"I *am* the guy."

She turned, spatula in hand. "Word to the wise, but I'm pretty sure there's not a woman alive who likes a man telling her he knows what's best for her."

He finished the orange and started licking his fingers. Her cheeks colored and she quickly turned back to the pan. For a cranky, prickly woman, she had the most expressive face. And she got embarrassed over the tiniest things. Almost as if she didn't know how to handle anything sexual.

"All right, I don't know a damn thing," he said. "But I think easing some of that tension you got going with a good orgasm or two might help you relax. I'm willing to sacrifice myself for the sake of your health—or you can do it yourself if you prefer."

She didn't say anything. Instead, she picked up a plate and slid an enormous omelet onto it. Then she set it on the counter between them. She took two forks from a drawer and handed him one.

"Seriously? After I pissed you off?"

"Just take it, for fuck's sake."

He did, and they dug in at the same time. She blew on the bite on her fork, then popped it in her mouth and chewed. He took a bite after she did, pretty sure now that she'd eaten it she wasn't trying to poison him for pissing her off.

"It's good." He meant it. He didn't know what she'd added, but it was more than just a cheese omelet.

"I'm sorry I snapped at you." She forked another bite. "You press my buttons pretty hard."

He wanted to say something about pressing the *right* buttons and how good that would feel, but he wisely refrained.

"Understandable. This isn't an easy situation for you. You're working for us, Black thinks you're working for him—and there's a terrorist out there who not only has your sister, but who's also tried to kill you recently. It's a lot to deal with."

"And you wonder if I'm still working for Black and setting you up, right?"

He wasn't able to hide his surprise. In fact, he nearly choked on the omelet and hot cheese. But he managed to swallow and followed it with a swig of water.

She was looking at him with an arched eyebrow, daring him to deny it.

"Yeah, I wondered that."

"If I thought Ian could get Emily for me, I'd have told you and your colonel to go fuck yourselves. He's had two years. It's your turn."

"Fair enough."

They ate in silence until the omelet was gone. She dropped her fork and stretched, her breasts pushing outward as she arched her back. Her skin was creamy and spotted with freckles. He wanted to see more, but he knew she wasn't going to show him.

"I'm going to take a shower, and then I'm climbing into that bed and sleeping for a couple of hours. Unless you object?"

He shook his head. "Nope. Best to catch up on sleep now since we have no idea how long we'll be here or when the target will appear."

"That's what I thought."

She sashayed away from him, and he turned and peered over his shoulder. She had a nice ass. He loved the way her hair fell to the middle of her back, a thick curtain he'd love to wind his fists into before burying his face in it and dragging her scent into his lungs.

He waited until he heard the shower, and then he went and tried the bathroom door just to make sure she was in there. Locked, of course. He laughed to himself as he pulled his phone from his pocket and powered it up.

He speed-dialed Matt Girard, making sure he could see the bathroom door in case she decided to creep out and listen to his phone call. It was a risk to call the team, but he needed to do so now while he had the chance.

His team leader answered on the first ring. "Brandy, thank God, *mon ami*. Been wondering about you."

"All's good for the moment." He'd already given his team the general address of this place, but now he added a report about their surroundings. He could hear keys tapping and knew that Billy Blake was hard at work doing what he did best.

"Kid says it's the Russian consulate across from you. There's oil in that part of Qu'rim, and the Russians are big players in the industry there."

Nick stared out the window. The consulate was surrounded by a tall stone wall with iron caps. There was a set of gardens leading to the house, which was about a hundred yards from the road. Not quite a football field in length. The windows running along the front of the building were tall and evenly spaced. But were they bulletproof?

"So Black could be targeting the Russians. Or bin Yusuf could, if Black's taking his orders from that quarter."

"Echo Squad is the closest to you. They're on standby if you need them."

Nick knew his own team remained in Baq, keeping a close eye on Ian Black, but he wished they were here. Not that another team wouldn't have his back, but still. These were his guys, and he hated flying solo. But, it was necessary if they were going to take down Black Security and put a stop to the shady dealings. Mendez trusted Alpha Squad more than anyone else in the unit, and they weren't going to let the colonel down.

"Copy." Nick sighed and sank onto a chair. "Can't figure out what we're supposed to be doing out here, but I still don't like it. We're sitting ducks."

"Echo Squad can be there in twenty minutes if need be. We're moving them into position now." There was a pause. "No sign of bin Yusuf in the Freedom Force's camp. We think he's on the move."

"Any word on Emily?"

"A white woman was seen within the past month. But she's being kept separate from the rest of the camp, so no idea if it's her or not."

"Shit," Nick breathed.

"We can't be certain it's Emily," Matt said, "but the description seemed to match. Still, I wouldn't tell Victoria if I were you."

"No, I don't think it'd be a good idea."

Because what if she got her hopes up and it was some other woman? Emily wasn't the only white woman to fall for an Arab man, surely. People fell in love with who they fell in love with—he knew that from watching his sister fight against her sexuality from an early age. She'd been told there was something wrong with her, and she'd tried to change what couldn't be changed.

The shower cut off, and he hurried to wrap up the call. When Victoria emerged about ten minutes later, her hair a dark auburn waterfall down her back, her face scrubbed clean, and her body encased in black pants and a black T-shirt, Nick nearly swallowed his tongue. Damn, she was sexy, and in a way that said she wasn't entirely certain of her appeal.

"Thought you were planning to sleep."

Her gray eyes had dark circles beneath them. "I was, but I'm too keyed up."

"Got a cure for that."

He couldn't help but tease her, mostly because he liked it when she flared up at him. And then there was the knowledge of that kiss they'd shared in the Land Rover and how they'd nearly combusted from that brief touch.

She glared at him. "Do you ever stop?"

He shrugged. "Can't blame a guy for trying. But yeah, I can stop. Just remember, Vic, how good that kiss felt. When you can't stop thinking about that, when you want to try a little more, all you gotta do is say the word."

TWELVE

THAT KISS *HAD* FELT GOOD, damn him. And the part where he'd been lying half on her, his hard cock pushing against her leg, had felt exhilarating in a way she hadn't expected. Victoria tried not to blush, but she knew it was useless. Her coloring gave her away every time.

Nick was watching her with that knowing expression he had that got beneath her skin and made her want to grab the back of his head and yank him down to her for a kiss.

Oh, he'd like that. The bitch of it was she would too.

She licked her lips and turned away, going over to her case and unzipping it so she could strap on her guns. The long rifle lay in pieces, ready to be assembled and set up just as soon as they had a target.

She let her gaze lift to the building across the street.

"It's the Russian Consulate," Nick said, and she turned to look at him, amazed he knew that already.

But then she realized that he must have called his people while she'd been in the shower.

"What else did they tell you?"

His gaze was steady on hers. "Nothing much. The

Russians are heavy into the oil industry here, but that's not criminal. Black is still in his compound, but that's no surprise. Bin Yusuf hasn't been seen in camp lately."

Her heart gave a little start. They had someone on the inside in the Freedom Force's camp? "What about Emily? Has anyone seen her?"

His eyes flickered and her hopes soared. "No."

She hadn't realized how much she'd wanted the answer to be yes until an involuntary whimper escaped her. Victoria bit down on the inside of her cheek as she turned away. She had to remain strong for Emily. Had to get her sister and clear her own name so she could have a normal life again. So she could make sure that Emily had a normal life, or as close to it as she would ever get after living with bin Yusuf for the past few years.

Nick put a hand on her shoulder and she stiffened, but all he did was squeeze before dropping his hand away again.

She turned back to him, arms folded over her chest. "I'm sorry."

He was looking at her with a troubled expression. "For what? Being upset about your sister? It's understandable, Victoria. If you weren't upset, I'd probably think you weren't human."

She dropped her gaze to the floor. "I am upset, but I, uh… Never mind. It's nothing."

She'd wanted to say she was sorry for being prickly with him, that she didn't know how else to be. But the words stuck in her throat.

The truth was he unnerved her, and she wasn't accustomed to it. She'd been pushing men away since she was a teenager, and she didn't quite know how to stop. She'd pushed because she had goals, and because Gramps had impressed on her that good girls didn't give away the milk for free if they wanted the man to value the cow.

She'd thought cows and milk were such a crude analogy, but she'd understood the point. And Gramps had said it with red ears and a throat he'd had to clear every ten seconds, so he'd clearly been uncomfortable. That was her sum total of the birds-and-the-bees talk from him.

Thankfully, she'd had her friends, romance novels, and cable television to enlighten her. But the lesson had stuck in her head, mostly because of Julia Gibson. Julia had gotten pregnant at age sixteen, left school to have the baby, and never came back. The father had been the star quarterback. He'd gone away to college on a football scholarship, but not before denying to everyone who'd listen that he'd ever had sex with Julia.

Victoria knew better because she'd been at the party that night when they'd disappeared into a parked car together and hadn't come out for a long time.

She was pulled against Nick suddenly, but it didn't frighten her. He opened his arms and wrapped them around her, but she didn't feel trapped. And she didn't feel like he meant anything by it except to comfort her. His hold was loose and he didn't make any moves to kiss her or pull her hips into his.

He just hugged her.

"It's okay, Vic. Don't worry about a thing. You don't have to tell me anything you don't want to tell me."

She thought she should push him away, but she really didn't want to. Instead, she put her arms around his waist and held him lightly. Something vibrated through him, but then he was still. He just stood there and held her, not speaking, not doing a thing other than rubbing his hand up and down her back.

She turned her cheek into his chest and closed her eyes. He was warm, and his heart thrummed hard and steady. After a couple of minutes, she felt a general stiffening in his body and she tilted her head up to look at him.

He shrugged and gave her a half smile. "Can't help it, sweetheart. You turn me on."

That's when she realized that a specific part of him was harder than the rest. She took a step back and let him go. "I'm sorry."

He laughed softly. "Don't apologize, Victoria. When it comes to you, I've learned it's gonna happen whether I want it to or not."

She could feel the heat creeping into her cheeks. His brows drew together, and she knew he'd seen it too.

"Does it really bother you that I'm attracted to you?"

She swallowed. Did it bother her? Hell, no. But it did disconcert her, because for once in her life she really hated that she had so little experience with this kind of thing. Who got to be twenty-five years old without having had sex with a man? And how in the hell did she ever admit that to a soul?

It sounded so stupid, so unbelievable. And there was no way he *would* believe her, so she wasn't exactly intending to tell him the truth.

"It doesn't bother me," she said, her voice a little rustier than she would like.

"I think it does in some way." His voice was quieter than before. Thoughtful. "I hope you know—really know—that I'd never use my strength against you."

Her eyes widened and she could feel her blush deepening. "N…no, of course not. I never meant to imply—"

"I didn't think you did. I just wanted you to know it. I don't know what kind of guys you've worked with before, but if any of them ever, uh, assumed anything… well, I don't. I've teased you up until now because you piss me off in so many ways that I can't quite believe it. But I'm not an asshole, Victoria. I'm really not."

The effects of that speech were still reverberating through her. Warming her and stunning her at the same time. Yes, she'd had to fend off some of the guys she'd worked with, though none of them had ever physically assaulted her. But they were men and she was a woman— and as the sniper on a job, she was in charge, and macho guys didn't usually appreciate that very much. She'd put up with her share of snide remarks, though she'd never felt Nick's remarks were meant to belittle her.

Dammit, she liked him. Too much. It hit her as she stared at him, at the hard, firm line of his jaw, the tanned features, the serious eyes that were mostly green but had a touch of brown that made them so mesmerizing to look at. His lashes weren't too long for a man, but they were long enough that she felt a little twinge of jealousy.

His dark hair was longer than it should be, but she liked the way it curled up at the ends and the tousled look he wore when he raked his hands through it. He was look- ing at her so seriously now, but it hit her that she liked it when he smiled. He didn't smile much, at least not with her, but the few times he had, her breath had caught and she'd had to remember to breathe.

Beautiful man.

"I know you aren't an asshole," she said, because she had to say something or she'd start to drool. "I think we piss each other off, probably, but that doesn't mean we're bad people, right? We just rub each other the wrong way."

She'd just given him the perfect line to say something about rubbing each other, but he didn't. Not that she'd intended to do that when she'd spoken, but always before now he'd tripped her up on her own words and made her sputter and fume. Not this time.

"We do piss each other off. I wish we didn't, but we can't seem to help it."

She hugged herself tighter. "Maybe we can make an effort to be civil then. Not assume the other one is trying to get under our skin just because."

"Sounds good." He went and grabbed a pair of binoculars before sitting down in one of the chairs and lifting them to scan the consulate across the street. She had the strongest urge to reach out and thread her fingers through his messy hair, to make him look at her one more time.

But he'd disconnected himself from the situation, and it left her feeling out of sorts and confused. Why, when she'd been so flustered by his interest, was she suddenly disconcerted by the lack of it?

Garrett Spencer sat in a chair and stared at the television over his head. The guys were laughing and talking about something, but he was watching the CNN commentator talk about unrest in the Middle East—except he didn't really hear a thing. It was just talking heads and words scrolling across a screen to him. His mind was back in Georgia, thinking about how his baby girl was celebrating her ninth birthday and he wasn't there to see it.

He didn't talk about Cammie to the guys. Or about her mother. *Especially* not her mother.

Though they'd been separated for years, Sara had finally asked for a divorce when she met someone else who could finance her lifestyle much better than he could. He'd given it to her and good fucking riddance. If not for Cammie, he'd have been happy never to have to see his cheating, manipulative ex again.

"Hey, Ice, what's got you all wound up today?"

Garrett looked up as Jack Hunter flopped down on a chair beside him. They hadn't seen Jack in a while as he'd been on special assignment somewhere else—no doubt due to that gorgeous pop star he'd married and the fact she wanted to keep his ass in one piece—but he was here now and everyone was more than happy to see him.

"Nothing much. Just chilling and waiting for the go order."

Jack took a sip of his beer. "Yeah, I get that. I've missed the fuck out of this kind of thing—and I haven't, if that makes sense."

Garrett snorted. "With that gorgeous wife of yours, I'm surprised you even think of us at all."

Jack grinned. "She keeps me busy. And Eli—holy shit, that kid never stops."

"No, they don't when they're young."

Jack just laughed. "You must have little nieces and nephews."

Garrett only nodded. "Yeah, right. Energetic little shits."

"Gina's pregnant." Jack's voice was soft, his eyes

shining with that faraway look that Garrett had never understood. He'd cared about Sara, but hell, they'd fought so much he didn't think he'd ever had the chance to feel dreamy about her.

"That's great, man. Fucking great."

And it was, but it also hit him in the gut in a way he hadn't expected.

"Yeah. She hasn't announced it yet." Jack shook his head. "I still can't believe I'm married to a woman who has to announce things to the press. It's fucking unreal how much they care about our lives."

"How's it working out for you, living in that little town on the Eastern Shore?"

"Waterman's Cove? We love it. They've gotten pretty used to us there. Hell, I heard from Cindy at the Crab Shack that Mr. Russell over at the body shop chased away a reporter who'd come to town asking questions. Disabled his vehicle and then said he didn't have the parts. Had the car towed to Cambridge, and the guy had to go with it or be without wheels." Jack shook his head. "It's funny, but I think the town feels protective of Gina."

"People surprise you, don't they?"

"Yeah, they do. She seems happy there."

The door opened and Mendez walked in. The guys all stopped what they were doing and came to attention.

"As you were," the colonel said.

Everyone relaxed, but no one sat down or turned away. They wouldn't dare.

"We've got a report that bin Yusuf is in the southern quadrant of Qu'rim. Is he going to the consulate in Ras al-Dura, or is he after Victoria Royal? No fucking idea, and nothing more on Black's organization."

The colonel looked ready to explode in that intense, subdued way he had. The man was like an IED waiting for the trigger. You had no idea how dangerous he was until it was too late.

"Brandy didn't have time to breach Black's server room, but we know where it is. We could infiltrate, sir."

This came from Flash. A couple of the other guys nodded. Mendez shook his head. "Black's got that place wired six ways to Sunday. If we bust in, he'll know it and he'll go underground. We'll never find him or figure out who he's working for. We have to leave it until Brandy returns and gets inside."

No one liked that option, but it was the only one they had if they wanted to stop Ian Black.

"Should we tell Brandy to get the fuck out?" Kev MacDonald asked. They all knew he meant the location where Brandy was holed up with Victoria. If bin Yusuf was on his way there, they could be in danger.

Mendez shook his head. "We'll send him a message and warn Echo Squad to keep an eye out. But no, he's got to stay until the last possible moment. We have to know who the target is in the consulate. That's the missing puzzle piece that might just help us take down Black once and for all."

THIRTEEN

NICK FROWNED AT THE PHONE in his hand. The text message was coded in such a way that anyone looking at it wouldn't understand. But he did. Zaran bin Yusuf was on his way to Ras al-Dura. No idea why, and no idea if Victoria was in danger.

But they had to stay put because to move would compromise the bigger mission, which was to learn Ian Black's secrets. Echo Squad was near, watching the building and ready to launch into action. That made things better, but not perfect.

Nick glanced at Victoria who sat in the chair beside him, scanning the consulate with her binoculars. Hours had passed and the sun was setting. They wouldn't turn on lights. Instead, they'd move closer to the windows, open one of them up, and start taking readings.

The life of a sniper was comprised of a lot of hurry-up-and-wait. They would rush to get to an objective, only to sit for hours sometimes, just waiting. Other times, the action was fast and furious and they worked until it was over and no more shots were fired.

This was one of the first types of jobs. Wait, wait, wait.

Not knowing the target made it frustrating, though Victoria didn't seem to mind. She might be used to working this way, but he wasn't.

"How did you decide to become a sniper?" he asked, realizing he didn't know the answer at all.

She turned toward him for a second before scanning the building again. "I told you my grandfather taught me to shoot. I think he probably did it to shut me up because I kept asking to go hunting with him. Then I think he was pretty surprised that I was good at it. But he was proud of me."

She paused. "I didn't join the Army with the thought of becoming a sniper. I thought I'd get into computers or something else that would translate well to a job on the outside. But my shooting in Basic was so good that the instructors kept challenging me to do more. It just kind of happened after that."

"And now you work for Ian Black."

He could feel her stiffening beside him. "I needed the money. And I needed to be in Qu'rim. A girl's gotta eat, Nick."

"Yeah."

She blew out a breath. "What about you? How did you end up here?"

He scratched the back of his neck. "Like you, I was good at shooting. Did a lot of hunting as a kid and just seemed to have an affinity for making difficult shots. I joined the Army to get the hell out of the Ozarks."

"And your sister?"

He hadn't forgotten he'd told her about Shelly, but he

was surprised she asked. "She's in Charlotte, running a restaurant with her wife. They're planning to have a baby in the next year."

She pursed her lips. "How do they decide which one...? Um, never mind. That's personal and none of my business."

It was personal, but he understood the curiosity. "It's a legitimate question. Jessica will be the birth mother. And I'm going to be the father."

The silence stretched and he began to regret he'd said anything. He didn't know why he'd wanted to share it with her, but he'd thought she might understand. Maybe she didn't. Not everyone would.

"That's amazing, Nick. Really amazing." Her voice was soft, a little thick.

He felt warm and his throat tightened. "Yeah, well, it makes sense, right? The baby will have both their DNA this way. Jessica is an only child. Maybe if she'd had a brother, they'd have done it the other way."

"You're a good man to help your sister."

Maybe so, but he couldn't fathom how or why he'd refuse. When Shelly had asked, he'd gone to the sperm bank as soon as he could and donated. With his job the way it was, they'd decided that putting his sperm on ice was better than him having to show up at a particular time and place. "Nah, my part was pretty easy. A few girly magazines, some porn, and a cup. I'll be the kid's uncle, but I won't be involved in raising him or her. Probably a good thing, considering."

"What's that supposed to mean?" she asked, a note of disapproval in her tone, and he almost laughed. She was defending him from himself. It was sorta sweet.

"Nothing much, just that I'm not sure I'm parent material. I don't have time right now—and I don't know the first thing about kids."

"I don't either. But I think I'd like one someday, when my life isn't so chaotic."

"A picket fence and a house with a dog?" He hadn't quite pictured her in that setting, but he could see it. After seeing her in that sweet dress a few days ago, he could definitely see it. Maybe even in an apron, baking some cookies…

No, wait. *Just* an apron. Bent over, ass bared, hands gripping a kitchen island…

Shit, not the image he needed in his head right now.

"Why not? And a cat too. A kid, a cat, a dog—and a man. That would be nice as well."

He tried to picture this shadowy man—but it only annoyed him to try. He didn't want some other guy touching her. Not when he hadn't touched her yet.

Jesus, dude, get a grip on yourself.

"If that's your thing, why not?"

She laughed. "You don't want to settle down someday? Have kids and a wife, go to a normal job?"

"I haven't thought about it."

"I thought everyone thought about it at some point. The future, I mean."

"I think about the future. I just don't think about being a nine-to-five guy with kids."

For him, family life was strict and defined. He'd grown up with such rigid expectations. And while he wasn't his father, he wasn't sure he had what it took to be a parent. His parents certainly hadn't provided a great example, though from the outside everyone would have said they had the perfect family.

Appearances could be deceiving.

Victoria didn't say anything else. The sun had slipped behind the horizon several minutes ago now. The lights of the city glowed against the desert sky. Across the street, the consulate's windows shined with light. Behind the windows, people moved back and forth, talking and... re-arranging furniture.

"Looks like they're getting ready for something," Victoria said, not lowering her binoculars. "Maybe a party."

He scanned the people inside, searching for hints of what they were doing. Yep, here came a huge table. A party was most likely when their target would appear, assuming *they* weren't the target.

"When did you last check in with Black?"

"A couple of hours ago. And no, still no information."

It didn't bode well for them that Black hadn't given them a mark. "Does he usually make you wait this long?"

"It depends on the client. Some are very secretive. Others don't care."

That wasn't exactly helpful. "The disadvantages of being a contract killer."

"And there goes the civility." Her tone was frosty.

Nick gritted his teeth. Yeah, he'd been the one to break the peace, but this situation pissed him off. She was in danger, and she didn't even know it. Worse, she seemed to trust that Black wasn't double-dealing with her.

"Bin Yusuf is coming." He decided she needed to know the truth of that at least.

She grew still. "All right." She sounded so calm when

he knew she had to be somewhat rattled over the news. "And yet there's not really anything we can do about it. Is there?"

It wasn't a question so much as a statement daring him to contradict her. He wished he could.

"No. He might not be coming for us at all. He might be on his way to the consulate, or on Freedom Force business in the city."

"But you think he's coming for me." It wasn't a question.

He blew out a breath. "I don't know. I have no fucking clue. It would be a terrible waste of resources for him to come for you—but if he's convinced himself you have to die, then maybe he thinks it's worth it."

The apartment was quiet, but outside, the sound of cars on the streets reached into the darkness. There were other sounds too—animals, people shouting and talking, and the milling of a city as people left the mosques now that the Mahgrib was done.

Victoria was still reeling from the idea that bin Yusuf was coming, but then they didn't know *why* he was coming. Nick was right that it wasn't a good use of resources to come for her. But the asshole wasn't precisely firing on all cylinders anyway—where was the logic in trying to kill her in Akhira, for instance? All he'd needed to do was deny her the chance to see Emily, but he'd specifically sent men to pick her up and dispose of her.

"We'll have warning, I presume?"

"Yes," Nick said.

She shrugged, though she didn't feel quite as unconcerned as she pretended. "Then we're safer here than we'd be on the road. And if bin Yusuf does come, then we'll know where Ian's loyalties lie, won't we?"

She let her hand glide over the butt of her pistol and then looked down at the gleaming rifle lying on a blanket on the floor. He might come for her, but she wasn't giving up without one hell of a fight. "Besides, we're heavily armed. It'd be suicide to bust in here after us."

Nick snorted. "Yeah, it definitely would."

She picked up her scope and went over to slide the window back. Then she sighted across the distance to the consulate, looking in each window, thinking about the shot it would take to fire through every one of them. She didn't know if there really was a target, but she'd act like there was until events proved differently.

It was all she knew how to do. If she let herself dwell on the topic—Zaran bin Yusuf, Ian, Emily—she'd want to scream. And that wasn't what she did. She worked hard, stayed serious, and took care of business.

But at least this time she wasn't alone.

"I'm glad you're with me," she said, not turning away from her task. And she was glad, because she knew she could trust Nick Brandon with her life. A man who cared enough about his own sister to cut ties with his family when they treated her poorly, who intended to give her a chance to be a mother to a child with her own DNA, was not a bad man to have at your back.

Even if you weren't sure what his goals were.

"I'm glad too," he said, and a little shudder rippled up

her spine.

She heard him get up and cross the distance between them. Her entire body went on alert, hoping he'd touch her again. Just put a hand on her shoulder like he had before, or slide his arms around her body and tug her back against him so she could feel his strength and his warmth.

But he didn't touch her, and disappointment rolled through her.

"Why don't you go and get some sleep?"

His voice was a velvet rumble in her ear, and another shudder rippled over her. "I'm not tired."

"Victoria, you have to sleep. We've been here since morning and you haven't slept yet."

"I'm fine."

He made a sound that was a cross between a curse and a growl. And then his hands were on her shoulders and her body lit up like a flame as he turned her.

"You aren't fine," he said, his body a big blur in the darkness. "You're operating on adrenaline and fear, even if you won't admit to being scared of any damn thing, and you're going to crash if you don't get some rest."

A strong urge to press her body against his swept through her. She trembled, unable to step away from him as she should. As she would have done only hours ago. Her resolve was crumbling, spurred on by exhaustion and that moment when he'd told her she was safe with him. What was it about that moment that had changed everything?

Until then, he'd been arrogant and cocky, and she'd been determined not to let him know how drawn to him she was in spite of how much he irritated her. But now her defenses were lowering, her determination cracking down the center.

His hands slipped down her arms and then fell away. She could feel the warmth coming from him, and the frustration.

"I'll keep you safe, Victoria. Just go and lie down. If it works and you sleep, great. And if it doesn't, you haven't missed anything."

"And who'll keep you safe, Nick Brandon?" she whispered.

"You'll get your turn to protect me, babe. Just not right now."

She suddenly had to touch him, had to feel his mouth against hers one more time. He'd made her feel safe when he'd kissed her, and he'd chased every other thought from her head. She wanted that again. Wanted to concentrate on nothing but him, wanted the million thoughts and fears whirling through her head to disappear for a while.

She stepped into him, wrapped her arms around his neck, and pulled his head down for a kiss. He stiffened with surprise—and then he dragged her closer with a groan, his mouth slanting over hers hungrily.

She opened her mouth and his tongue met hers, sliding and stroking and setting up an answering throb of heat in her belly. And lower. Her pussy ached with the need to have him, and yet she feared him too. To take that step—that ultimate step—here and now had to be insane.

But an animal part of her wanted it. Because she'd gone for so long—her entire life—without knowing what it felt like to make love to a man. What if bin Yusuf killed her before she ever experienced it?

It was an insane thought, because she'd spent the past two years putting her life on the line, but she suddenly couldn't stand the idea any longer. She had to *know* what it felt like, what made women lose their minds over a man.

Nick's hands went to her back, squeezed her shirt in his fists as if he were trying not to touch the rest of her.

"Touch me. Please touch me," she said between kisses.

He did touch her, but not the way she expected. He swept her into his arms as if she weighed nothing, his mouth still on hers. And then he broke the kiss and carried her into the bedroom while she clung to him. She put her mouth on his throat, tasted the salt of his skin. She could feel his pulse throbbing hard, and a surge of power went through her to know she could affect him this way.

He lowered her to the bed and she clung to him, wanting him to stretch out on top of her and dominate her. To take charge of the situation and give her everything she'd been missing out on.

But he wasn't lying down. He was trying to disentangle her hands from his neck, gripping her wrists gently and pulling.

"Victoria, sweetheart, you have to sleep."

Sleep? Her brain struggled to catch up, to penetrate the sensual fog surrounding her ability to reason. She'd finally decided she wanted a man—and he wanted her to sleep?

Oh God, she was clinging to him like some kind of octopus, arching her body into his and trying to get him to strip her naked and make her forget everything for a while.

And he didn't want to. Didn't want *her.* No matter what he'd said the past few days, no matter that he'd teased her and kissed her and told her he wanted her—

He didn't.

It hurt, more than she'd thought it would. She let him go and curled on her side, turning her face into the pillow to hide the stupid tears threatening to break free.

He touched her shoulder and she jerked. He didn't pull away, however. He slid his fingers down her spine, over her ass, and along her hip. Then he stopped touching her altogether.

"I want you, Victoria. Believe me, I do. But not like this. Not when you're overtired and your defenses are down. Ask me again when you've slept a few hours."

She kept her face turned into the pillow. He stood, and she heard him moving across the room. The door shut softly, and she was alone.

Alone and mortified.

FOURTEEN

NICK SETTLED A BLANKET AND pillow on the floor of the living room. He had his guns and his early warning system in Echo Squad, so he was going to take this chance and get some sleep too. He thought of Victoria lying alone, her body curled up tight, her face turned away from him, and his gut clenched hard. He'd wanted her so bad.

Wanted to strip her naked and fill her with his cock while she moaned and begged him for release. He could still feel her body pressed against his, her tongue caressing his so desperately, and his dick grew harder than it already was.

He had half a mind to do something about it, but a hard-on had never killed him before and it wasn't going to now.

Except, fuck, he wanted to be inside her. Thrusting again and again, her legs wrapped around him, her tongue in his mouth. He wanted to feel her sweat and tremble, and he wanted to hear her fall apart as she came.

Damn, he had it bad. He was used to wanting, but he was also used to getting what he wanted. And he wasn't sure, after he'd turned her down just now, that she'd ever want him again. Screw him and his sense of nobility anyway.

But he couldn't take advantage of her emotional turmoil. He knew she was upset about her sister, keyed up about Zaran bin Yusuf and Ian Black, and worried about what the future might bring. She'd wanted escape, not him.

Perversely enough, he wanted her to want *him*.

Yeah, he could be naked with her right now, but it wasn't right. He lay on his back and put his hands behind his head. The room was dark, but the city lights filtered inside, flickering on the ceiling when cars rolled by on the streets below.

He wanted to know what the fucking target was. And then he wanted to get back to Black's HQ and get inside that server room. He imagined the server was portable, probably a hardened shipping crate on wheels, with the equipment tucked inside and maneuverable. There was quite possibly some sort of destructive device attached. A thermite grenade would do the trick, but it would destroy far more than the server. Would Black take that kind of chance? Or was he certain he could control access?

There was no way of knowing until Nick got back there. Assuming this wasn't a suicide mission and the Freedom Force wasn't bearing down on them even now. He picked up his phone and checked it. Nothing from HOT, no warnings or directions.

He put it down and lay there, his body throbbing for what seemed a long time. Eventually he must have slept, because he was jolted awake by a noise. He lay very still, listening for whatever had woken him. A glance at the door told him no one had broken in. The only windows were along the front of the apartment, where he currently lay, and none were shattered. They were on a high enough floor that someone would have to rappel down the building to get to them, but there was no evidence of that either.

The noise came again, and he realized it had to be Victoria. He thought maybe she was talking to someone, so he got up, slipped his phone in his pocket, grabbed a gun just in case, and crept toward the bedroom where she was supposed to be sleeping. He stood outside the door, listening.

She cried out and he pushed the door open, his heart kicking up. She wasn't on the phone. She lay in bed, the covers thrown off, whimpering.

He went over and touched her shoulder. "Victoria."

She cried out, and then her eyes snapped open, clashing with his. She scrambled upright on the bed before flipping and reaching for the table.

Holy fuck.

Nick dropped to the floor, knowing instinctively that she was going for her gun. He was armed, but that wasn't going to help the situation when he was pretty sure she was just reacting to him surprising her.

"Victoria, it's me. It's Nick Brandon."

"Nick?"

His heart thumped as he lifted his head. She stood on the other side of the bed. He could see the gleam of the pistol as she lowered her hand to her side.

"Yeah, it's me. Promise not to shoot?"

He heard the clatter of the weapon on the table and he got to his feet.

She was standing there with her hands on either side

of her head. "Oh God, I'm sorry. I don't know what happened... I was dreaming, and then you were there and I thought he'd found me..."

His pulse was racing like a frigging Formula One car as he tucked his gun into his waistband. "It's okay. I guess I should have woke you up another way."

She laughed softly, brokenly. "How could you predict I'd forget where I was or who I was with?"

The emotion in her voice made him want to reach for her, hold her tight, but he didn't move. "Couldn't have been easy to wake up from a nightmare and see a dark shape standing over you."

"No, definitely not." She chafed her arms as if she was cold. "What time is it?"

He pulled his phone from his rear pocket. "Three o'clock."

"Is that all? It seems later." She made a soft noise. "I feel like I've run a marathon."

"Night terrors will do that."

"I don't usually dream like that. It was... very realistic."

"You were taken to a remote location and almost killed. It's natural to feel some delayed stress."

"Yeah, I guess so. I'd thought I was over it already."

He snorted. "Not likely. And that's fucking normal, so don't beat yourself up over it. You'll probably dream about it some more before you're done."

She studied him. "You seem to know a lot about it. What's your story?"

The curved scar on his torso seemed to throb for just a moment. It had happened so long ago now that he never really thought of it much—but he'd thought of it a lot at the time.

"I was mugged when I was seventeen. Visiting Chicago on a school trip and stayed out late, in spite of being told not to by our chaperones. I was walking the streets past curfew with a couple of friends when some guys stepped out of the shadows and demanded our money. I resisted when I probably shouldn't have, and I got knifed for the trouble."

"The scar on your side?"

"Yep." He wasn't surprised she'd noticed it. "It wasn't life threatening, but it sure hurt like a motherfucker at the time. Not to mention the trip to the hospital got us busted for sneaking out, and my parents were pissed as shit that I'd embarrassed them that way. The preacher's kids were supposed to be models of good behavior and upright moral standing."

He could still remember the looks on his parents' faces when he'd got home. His mother had worn that combination worried/disappointed look he knew so well. His father, however, was royally pissed. And he definitely believed in not sparing the rod. Hadn't mattered that Nick was seventeen and too big to get beat. His dad had been so angry he'd hit him again and again across the butt and back with a belt while Nick stood there and took it, his insides churning with fury and hurt.

That's when he'd vowed to get the fuck out just as soon as he could. The minute he turned eighteen, he'd gone down to the recruiter's office and signed up. He'd had to sign up for the Delayed Enlistment Program since he'd still been a senior in high school, but as soon as school ended, he was on his way.

His parents had been furious about that too.

"That must have made it even tougher for you."

"Didn't make it easy."

Shelly was gone by then, and he'd been the only one left. He'd already been angry with his parents over their continued refusal to accept Shelly unless she changed to suit them, and the knifing hadn't exactly made them confident in *his* ability to do the right thing. He could still remember how shocked he'd been that his father was more furious that Nick had disobeyed a rule than the fact he'd been hurt and could have died if the attacker had jabbed him a little differently.

That's when he'd realized that his parents considered appearances more important than anything else. Not only had they chosen to cut his sister from their lives, but he knew they'd also do it to him in a flash. It was a sobering realization as a seventeen-year-old that your parents cared more for their ideals than they did for you.

"Did you have nightmares?"

"For a while. Eventually they went away."

She seemed to hesitate. "About earlier. I'm sorry."

"For what?"

"I threw myself at you. It's embarrassing."

He didn't quite know what to say. "You didn't throw yourself at me, Victoria. And even if you did, I was a dumb ass not to take you up on it. Been kicking myself all night."

He could see her shaking her head in the darkness. "You're too nice to me. I was all over you."

"I'm not at all fucking nice, sweetheart. In fact, if you'd like to kiss me again, I definitely won't be nice. I'll take everything you have and ask for more. Your choice, but believe me, I'm more than ready."

Victoria couldn't breathe for a second. He had no idea how much she wanted to do just that.

She could still feel his tongue against hers, still feel the hard knot of desire low in her belly now that her terror from the dream had dissipated.

But she *was* embarrassed by how she'd acted earlier—by her lack of control, by how inexperienced she was, by his rejection, even if it had been for noble reasons. She felt like he must have certainly known she had no idea what she was doing, and he'd been trying to let her down easily.

But this statement, that he was ready if she wanted to try again, knocked her for an emotional loop. Worse, now that he'd tossed the ball back into her court, she had no idea how to hit it out again.

"I don't know what to do."

"Just kiss me, Vic. The rest will happen."

She swallowed. Her heart was thrumming fast, and she felt a little dizzy with it. "No, I mean I don't know what to *do*. I... I've never done anything like that before, and I just..."

She felt like an idiot. Why was she admitting such a thing? Why was she even talking about this? She should tell him no thanks, she'd changed her mind, please go away.

But some little part of her—the small, girlish part that wanted to be loved—refused to let her do it. Instead, it made her embarrass herself further by admitting she was a clueless virgin.

She was glad it was dark and she couldn't see his expression as well as she would during the day. He stood there, not speaking, and she imagined he was trying to think of how to extract himself from this situation.

"I... Are you saying what I think you're saying?" His voice was tightly controlled, and her heart sank a little more. He must think her a freak.

Goddammit, she was tired of this shit. Tired of pretending to be something she wasn't, tired of hiding the truth because it made her feel stupid and unattractive. And abnormal. Never forget abnormal.

"Yes, Nick, I'm a twenty-five-year-old virgin. I've never had sex before. I know how it works, for fuck's sake, but I've never done it. I don't quite know why, except I just haven't found anyone I wanted to do it with before. I've been too busy taking care of my sister—*worrying* about my sister—to spend a lot of time dating or screwing random men."

"Damn, Vic," he said softly. "You sure know how to make a speech."

Humiliation was her old friend by now. "Screw you, Nick Brandon. Screw you and get the fuck out."

He moved toward her then. "Hey, sweetheart," he said, stopping in front of her, taking her by the shoulders and then tilting her chin up and forcing her to look at him. "That wasn't an insult. Honestly, I haven't a fucking clue what to say to you right now, other than I think you're probably the toughest, most single-minded person I've ever known. You had a goal, and you didn't let a damn thing get in your way."

"I let Zaran bin Yusuf get in my way."

He tugged her against him, pressing her cheek to his chest. His fingers stroked her hair and little tingles of sensation began to drip through her system.

"You were trying to make a better life for you and Emily. You did the best you could. The fact she fell for an asshole like bin Yusuf isn't your fault."

"Maybe it is," she said, her throat clogging with old regrets. "Maybe I should have stayed home and tried harder."

He pushed her away, holding her by the shoulders again. Then he bent until his face was level with hers. "You aren't at fault for another person's actions. Your sister made choices, and while those choices worry you and you're here trying to find her again, frankly I'd be more than a little pissed off that she's put you through hell like this. In fact, I *am* pissed off, and I don't even know her. But I'll do everything in my power to help you find her. And when you get her home again, I hope you realize you aren't responsible for her entire fucking life. She's an adult, Victoria. Like you, like me. She might have made a bad choice, but once you have her back again, you'd better realize she's capable of making more of them. And they won't be your fault either."

His words made her uncomfortable in a way, and yet she knew he was right. "I am pissed at her," she said softly. "I've been pissed for a very long time—but I also think she wants to come home and that he's keeping her locked up against her will. I can't abandon her. No man or woman left behind. Gramps said we had to look out for each other because no one else would. He was right, and I can't do anything less than what I'm doing right now."

"I know you can't."

He ran his hands down her arms and let them drop away. She wanted to ask him to hold her again, but she was too shy to do it. Which was ridiculous considering she wasn't precisely timid about a lot of things. But this—him—she was out of her element.

It had come on fast. Too fast.

This crazy pull between them was disconcerting and exciting all at once. She'd known it was there before, in sniper training, but she'd been unable to give in to it. Not to mention she'd thought he was unaffected and it was all her. Silly her, mooning over some guy because he was handsome and made her tingle.

Now she wanted more—and she wanted nothing because she was afraid of how it would change her life if she got it. They were mostly strangers to each other, and just because he was basically a decent guy didn't mean there was a future beyond however long they had to work together.

Not that she expected there to be. It was certainly premature for that. But she liked him, and she wanted to know if she would still like him in a month. Two months. A year.

"For the record," he said, "I think you're pretty amazing. Gorgeous, sexy, determined, talented. Amazing."

She could feel the heat creeping beneath her skin. It made her glow warmly when he said it, and yet it embarrassed her too. "If you're trying to get in my pants, you're doing it wrong."

He snorted. "So prickly. I like that about you." He let out a long sigh. "I want in your pants, Victoria. Desperately. But in light of what you just told me, I can't help but feel you deserve better than to lose your virginity while staking out a Russian consulate. You should be wined and dined and made love to on a bed with satin sheets. It ought to be a memorable experience."

She rolled her eyes. "You're kidding, right? Satin sheets are such a cliché. Besides, how many women lose their virginity staking out Russian consulates? I'd venture to say precisely none. Why can't I be the first?"

"Goddamn, you tempt me," he said, his voice a low growl that made a shiver roll over her. "But I feel like I'd be taking advantage of the situation. Of you."

She folded her arms over her chest, hugging herself. "I'm a twenty-five-year-old virgin, Nick. If I've never done it before now, do you really think I don't know my own mind? That I'm weak willed enough for you to take advantage of just because we're out here alone together and I find you sexy? Do you really think you're just too irresistible to me and I don't know what I'm doing or saying?"

He reached out and caressed her cheek. "You're incredible. Seems to me if you've waited this long, you might want it to be special. With a man who loves you. You..." He sucked in a breath. "You have to know that I don't. That I'm a horny bastard who desperately craves you. It'll be special for me because I'll be your first, but not the way it'll be special for you."

His words made her shiver deep inside, but they also made her angry too.

"For fuck's sake, Brandon, do you honestly think every girl's first time is with a guy who loves her? That *that* makes it special? I'd think the most important quality is a guy who knows his way around the female anatomy. Can you make me come? Can you make me cry out and beg for more? That's what I want, not some declaration of love and devotion."

FIFTEEN

COULD HE MAKE HER COME? Holy hell, was this some kind of torturous payback for all the things he'd done wrong in his life?

Victoria Royal was just about the sexiest woman he'd ever known. She was strong, determined, loyal, had a deadly accurate eye and nerves of steel—and she'd never had sex before.

Twenty-five, with a body like that and a mouth made for kissing, and she'd never had sex.

It was more than a little bit tempting to be her first. And yet it was a huge responsibility too. He knew he could make her come. Hell, he could make her first time good— but he couldn't fight the idea that she should be with someone who cared.

He knew he didn't care.

Well, fuck, maybe he cared a little bit—but that's because she was sweet beneath the sass, innocent in this one thing, and he couldn't help but care about that.

And maybe he even cared about her as a person because he certainly couldn't seem to stop thinking about her well-being lately. But that wasn't good enough. It wasn't the kind of all-encompassing caring he should have for a woman who wanted to give herself to him for her first time.

He was a dog. He loved sex, like most men, and he loved the release it gave him for a little while. He could lose himself in her—but it wasn't the same as when he'd thought she was experienced. Everything they did would be her first time, while for him it would be numberless.

He didn't have mindless sex, but he didn't stick with any one woman for long either. He did quick relationships, if you could call them that, where he was faithful to one woman for a few weeks or so. Then he just got tired of dealing with the questions and the demands for more emotional commitment, and he moved on.

He didn't do long-term. He knew that long-term didn't last. If your own parents couldn't commit to you for a lifetime, why on earth would anyone else?

"You didn't answer the question, Nick. Can you make me come?"

Her voice was soft and sultry, but there was an underlying current of uncertainty as well. It was the uncertainty that undid him. If he told her no, if he turned and walked away now, he'd leave her feeling as if she weren't good enough for him. As if she weren't sexy or desirable.

How could he do that? This beautiful, innocent woman was asking him to be her first, and though it scared the shit out of him in some ways, it also thrilled him in a deep, primal way that shocked him.

"Yeah, I can."

"I'm scared as hell, I should admit that to you... but I want to do it. I want you to be first."

He reached for her, pulled her against his chest, and tilted her head back with both his hands on her face. He was a fucking goner. He was like an addict being offered a fix, and he couldn't say no.

He told himself it was just sex, but he knew there was something else driving him too. Something he didn't know how to quantify.

"If you change your mind at any point, tell me to stop. Don't endure because you think you have to. Don't let it go too far if it feels wrong."

"Okay." Her voice was soft and breathy, so different from when she was giving him hell. It was such a turn-on.

"And if you don't like the way I'm touching you, for God's sake tell me. I'm not a mind-reader, and everyone is different."

"All right."

He could feel her trembling, and a wave of answering tenderness washed over him. He didn't think Victoria was scared of anything, yet she was clearly nervous about this.

"Sweetheart, we don't have to do this. You don't have to prove anything to anyone."

"You're going to give me a complex if you keep trying to back out."

"You're shaking."

"Anticipation."

He laughed. "More like adrenaline."

"That too." She ran her hands up the front of his chest and put them around his neck. "Just kiss me. Let's see what happens from there."

He tossed up a silent prayer, asking for the patience he'd need to do this right—and then he lowered his head and claimed her mouth with his own.

There was something about kissing him once she'd decided to go all in that was different. Oh, it was every bit as exciting and arousing as it had been before. But knowing she'd given herself permission to let anything and everything happen, she felt a certain wild joy that she'd never experienced before.

Flame roared through her veins, ignited in her belly, made her tremble even more than she already had been. Her pussy throbbed with need, the walls growing slick with moisture.

She was the sort of person that when she made up her mind to do a thing, she wanted to do it immediately. She tugged his shirt from his pants and slid her hands beneath the fabric, her palms against his warm skin. She could feel his scar, that indentation that ran in an arc beneath his breastbone, and it made her heart squeeze to think of him on a Chicago street as a teen, getting knifed and then going home to censure from his parents rather than love and gratitude he was alive.

She didn't know his parents, but she took a rather dim view of them, considering how they'd treated him and his sister. Since she'd lost her parents so young, she'd never thought it possible they might not love her enough to accept her no matter what she did. It was a shocking truth to find out that some parents were capable of such a thing. Though logically she knew it happened, she'd never known a soul who had experienced it.

Nick's mouth was another world, a revelation to her

senses. She'd been kissed, but not quite like this. Not with this kind of all-encompassing attention to detail. His tongue stroked against hers one moment, delicately explored her mouth the next, and then strongly demanded a response from her.

She was helpless to do anything but kiss him back exactly as he taught her. He dropped his hands lower on her body, took her by the hips, and pulled her into him. The hardness against her belly made her stomach flip. He was big and ready, and she was afraid she'd be a disappointment to him.

What if she sucked at this? What if she did everything wrong and he thought she was a lousy lay? He wouldn't tell her. She knew that as sure as she knew her name. He was too gentlemanly to tell her she sucked.

She pushed him back suddenly, breaking the kiss, and he immediately lifted his head and relaxed his hold on her.

"Change your mind? It's okay if you did. Just let me know."

She swallowed. God, she was already so bad that he'd just walk away if she gave the word. In the next heartbeat, she told herself that was ridiculous, that he was being kind and making sure she hadn't decided against doing this.

"No. I… I just wanted to say that you have to let me know if I'm doing something wrong. If I'm horrible in bed, you owe me the truth. Don't sugarcoat it."

He snorted. "That isn't going to be a problem, honey. Trust me."

Funny, but he still had the ability to irritate her. She was trying to be honest, and he was dismissing her fears as if they were silly. "How do you know? I might be terrible. And you're going to lie about it if so. Just don't; that's all I ask."

He gathered the bottom of her T-shirt and started to push it up and over her head. She let him remove it, her skin prickling with goose bumps that had nothing to do with the coolness of the AC.

He dropped it on the floor and went for the button of her pants. "Victoria, I'm not going to let you be terrible. Trust me. And stop thinking so hard. Just feel."

He slid her zipper down and pushed the pants over her hips until they fell on the floor and she stood there in her bra and panties.

Then he dropped to his knees, pressed his open mouth to her belly, and her goose bumps intensified. Her fingers slid into his hair automatically, clutching him to her as his tongue danced and teased its way over her skin. He cupped her breasts in his hands and then took the edges of the cups and pulled them away until her nipples were bared and her breasts sat high and firm.

Victoria didn't think it was possible for her to get any wetter than she already was, but when Nick licked a stiff nipple, she gasped at the sensation rolling through her. She grew so slick and swollen that she thought she might die if he didn't touch her there soon.

Her fingers tightened in his hair as he sucked her nipple into his mouth, rolling it between his teeth and flicking it with his tongue. Every sweet pull on her breast sent sensation streaking down into her pussy, making her ache and throb with need.

As if sensing that she needed more, he slid his fingers beneath her panties, down into the seam of her body and the hot slickness of her desire. He rolled a finger over her clit, and she let her head fall back, a moan escaping her.

She spread her legs to give him better access, and he made a noise against her skin that might have been a laugh or a groan.

But he dragged his fingers through her wetness, then inserted one inside her. The walls of her pussy gripped him tightly, craving the invasion. His thumb circled her clit while he slowly moved a finger in and out of her slick core. It wasn't a completely new sensation, but it was different because it was someone else doing it.

"Nick," she gasped as her body wound itself tighter and tighter. She could come this way, standing here with his fingers on her body and his mouth sucking her nipples. She clutched at his shoulders, giving herself over to the decadence of his touch.

And then he stopped and she cried out. But he simply pulled her panties down her hips and she stepped out of them. Then he pushed her back onto the bed and pulled her to the edge, her legs spread wide.

"I have to taste you," he said, his voice a low growl that sent a shiver of need rolling through her.

He put her knees over his shoulders and licked into the heart of her as she gasped.

"You're so wet for me," he said. "Fuck, what a turn-on."

"Don't stop this time. Please don't stop."

"I'm not stopping until you scream my name, baby."

She didn't think that was possible, really, but then he started licking her again, his tongue swirling around her clit, his fingers sliding in and out of her body, and every nerve ending she had lit up like a flame. He played her body with an expertness that stunned her. Oh, she'd expected him to know what he was doing—but to know her body so well, as if they'd had sex a hundred times already, wasn't something she'd anticipated.

He knew just when to increase the pressure and just when to ease off to stop the wave building inside her from breaking. She could see her release hovering so close, could taste it, and yet he kept her from throwing herself into it.

She wasn't sure whether she was grateful or frustrated that he kept the tension building. But oh, his tongue. It did magical things to her, swirling and licking and tasting until she was panting from the overwhelming sensations churning inside her.

She'd imagined this, of course. Imagined what it would feel like to have a man give her pleasure this way. But imagining and experiencing were two entirely different things. It made her wonder how she'd resisted sex for so long if it was always this way.

She threw her hands over her head, grasping handfuls of the sheets, and arched her hips, seeking release from the torturous cycle of pleasure kept on the edge for too long.

And Nick let her go this time. Victoria heard her voice, heard his name breaking in her throat, but she had no time to marvel at the fact he'd done what he'd said he would do.

No, she was overwhelmed with a bright, hot euphoria that exploded inside her and raced through her veins like a brush fire. Everything centered on that one spot of pleasure—and then it didn't. It flowed over her and through her while she broke apart, clutching the sheets and gasping for breath as her body disintegrated.

When she came back to herself, Nick was still there, stroking her sides with his hands—roughened hands, but soft and tender too—and a wave of embarrassment flooded her suddenly.

He'd just witnessed her losing control, and she wasn't sure how that made her feel. Plus she was naked, disheveled, and he was still dressed.

"You okay?" he asked, and fresh heat flared inside her.

"Yes." She sounded hoarse. Probably from all that moaning and screaming she'd done.

"You're beautiful, Victoria. Amazing. If you still want more, I want to be the one to give it to you."

She blinked. He was asking her if she wanted to continue? After what he'd just done to her? He must be aching with his own need for release, but he'd still asked her if she wanted to continue.

"I do," she said, and she meant it. Yes, she was embarrassed by what had just happened—but she was amazed too, and she couldn't imagine stopping now. "All in, Brandon. I told you that."

He got to his feet slowly. She thought about getting up and helping him undress, but then he dragged his shirt up and over his head and her breath caught at the bulge and ripple of his muscles. He was in phenomenal shape, of course, and it was utterly breathtaking.

"Wait," she said when he reached for the button of his cammies after setting his gun on her night table.

He stopped, his fingers hovering just over the fly, and her heart thumped. He would stop, right now, if she asked him to. She knew it, and it made feelings swell inside her that she didn't quite understand.

"Take them off slowly."

Nick grinned. He flicked open the first button and

then reached for the next. "You like a little show, Vic?"

She raised herself up on her elbows. She was self-conscious about being naked in front of him, but the room was shadowed and she told herself it was okay. "I do want a little show. I want to remember this."

He undid his pants and pushed them down his hips. He must have taken his boots off earlier because the pants disappeared, and then he was standing there in his briefs. Tight, white, bulging briefs that made her heart skip. Her gaze roamed over him, taking in every delicious inch.

With abs and thighs like that, he could be an underwear model instead of an elite sniper.

He hooked his thumbs in the wide band of the briefs. And then he stood there for a long minute, watching her.

"You really want to do this? We're in the middle of a fucking war zone, we've got an unknown target, a terrorist who might be coming for you even now, and it's very likely your adrenaline is kicked up so high it's making you do things you wouldn't otherwise do—"

She got to her feet and pressed her hand over his mouth before he could continue.

"I want you, Nick Brandon. I don't know why, but I do. Badly. You've been under my skin since the first moment I saw you back in training, and while I have no fucking clue what I'm doing, I think I'd regret it for the rest of my life if I didn't do this with you. I want you inside me, taking me over the edge. I want your tongue in my mouth, your hands on my body, and your cock inside me. I *need* it, and I feel like I'll die if you don't give it to me."

He let out a breath when she slowly lifted her hand away. "Fuck, you sure do know the right things to say to a man."

He took her hand and pressed a kiss into her palm. It was a tender move when they were both aching so badly for something far more raw and primal.

"You're special, Victoria. Incredibly special."

Tears gathered in the corners of her eyes at his sweet words. She couldn't remember the last time anyone had told her she was special and meant it.

But she wasn't about to cry. She knew if she did, it was over. He would think she was too emotional, not thinking straight, and he would end this. And then she'd never know what it felt like to be with him. Sure, her body was sated after the way he'd just taken her over the edge with his mouth, but it wasn't quite enough.

She wanted more. Much more. And so she slipped her fingers into his briefs and pushed them down because she needed something to do.

His cock sprang free, big and full and ready, and she dropped to her knees in front of him. Her nipples were tight, aching buds, and her belly flipped even as her core throbbed with need.

"You don't have to—" he began. But he didn't get to finish because she took him in both hands and sucked the tip of him into her mouth.

Another first.

She closed her eyes, enjoying the foreign feel of him on her tongue. He was firm but soft, and he tasted salty. Not unpleasant, but not quite expected either. Victoria opened her mouth a little wider, took him deeper, just to the edge of where she would gag if he went farther.

She swirled her tongue around him, learning the texture of all that velvety skin.

"God, Victoria."

She opened her eyes and looked up at him. His eyes were shadowed, but she could see the intensity on his face.

"I used to dream of this," he said, his voice rough. "Your mouth on my cock. Made the nights in training so fucking miserable, I have to tell you."

She removed him from her mouth, ran her tongue up the underside of his penis. "Tell me what to do. Tell me how to make this good for you."

His laugh was broken. "It's already fucking fantastic." He reached down and tipped her chin up gently. "You've never done this before either?"

She shook her head. She supposed it was something she could have done, but she'd honestly never been motivated to try it before.

He showed her where to grasp him. "Stroke while you suck. But not too much because I've got to tell you I'm pretty much on edge. Too much and this is over too soon."

Victoria's pulse hammered in her veins, her throat. But she loved the intensity in his gaze and the way he swallowed hard when she took him into her mouth again. She pumped him the way he'd showed her, swirling her tongue around the head of his cock as she did so. She moved her mouth up and down on him, taking him as far as she could before she had to back off again.

It was exciting in a way she hadn't considered it could be. It was all about him and his pleasure, but feeling the twitches and jerks of his body, hearing the sharp breaths and harsh groans he couldn't contain, she felt a power she hadn't known existed. She was pleasuring him, and it made her feel powerful and beautiful.

And excited. If she weren't using both hands on him, she'd use one on herself.

Suddenly Nick swore. And then he reached down and pulled her to her feet. His eyes were bright as he searched her gaze.

And then he crushed her to him and kissed her.

SIXTEEN

THE KISS LIQUEFIED HER BONES. Nick's tongue swept into her mouth, his lips firm and demanding against hers as he walked her backward. Her knees hit the side of the bed and she stopped, clinging to his shoulders before she fell.

But that's what he wanted, because he gripped her hips and lifted her onto the bed before coming down on top of her. Automatically her legs went around his waist. His cock slid firmly against her clit and she moaned into his mouth.

"Condom," he said, breaking the kiss. "Need a condom."

"I'm on birth control. An implant under the skin."

He blinked and she felt herself reddening.

"It was in case… I'm a woman in a war zone. I had to protect myself."

His grip on her tightened, and she felt the tremor of anger roll through him. "In case of rape, you mean."

She swallowed. "Right."

It hadn't been something she'd wanted to take a

chance with, though God knew she would have fought tooth and nail if any man had tried to force her against her will. But she knew she was a woman in a man's world out here, and in a man's profession, and the possibility existed. She'd decided to protect herself.

"Obviously, I'm healthy," she added, though it was unnecessary.

"We get tested regularly in the Army. You know that."

"Yes."

He lowered his forehead to hers. His skin was hot. "You're turning me inside out, Vic. Every time I think I know which way is up, you flip it on me."

"I'm sorry."

He ran a hand down the side of her body, under her ass, cupping her. "You're fucking beautiful, you know that?"

She felt suddenly shy. Here they were, skin to skin, his cock poised to enter her body, and she was shy whenever he complimented her. Sassiness was her default setting when she was embarrassed.

"Are you going to fuck me or talk to me all night?"

He dropped his head and sucked one of her nipples into his mouth. His tongue rolled around the tight peak and she arched her back, amazed at how she always seemed to want more.

And then he moved his hips and she felt him, right there at her entrance, hard and relentless, and her pulse shot into the hot zone.

"Relax, sweetheart," he crooned. "It might hurt at first, but it gets better. I promise it does."

He began to move, the head of his cock slipping into

her wetness, spreading her wide. It was a foreign feeling—and an amazing feeling.

He sank deeper, slowly deeper, and she moved her hips to try to accommodate him.

"Are you okay?"

"Yes." She didn't have a hymen after a couple of pelvic exams at the doctor's office, but she still expected it to hurt. Nick wasn't a rubber vibrator, after all.

And it did hurt, but not badly. It was the stretching of tissues that were unaccustomed to such an invasion, the foreignness of a large male entering her for the first time. Maybe she should have used a bigger vibrator…

"You're so tight," he said after a few moments of not moving at all.

"No miles on this thing, remember?"

He busted out laughing, and she felt it reverberate through her. What a sensation to be joined so intimately and feel your partner laugh.

"Jesus, how can you make me laugh when this is serious? And why are you cracking jokes anyway? You're supposed to be incoherent with passion right now. Not doing my fucking job right if you aren't."

A wave of emotion washed over her. He made her happy. He made her feel as if she were important. And he made her forget, for the time being, everything but what it was like to be with him.

"Maybe you aren't as good at this as you thought." She loved teasing him, even when her nerve endings were raw and her body was on fire.

He lifted her to him with that one broad hand on her ass and slid the rest of the way home. Victoria gasped and Nick made a sound that was half growl, half groan.

"Not good at this?" he said tightly. "You'll pay for that, Vic. With a lot of begging, I might add."

She was still panting at the invasion, at how full and stretched she felt. It hurt, but in a good way.

He dipped his head and kissed her softly. "I'm sorry if I hurt you."

She put her hand on his cheek, then slid her fingers into his hair. "It's a good kind of hurt. Now please make it better. I want to get to the good part."

He shifted his hips, moving gently, and the nerve endings in her entire body sat up and took notice. It was as if Nick were an electric storm, and she were a conduit for his energy. Her skin lit up with pings and sizzles in places she hadn't realized could be so sensitive.

Nick slid almost all the way out and then pushed deep inside her again. Victoria gasped his name as she clutched his shoulders, seeking an anchor in the storm. He didn't give her any mercy after that, moving inside her faster and faster, his body demanding everything she could give in return.

She lifted herself to him, opened herself, took him as deeply as he could go, her body melting and reshaping itself to accommodate his. The tension she'd felt earlier began to spin up again, coiling tighter and tighter inside her until she thought if she didn't get some relief, she would scream.

Victoria closed her eyes and arched upward, wanting more. She wanted to remember everything, experience everything, but she knew it wasn't going to last. Her orgasm was a wave just out of reach, a wave that would annihilate her when it arrived.

She wanted to come, but she also wanted to control

her reaction.

Except she knew there would be no control. When she shattered, she would lose herself in the bliss of the moment. Nick owned her body right now and he would accept nothing less.

He drove into her with more force than before, their bodies slapping together, their sweat mingling. And it didn't hurt anymore. It felt astonishingly wonderful.

Why had she waited so long? *Why?*

And then her heart whispered to her. *He* was why. Nick Brandon. The thought disconcerted her. She couldn't let herself get emotional over this man. Emotion was vulnerability, and she had no room for vulnerability. Not out here. Not now.

"Come for me, Victoria," he rasped in her ear. "Let yourself go."

It was as if he'd given her the key, because her breath caught and her body flew over the edge as the tension inside her exploded in a single blinding flash. She heard herself cry out his name, her voice broken and breathless.

She'd had orgasms before, but never like this. Never with a man inside her, driving her over the edge. It was different; it was a revelation. There was something about experiencing such a supremely intimate moment with another person that was both frightening and comforting.

Victoria closed her eyes and gave herself up to the sensations vibrating through her. Nick followed her over the edge, shooting warm jets inside her. That was also a revelation, to know she could feel the moment when he came.

He didn't collapse on top of her but held himself up on his elbows. He was still inside her, still hard, and she pressed her forehead to his shoulder and concentrated on breathing.

"Hey," he said softly, and she looked up to find him watching her with a look of concern on his handsome face.

She didn't know why until he reached out and smoothed his fingers over her cheeks. Her skin was wet.

"Did I hurt you?"

She gulped, suddenly uncertain she could maintain her composure. Her emotions were a whirlwind and she wasn't quite sure why. "No. I... I'm fine."

He pushed her hair from her face. "You don't look fine."

"It's just a bit overwhelming."

He gave her a smile. "Yeah, it can be."

"Is that a commentary on your awesomeness or just a general statement?"

He snorted. "Whatever you want it to be."

His hips flexed, and she gasped, both at how sensitive she was and at how eager her body was for more. She dropped her gaze to his chest, unable to look at him for more than a few seconds. Her heart still pounded, and little aftershocks of nerves zipped through her body. Her brain raced with conflicting thoughts.

What had she done? Why had she chosen a man who got beneath her skin to be the one to initiate her? Was it a mistake? How would she ever regain her balance? How would she ever look him in the eye again?

He tipped her chin up and forced her to look at him, putting an end to that question. His hazel eyes searched hers. "Regrets?"

It was strange to be asked such a thing when he was still buried inside her, when her body hadn't quite pieced itself back together again.

She swallowed. Her throat hurt. "I don't know."

She felt him stiffen slightly, but then he sighed. "Believe it or not, I understand."

A tiny sliver of pain lanced into her. Because if he understood, he must be feeling some regret of his own. And that was a thought she couldn't stand. It might be hypocritical, but it hurt. She pushed at his shoulders, but it was like trying to move a brick wall. He wouldn't budge.

"Get off," she said as the hurt threatened to turn into a deluge.

"You aren't pushing me away, Victoria. Not like this."

Fresh tears trickled down her cheeks. Crying was an unbelievable breach of her usual control, but then nothing about tonight had been normal.

He swore. She thought he would get up and stalk out of the room, but he took her hands in his and pushed them above her head. His mouth captured hers almost savagely. She had a brief moment of shock—and then her belly clenched and a hard wave of desire rolled through her.

His body bore hers down into the mattress, his cock swelling inside her.

"Do you still want me to go?" he demanded, his mouth at her ear.

She heard herself moan—and then she wrapped her legs around his waist and he started to move. It was faster this time, more frantic. They moved as one, rocking the bed hard against the wall—and then she came, biting down on his shoulder as she did so. She was still coming when he stiffened and groaned his release.

This time he rolled away when it was over. The cool

air on her body was a shock after being beneath him for so long. She pushed onto her elbows and looked at him. He'd flung an arm over his face and his chest rose and fell more rapidly than before.

"I shouldn't have done that," he said after a long moment.

"Which part?" Because she had to know what he meant.

He moved his arm and turned his head toward her. "Just now. You thought I regretted having sex with you. The only way I knew to prove differently was to do it again."

She lowered her gaze even as she felt her face flushing. Her damn coloring showed everything. "I did think that."

He reached out and tangled his fingers with hers. "The only thing I regret is that I was too weak to tell you no."

She didn't know what to say to that. She wanted to curl against him and go to sleep, but she felt awkward and uncertain. When would she stop feeling this way?

"I didn't want you to tell me no. I think I made that clear."

He snorted softly. "Yeah, you did."

He reached for the nightstand, checked his phone and his gun. She thought he would get up and go now, but he didn't. He lay back and then dragged her down and wrapped an arm around her. She put her head on his chest, her cheek against his warm skin. He smelled like soap and sex and she closed her eyes, sighing.

"I have a feeling tomorrow's going to bring news, one way or the other. For now, we're safe, so let's sleep while we can."

She wanted to stay right here with him—and yet she needed to stay in control of the job as much as possible. She pushed herself up. He let her go.

"I know your guys are watching, but maybe one of us should stay on alert. I'll take this shift."

He sighed. "It's not necessary, Victoria."

"I think it is."

"You just have to argue with me, don't you?"

"I'm not arguing. I'm following procedure."

She knew it sounded hollow when she said it, but she had to wrest back some of the control of this operation—of herself—where she could.

Nick turned onto his side and punched the pillow. "When you get tired of sitting up alone, come back to bed."

She fumbled for her clothes in the darkness, cursing herself the entire time she got dressed. Was she insane? She could have stayed right there, curled up in his warmth, but she'd had to be stubborn.

And now she would pay the price, sitting in the dark until dawn and wishing like hell she could explore his body one more time.

Nick slept soundly, only waking when the sun sent a shaft of light streaming into the room. It fell across his face, warming him. For a moment, he was disoriented. But only for a moment. The night before came back to him with blinding clarity.

Skin to skin, breaths mingling, bodies straining, soft limbs tangling with his own. He'd been so lost in her. So overwhelmed by the sweetness of her body. He'd thought he would wake up this morning and feel pleasantly sated.

Instead, a hot, hard hunger swept through him. His cock swelled, remembering. He wanted her again, and just as badly as he had last night.

He turned his head, intent on waking her and indulging this need, but Victoria wasn't there. She'd stayed away all night.

He bolted upright, uncaring that he was naked, and grabbed his phone. Though it was late morning, there were no messages, no missed calls.

He tracked toward the open door.

He could hear Victoria's voice. He stopped in the doorway and watched her. Her back was to him, her red hair flowing over her shoulders and almost to her waist. She was wearing the same clothes she'd worn last night. He remembered peeling those clothes off her, tasting and touching her before burying himself inside her.

He wanted to do it again. And again. His dick ached with the need to do so. He could go over, nibble the skin on her neck, strip her slowly before spreading her out for his pleasure…

She raked a hand through her hair, but she didn't turn.

"Everything's fine, Ian. It'd be better if you'd give me the target. … No, I'm not having fun. … I don't give a fuck about Nick Brandon! He's just a guy I once knew. … Yes, fine. … Roger."

She dropped the phone to her side but still didn't turn. Nick walked out into the living room, naked as fuck, and she turned when she heard the movement. Her eyes widened. And then she reddened and turned her head as if she were embarrassed.

What a fucking turn-on. She was hot and sassy, bolder than hell—and still virginally embarrassed.

"Don't give a fuck, huh?" he said, his pride stinging just a little bit more than he would like. "I'm afraid you had me fooled last night, sugar."

"You were listening to my call?"

"It's a small apartment. Couldn't help but hear it." He walked over to the fridge and opened it. Taking out a bottle of water, he twisted the cap off and took a long swallow.

"Maybe you should put some clothes on."

He leaned against the bar and grinned. His dick stood up like a flagpole. "Why? You saw it all last night. Licked quite a bit of it too, if I remember right. Would have sworn you gave a fuck then."

"It's none of Ian's business, all right? I don't want him knowing… uh…"

"That we've fucked? Yeah, probably not a good idea. He might get jealous over that one."

The thought of her and Ian Black definitely made him feel a twinge of something that pissed him off.

She sucked in a breath. "He's not getting jealous. Why would he? But he might just think there was something more to the story about how you came to be in the right place at the right time if he knew we were, uh, having sex."

"Do you have any idea how red you get when you try to say what we did together? Yet you asked me if I was going to fuck you or talk all night. How did you manage that?"

She lifted her chin. "It was dark." She waved a hand and then turned away. "Jesus, can you just put some clothes on?"

He sauntered toward her, stopping when he could feel the heat of her reaching out and burning him up. His hands itched to grab her, to turn her toward him and make her his again.

But there were other considerations, and he was decent enough to remember them.

"I'll put on some clothes, but only because last night was your first time. But tell me you aren't sore, even a little bit, and I'll have you naked in about ten seconds."

Her throat moved as she swallowed. "It's not too bad, but yeah, I'm sore."

"Figured that, unfortunately. I think we got a bit carried away. Or I did."

She met his gaze again. Her cheeks were so delightfully red. He loved that about her.

"I wouldn't have wanted it any other way."

He grinned. "Guess I should get dressed. We have work to do."

"Yes."

He went back into the bedroom and dragged on his pants and T-shirt. When he returned, Victoria was standing with binoculars and looking across to the consulate. The guns were in position on the floor below the window. All they needed was to know who they were here for and why, and they'd be in business. He prayed it wasn't something he couldn't do, like let a Freedom Force terrorist walk when he had one in the scope.

Then again, that's why he wasn't the one taking the

shot. He cast a glance at Victoria, wondering again how she could so easily take orders from Ian Black. The man was dirty through and through.

But Nick knew why she did—or why she said she did. *Emily.*

If HOT found Emily for her, then she wouldn't have to take orders from Black ever again. She could go back to the States and start a new life. A life that didn't involve Qu'rim, Ian Black… or him.

That thought sent a sharp feeling slicing into him, though he wasn't sure what it was or why. She was just a woman he'd had sex with—a hot, amazing woman—and not anyone he needed in his life. Though he'd like to keep her for a while and have a lot of sex with her, no doubt.

He was thinking about when he might possibly be able to get her beneath him again when Victoria's phone buzzed. She glanced at it tiredly—and then she made a little sound of shock as she swiped the screen and pressed it to her ear.

"Emily! My God, where have you been?"

SEVENTEEN

VICTORIA'S HANDS SHOOK AND HER heart had shot into the danger zone the second she'd looked at her phone and seen Emily's name. For months, Emily's phone had simply rang and rang whenever she dialed the number, but now she was taking a call and praying it was really Emily on the other end.

The silence dragged on for long moments, but then there was a voice, very quiet and still.

"Victoria?"

"Yes, Em, it's me! Where are you, sweetie? Where have you been? I've been so worried!"

"I'm fine. I just… I wanted to talk to you. It's been so long, and I've been scared. Zaran…"

Victoria's heart thumped. She glanced at Nick. He looked stony-faced. So different from the sensually teasing man who'd stood there a few seconds ago. "What about Zaran, Em?"

"He's… different these days." Her voice broke off in a sudden sob. "I want to leave, Victoria. But I can't get away. He took my phone, but I found it this morning, and I had to call you."

"Where are you?"

"I don't know. We've been traveling. We reached a city, but I don't know where it is." Emily sniffled. "I just want to go home. I want to go back to New Orleans and start again."

Victoria gripped the phone tightly. "We're going to do that, baby. I swear we are. I'm going to get you away from him."

"I don't know how you can." Her voice sank to a whisper. "He hates you, Victoria. He keeps telling me he'll kill you if I don't stay with him. So I stay—but I want to go."

Victoria closed her eyes. She felt a tear slide down her cheek. Nick's arms snaked around her from behind. He held her close, his solid body pressed against hers, and she felt his strength seep into her. It was just what she needed right now. She always handled everything alone, but it was nice to have someone hold her. Be there for her.

"Don't worry about me, Em. Just walk away whenever you can. He won't hurt me."

"You don't know him. He'll kill you if I leave. And then he'll kill me."

Victoria's throat ached. "Not if I kill him first. Just hang on, Emily. I'm going to find you, I swear."

"I wish you could, but— Shit, I have to go!"

The line went dead and Victoria's blood turned to ice. "Emily? Emily!"

She knew her sister was gone, but the adrenaline rush made her furious and jumpy. Her eyes blurred with tears—there was no holding them back now. They welled and spilled over, and she turned in Nick's arms to bury her head against his chest. All the tears and frustration she'd felt for so long came rushing out. She fisted her hands in Nick's T-shirt and cried while he rubbed her back and didn't say anything.

She didn't know how long they stood like that before she lifted her head and gazed up into his eyes. His brows were drawn low, and his expression was thunderous. It made her heart catch and then speed up again.

"I'm sorry, Victoria."

She pushed herself away from him and swiped beneath her eyes. Fresh embarrassment set in, heating her skin and making her wish she could go hide in the other room for a few hours. But hiding from Nick was impossible. She'd learned that last night.

"It's okay. She's alive, and that's a good thing." She pulled in a deep breath and let it out again in a rush. She had to get her equilibrium back. "We have to find her, Nick. She's in danger—and your colonel promised he'd get her out of here."

He looked torn, and her belly began to ache. Nothing had changed after last night. She'd known it was the truth, but to see it so blatantly after all they'd done together in the darkness of the night—after all they'd shared—made her feel more alone than ever.

"Victoria—"

"No!" Because she couldn't stand it. She couldn't stand here and listen to him tell her that until they knew what Ian was doing and who he was working for they wouldn't do a thing for Emily. She knew what the bargain was, but dammit, they could alter it. She'd do anything they wanted if they just got Emily away from Zaran bin Yusuf. "She's scared and she wants to leave, but he's threatened to kill me if she does—and her."

"Did she tell you where she's being held?"

"She doesn't know. She's with him, though. Traveling with him. They could be anywhere…" Her gut churned as sudden understanding rocked through her. "They could be *here*, Nick! Right here in Ras al-Dura! You said he was coming this way."

It wasn't impossible. If Zaran were coming to meet with someone, then why not? Emily could even now be nearby. It made her frantic, but there was nothing she could do. She didn't have the technology to find Emily.

But Nick did. His people did.

Nick took his phone from his pocket and dialed. She had no idea what he planned to say to his people, but her pulse skipped and fresh adrenaline swirled through her, making her tremble with the desire to act *now.*

His eyes didn't leave hers as he started to speak. "Got a situation here, Richie. Emily Royal just called—and she's in danger."

Victoria waited while he filled in the guy on the other end of the phone. She didn't know what she expected, but for him to say "Copy" and hang up a few minutes later wasn't quite it.

She balled her hands into fists at her side. "That's all?"

Nick's hazel eyes were somber. "There've been no new reports on bin Yusuf's whereabouts. We're keeping an eye out for him, but he's not surfaced yet."

Victoria wanted to scream. "So basically it's business as usual and never mind that my sister is scared and wants to go home."

Nick blew out an explosive breath. "It's the best I can

do! The team knows Emily's with him instead of in a camp somewhere, and that's a good thing. But we don't know what he's planning, so there's nowhere to look for him. We just have to wait for him to reveal himself. When he does, they'll move."

Bitterness swelled in her throat. "Will they? Or is that just what you've been told to say in order to keep me compliant?"

He took a step toward her, his expression angry. And then he grabbed her arms and yanked her toward him. She should fight him, but a part of her didn't want to. A part of her wanted him to touch her, no matter what.

"Goddammit, I'm on *your* side, Victoria. I'm trying to help you. I've been trying to help you since the moment you dropped your ass into the middle of my op and shot it all to hell."

She searched his gaze, her breath hitching. He'd been so furious with her that day. But he'd helped her get out, and she'd been wondering why ever since.

"Why? Why would you do that?"

He'd been asking himself the same question for the past couple of weeks. He'd been pissed as shit with her and ready to haul her back to Mendez and HOT HQ when she'd fucked up his mission, but somewhere along the way he'd lost his conviction. Instead of wanting to punish her, he'd wanted to know what the hell was going on with her.

If he thought about it, he knew the moment it had

happened. When they thought the roof was coming down on their heads and he'd rolled her beneath him to protect her. She'd been so tough and hard up until then, but in that moment she'd been small, soft, and she'd trembled as he'd held her. She'd tucked her face against his chest, and every last protective instinct he'd had—as well as every last ounce of testosterone—had roared to life inside him.

He'd wanted to spank her ass for what she'd done— and then he'd wanted to kiss her senseless and hold her close. When she'd pulled a gun on him and Dex, a tiny part of him had silently cheered her fighting spirit. He'd known it even if he hadn't wanted to admit it then. He could have tried harder to disarm her without getting himself or Dex killed, but he'd walked away and given her the chance she needed.

He still didn't know why he'd done it. But he had, and now they were here, together, and this need he had for her hadn't abated one bit. If anything, it was growing worse.

Which made absolutely no fucking sense.

"Why?" she repeated.

"Because I think you need help. Because I think no one has been on your side for a very long time."

Her rain-gray eyes glittered, but he wasn't certain if it was anger or hurt or even sadness he saw reflected there.

"I'm a traitor, Nick. I shot the wrong guy, remember? And I don't regret it, just so you know. If I'd killed bin Yusuf—or if you had—Emily might be dead too."

His gut clenched. He'd called her a traitor. He'd even believed it at the time. He didn't anymore. "I know."

Her phone buzzed again and she gasped. But then her expression fell and he knew it wasn't her sister calling back. This time, she punched the Speaker button and Ian Black's voice filled the silence as he spoke to someone in the background.

"Hello, Ian."

The conversation abruptly stopped. "Victoria... Am I on speaker?"

"Yes. Do you want me to take you off?" Her eyes met Nick's. She looked determined, angry, and even a little bit lost.

"No, it's fine. How's it going out there, Brandon?"

"Boring," Nick said in his best Ozarks drawl.

"Aren't snipers used to that?"

"Yeah, but it doesn't mean we have to like it."

"Tonight there's a garden party at the consulate," Ian said, launching into the briefing. "There's a scientist supposed to be there. Igor Chernovsky. He works at VECTOR. Or did work."

The hair on Nick's arms prickled. VECTOR was the Russian laboratory in Koltsovo that housed some of the few remaining stocks of smallpox. The only other place the virus existed was at the CDC in Atlanta, Georgia.

Victoria seemed to know what that meant as well because her eyes widened. She mouthed the word *fuck*.

"Chernovsky is reputed to be trying to negotiate a deal to sell smallpox to the Qu'rimi Opposition. He has to be stopped. I'm sending over photos—"

"Wait a minute," Nick said. "How do we know he doesn't have any vials with him? If he does, and we kill him, we're leaving those vials in the open."

"Don't worry yourself about that part, Brandon," Black said coolly. "Your job is to kill Chernovsky before the deal is made. Understood?"

Nick clenched his fingers into fists. "Copy that."

"Good. Victoria, I don't have to tell you how critical this is. Take Chernovsky down and get out immediately. Return to Baq as quickly as you can."

"Ian…"

"Yes?"

Victoria shot Nick a look. "Emily called. She's with bin Yusuf. Is he in Ras al-Dura?"

Ian huffed a breath. "I don't have that information, Victoria."

"Would you tell me if you did?"

There was silence for a long moment. "If it didn't compromise a mission, yes. But I don't know. I honestly don't. Now get the job done and get back here."

"And what happens if I don't?"

There was a stunned silence on the other end. Nick's chest swelled with pride at the militant look on Victoria's face. She had power, and she wasn't afraid to use it.

"If you don't, you don't get paid. Not to mention the Qu'rimis get smallpox, and that's not a good plan for anyone, believe me. What the fuck is this?"

Her eyes flashed. "I'm sick of being used, Ian. For two years, you've promised me you'd find my sister. And then you sent me to protect the man who turned her against her family and her country. If you're working for those terrorists, then I'm not working for you. I quit."

Nick knew he should be pissed—and he should be giving her the signal to stop, because if she quit and they didn't do this, then HOT wasn't getting answers to who Black was working for and where the intelligence leak was coming from. But the truth was that he was elated she was telling this asshole off. Elated she was standing up for herself.

"Goddammit, Victoria, we don't have time for this shit. I'm not fucking working for terrorists. There's a bigger picture at stake here, but trust me when I tell you I'm on the right side of this thing."

"Why should I trust you? How do I know you aren't lying to me?"

He was silent for a moment. "You don't. But if you let Chernovsky get away with this, then ask yourself if you can live with a smallpox outbreak. Because that's what will happen. The Qu'rimis will weaponize it—or the Freedom Force will. Do you want to be responsible for that?"

Victoria's brows arrowed down. "No, I don't. But Ian, if I find out you've lied to me and dragged me into something my gramps would be ashamed of me for, I'll hunt you down like a rabid dog and kill you. You got that?"

"Get the job done. I'll be waiting for you when it's over."

The line went silent and Victoria gripped her phone with a growl. "Son of a bitch."

Nick pulled her into his arms. She came willingly, her small frame shaking with anger—and maybe a touch of fear too, though she'd never admit it. He stroked her hair.

"I'm glad you did that."

"Are you? It's not what your colonel wanted."

Nick shook his head. "Can you believe that right now I don't give a shit what my colonel wants?"

She pushed away from him, her hands on his arms, and searched his gaze. "Don't get in trouble for me, Nick."

It touched him that she cared. "Hey, what happened to the woman who thought I wasn't doing enough to find her sister? I thought you were pissed at me too."

"You said you were on my side. I'm choosing to believe you. I know you want to help me find Emily." She took a deep breath. "After what you've done for your own sister, I don't think you'd let mine suffer if you could help it. It's not just that blood is thicker than water with you. You're wired to take care of people—and you can't ignore the fact Emily is being held against her will."

He blinked. She'd pretty much gotten it right. He did want to find Emily. But he was afraid he wanted to do it for Victoria more than he wanted to do it for Emily. He didn't quite know why that was, but he thought that right now he'd do nearly anything for her.

Before he could speak, she pulled his head down and kissed him. It was a sweet kiss, a hot kiss, their tongues tangling urgently. His dick went from zero to sixty in half a second. He wanted her badly, but now wasn't the time. Carefully, he ended the kiss and set her away from him.

Her skin was flushed, her eyes filled with passion, and it took everything he had to push her away.

"I have to call my guys," he said, his voice hoarse. "They have to know what's happening."

"I know." She stepped back and went over to check the equipment.

Nick walked over to the window. The consulate hummed with activity, cars coming and going, guards checking identification carefully before letting delivery trucks inside. Outside in the gardens, there was a tent being set up. It was far too hot to do anything out there now, but when the sun went down, it would be perfect.

Both for a party and for an assassination.

Nick took his phone out and texted Matt Girard. He

had to let them know about Chernovsky. If it blew his cover when HOT landed in the middle of Ian Black's mission, then so be it. But a rogue scientist with access to smallpox was not something to take lightly.

As expected, his phone lit up a second later.

"Brandon."

"Tell me everything."

But it wasn't Matt. It was Colonel Mendez, and he didn't sound in the least bit happy.

Nick gave Mendez all he knew—Chernovsky, smallpox, the party at the consulate, and the kill order.

Mendez swore long and low, and Nick knew this was news to the colonel. Which definitely didn't make the man happy, considering Ian Black was disavowed and shouldn't have access to such sensitive information. But he clearly did.

And HOT clearly didn't.

"Don't do a damn thing until I get some answers, Brandy. You got me?"

"Yes, sir," he said, though one look at Victoria told him that wasn't going to be easy. She was scanning the consulate through her scope, and she wore a look of determination. He didn't know what she was thinking, but he was pretty sure it didn't involve standing down at the moment. She'd been given her orders, and she was going to complete them like the professional she was.

And then she was going to rip Ian Black limb from limb, at least metaphorically. He almost felt sorry for the guy. Except, of course, he'd really like to rip the man apart himself—and not metaphorically.

He finished the call and walked over to where Victoria was peering through the scope. She glanced up at him, her lips set in a hard line.

"We've got a few hours until dark," he said softly. "We've been over this again and again. There are no more calculations to take."

Her fingers tightened on the grip. And then she sighed and lowered the scope.

"I don't want to just sit here and do nothing when Emily's out there," she said. "I feel like I need to be looking for her, not waiting here for some asshole Russian."

"I know. But there's nowhere to look. We don't know where she is."

"Can't your people trace the call? Something? I thought you were super soldiers."

"They're working on it. These things take time, especially since we're dealing with a country in the midst of a civil war. The Qu'rimi networks aren't precisely stable right now. Our phones are sat phones. Hers isn't."

She bowed her head. "I know. Shit, I just feel so helpless!"

"Let's power up the computer and see what Black's sent us. We need to know who this guy is."

EIGHTEEN

JOHN MENDEZ WAS NOT A happy camper, as the saying went. All these years in the Army, busting his ass and putting his country first, and some disavowed CIA asshole had information he didn't. It was enough to send his blood pressure into the danger zone.

He was on a secure sat link back to DC, waiting for his contact to come back on the line. A Russian scientist with fucking smallpox. How had they let this get out? And what the fuck was Ian Black doing, sending his mercenary snipers after this man? Did he even fucking know if Chernovsky had the virus with him?

If he did and Brandy and Victoria Royal took him out, that would leave the virus vulnerable.

Though maybe that was the plan. Kill Chernovsky and get the virus without paying for it. It was just the sort of deal the Freedom Force would make.

Echo Squad was in place in Ras al-Dura, but until he had more, he couldn't send an American special ops team into a Russian facility to kidnap—or kill—a Russian citizen. Did the Russians even know what Chernovsky was doing? It didn't strike him as the kind of thing they'd care for.

Since the end of the Cold War, the Americans and Russians had done a diplomatic dance based on mutual mistrust and suspicion. Russia had smallpox stocks because America had them and vice versa. Even if it was best for the planet to destroy them—and he in no way knew whether it was or not—it wasn't likely that either side ever would.

Smallpox was here—in the lab, anyway—to stay. And sensible people really wanted to keep the virus confined to a lab, whether they were Russian or American.

But take a scientist who was disgruntled or in need of money, some lax security, and it all fell apart. Hell, not that long ago, there were vials of the virus found in a lab in Maryland. Fucking Maryland when they were supposed to be in the CDC in Atlanta.

Not that it surprised him, really. If DARPA wasn't up to something, then someone else was. Someone always was.

"Thanks for waiting, John."

"So what have you got for me?"

"Not much. Our guys know who Chernovsky is, but we've got nothing on him trying to sell the virus. Of course, it would take days to sift the intel."

"That's not good news, Bill. If Ian Black is to be believed, Chernovsky's in Qu'rim trying to make a deal."

"I've got people on it, but I don't know where Black's getting his intel…"

Mendez snorted. "If we knew that, we'd know a lot more about the man, wouldn't we?"

"He was always a quiet sort. Intense. I didn't dislike

him… but then I didn't like him either. No idea what he did to get on the wrong side of the agency. The record is carefully blank on that score."

Mendez raked a hand through his hair. His eyes were gritty, and he was pushing about forty-eight hours without sleep. "Take it as far as you can go. But be careful. Whoever's feeding him information knows a lot more than we do. I don't think it'd be a good idea to get their attention."

"I hear you, man." Bill sighed. "You be careful out there too, Johnny. Qu'rim's a bad place to be these days. You're getting too close to retirement for this shit."

Mendez snorted. "I'm forty-nine, old man. Younger than you. And I'm not ready for retirement yet. I'd still like a star one of these days."

"Hell, you already run the most elite unit the military has. Why do you need a star? There are generals with less power than you have."

"Yeah, but I'm never satisfied with where I am. There's always a new mountain to climb."

"I'll call if I hear anything."

"No matter the hour. I'm here."

"I know it."

Mendez ended the call and sat with his eyes focused on the far wall. What the fuck now? Let Brandy take out this scientist? Send in Echo Squad? Storm Ian Black's headquarters and take him into custody?

Fuck, so many options. And none of them good. He picked up the phone and made another call. He needed transport—and he needed it fast.

The party was in full swing across the street and had been for over an hour. There was no sign of the target, and no word from Mendez or HOT. Nick watched the crowd with mounting frustration. It had been about four hours since Mendez told him not to act, but there'd been nothing since. He'd sent a text message. All he'd received in return was a simple acknowledgement.

Victoria was on edge. He'd watched her prowl the apartment for hours now, her slim body encased in black, her hair swept back in a ruthless ponytail. He'd wanted to strip her naked and make love to her more than once, wanted to calm her with his mouth and body, but every moment was crucial and there was no time to take away from the task at hand.

They'd gotten the dossier on Igor Chernovsky from Black. The most current photo of the scientist was only a week old. He was tall and lean, with the gaunt look of a man who lived off caffeine and cigarettes and probably forgot to eat half the time. Chernovsky didn't look like a well man, that's for certain, though there was nothing about him being ill in the dossier.

Nick scanned the crowd again, but there was still no sign of Chernovsky. If the man was here, he wasn't coming outside. Nor was he walking in front of any of the many illuminated windows of the consulate.

Nick scrubbed a hand through his hair and growled in frustration. Beside him, Victoria looked up from the weapon she'd been cradling against her cheek. The long rifle was sleek and beautiful, ready to kill with a single squeeze of the trigger.

Victoria was much the same, he thought, without a trace of irony. He'd worked with other snipers before, but none had been quite so intense as she was. Then again, none of them were dealing with the emotional turmoil of a sister being held by a terrorist. Victoria had been quiet since the call from Emily. It killed him that he had no information for her, but the best he could do was hope that HOT figured out where her sister was before it was too late.

He didn't know what to say to her other than to tell her that he believed in the colonel's ability to deliver. And that he usually did.

But he wasn't as certain this time. And there wasn't a fucking thing he could do about it, though he kept trying to imagine how he could create the outcome Victoria wanted. He had no answers, and it pissed him off.

"You okay?" she asked, her voice a little rusty.

"Yeah. You?"

She shrugged and turned back to her weapon and the scope mounted on top of it. "I'm all right. I just want to get the fuck out of here."

"I know." They'd argued about who was going to take the shot. He'd said she was too upset and angry. She'd said he was too arrogant and too used to getting his way. In the end, he'd suggested they flip for it.

She'd told him to fuck off and stationed herself at the weapon. He'd finally decided, after fighting the urge to drag her up bodily and prove to her that there was at least one area of life in which she obeyed him without question, that fighting about it would serve no purpose other than to piss them both off. And cancel out any chance he stood of getting in her panties once this was over.

He scanned the crowd again, almost bored with the routine—but this time a chill shot through him as the binocs landed on a new arrival. A tall, gaunt man in a tuxedo emerged from a car that had just pulled up in front of the consulate. The man held a lit cigarette in one hand and a briefcase in another. He turned and looked toward the road, almost as if he were looking at the apartment where they were hidden, and then flicked the cigarette from his fingers before ducking into the building.

Fuck. The fact the man had a briefcase did not bode well for the idea that Chernovsky didn't have vials with him. Maybe it was papers, but maybe it wasn't.

"Chernovsky's arrived," he said, and he felt Victoria tense beside him for a split second. "He's carrying a briefcase."

"Shit… I should call Ian."

Nick started to tell her not to do it just yet when the next car disgorged its passenger. Nick was still watching, out of habit, when Ian Black stepped out into the open. Nick's eyes bulged as Black moved away from the car. His face was wreathed in smiles as he greeted someone who hurried over and shook his hand.

"I don't think you should call Ian."

"Holy shit," Victoria said, and he knew she'd seen Black. "Why didn't he fucking tell us he'd be here?"

"I don't know. But I don't like it." Nick whipped out his phone and pressed the button to speed-dial HQ. Mendez answered on the first ring.

"Chernovsky's arrived and he's got a briefcase. Ian Black is here too."

Mendez swore. Nick held the phone away from his ear for a long minute while the colonel turned the air blue.

"That wily son of a bitch," Mendez said when he could form a complete sentence. "He's the fucking buyer, and he needs you to kill Chernovsky so he either doesn't have to pay or the scientist doesn't make another deal. Goddammit!"

That's pretty much what Nick was thinking too. Why else would Black send them on this secretive goose chase and not tell them he was also going to be in Ras al-Dura at the appointed time?

"Do we take the shot or not?"

Mendez didn't answer for a moment, though Nick could hear the man swearing under his breath. "Take the shot. Let Black win this round, but only because we're fucking going after him next."

"Copy, sir."

"And Brandy?"

"Yes, sir?"

"Your team is there along with Echo Squad, but there's no time to get you wired in. You'll have to go this alone, son."

"Not a problem, sir. It's what I do."

"Good luck."

Victoria couldn't believe what her scope was showing her. Ian Black chatted with another man, smiling and laughing as he held a drink in his hand. Periodically, he seemed to look toward the apartment building. He knew they were there, of course. And he knew they were watching.

She kept expecting him to take his phone out and text her or something, but her phone remained silent. She'd threatened to quit earlier. For all he knew, she had. Was he here to do the job himself? Or was he here because he was the buyer?

If so, why the fuck did he need her to kill Chernovsky?

Colonel Mendez had told Nick to go through with the job, so that's what they were doing. If Ian was the buyer, then they had to stay on target and eliminate Chernovsky. And if Ian wasn't the buyer, they still had to stop the scientist. Maybe Ian was there to prevent the vials from falling into rogue hands. That's what she hoped, anyway.

Because no matter how pissed she was at Ian for various reasons, she'd always thought he was honorable. She'd never wanted to believe he'd set her up, and when he insisted he hadn't, she'd been relieved.

But what if she was a fool? What if she was a poor judge of character and Ian was as dirty as seven-day-old socks?

She told herself that she'd pegged Jonah right, and Rascal—and hell, even Zaran bin Yusuf since she'd never liked him. But what if she'd gotten Ian wrong?

"No sign of Chernovsky," Nick said from his position beside her. "One mil right."

She dialed as he said, but she searched Ian out again. Still talking, still laughing and acting like he was right at home. Disavowed CIA. Russian spy? Double agent?

God, Gramps had to be spinning in his grave at the

idea she'd worked for this man for two years.

Victoria chewed the inside of her lip. She was hurt and angry, and she wanted to call Ian and ask him what the fuck. But she wouldn't. She'd do this damn job, and she'd walk right back into his compound and pretend she was a happy little soldier.

Because, more than anything, she wanted answers. If she had to help Nick break into Ian's server room herself, she'd do it.

"Chernovsky. Twelve o'clock."

Victoria's breathing slowed as she found her target and concentrated on him. Once she pulled this trigger, the party would descend into chaos. She and Nick would have seconds to get out before the apartment was swarmed by Russians or Qu'rimi authorities—or both. They'd planned their escape route to the second. All she had to do was pull the trigger to set it into motion.

Chernovsky didn't have the briefcase this time. Not that she'd expected him to. Her finger rested over the trigger, but she couldn't shoot just yet. Chernovsky was standing too near a group of innocent bystanders.

"Black's on the move," Nick said, and Victoria's heart squeezed tight. She couldn't follow Ian when she had to follow Chernovsky.

But Ian passed into her field of view. He didn't speak to Chernovsky. He simply walked by the man.

Chernovsky bent to pick something up off the ground. The crowd slid in front of him and Victoria made a sound of frustration. But then his tall head rose above the rest and he turned and walked toward the edge of the gathering, moving in the same direction Ian had gone.

"This is it, Victoria."

"I know."

She followed him away from the crowd. He didn't go far, but he moved into a place where no one else was around. She thought Ian might appear, but he didn't.

"Now. It has to be now."

She heard the urgency in Nick's voice, but she had her own rhythm of doing things. She pulled in a breath—and exhaled slowly, her finger squeezing the tight trigger back toward her body. She said a prayer for Igor Chernovsky's soul as she took the shot that would end his life.

She always said a prayer. She didn't doubt that the killings were necessary—kill one, save thousands—but they were still husbands, fathers, sons, and brothers to someone. Someone, somewhere, must have loved them at one time even if others feared the destruction they could cause.

The shot hit its target. Igor Chernovsky dropped to the ground, and the crowd erupted in screams.

Nick bolted to his feet and began breaking down his equipment. Victoria disassembled the sniper rifle and stowed it quickly. They'd wiped the apartment for prints earlier, packed everything they didn't need, and set the bags near the door. All they had to do was grab their gear and go.

Across the street, the consulate erupted in pandemonium. Somewhere a siren blared into the night. Victoria slung her pack over her shoulder, grabbed her case, and shot for the door behind Nick.

They shouldered the rest of what they needed and then burst out the door and down the hall. Alarms were sounding in the night as they raced into a utility stairwell and started pounding down the stairs. If they encountered anyone, they'd have to determine quickly if it was friend or foe and act.

But no one got in their way as they ran into the parking garage and raced for the Land Rover. Nick had moved the vehicle earlier, putting it near the exit. There were other cars in the garage, but no one else was there. People were home, for the most part, and settling in for the night. Except now their night was interrupted by the sounds of sirens and screaming.

Nick threw their gear in the car and covered it with blankets; then he got into the driver's seat while she took the passenger's after whipping a burka over her head and settling it over her clothing. They'd determined he'd be the driver earlier, and she was actually glad of it, considering how drained she felt.

The street in front of the consulate was blocked off as the Russians quickly took charge of the situation. Nick turned the opposite direction from the consulate and started down the street. If they could just reach the end, they'd slide into the city traffic and become anonymous.

But an armored car shot across the intersection and blocked the road.

"Fuck," Nick muttered as he slammed on the brake. There were other cars caught in the jam besides them, so it wasn't immediately dangerous.

But it *was* dangerous. If the Russians insisted on searching their car—and they likely would since neither one of them was Qu'rimi—they'd be discovered.

Victoria reached inside her burka and put her hand on her Sig. Her heart thumped, and sweat rolled between her breasts. If the Russians took them into custody, she didn't have high hopes for their fate once the guns were found.

A helicopter suddenly appeared overhead, its rotors whipping frantically. For a scant moment, Victoria thought it might be Nick's people coming to help them—

But a searchlight flicked on and began sweeping over the traffic as if searching for something.

When it stopped on their car and lingered, Victoria had to shield her eyes from the glare. She prayed it would go away again, that it was temporary.

But the glare stayed—and a voice boomed from a loudspeaker.

NINETEEN

"FUCKING HELL, THIS IS GOING to shit fast." It was Big Mac who'd spoken.

No one disagreed with him.

"We've got to get them out of there," Garrett said. "If the Russians get them…"

He didn't need to say what would happen then. If the Russians got Brandy and Victoria, it was over. Because HOT wasn't going to be allowed to charge in and take their teammate from the Russians. The Cold War was a long time ago, but even though missiles weren't pointed at each other's cities anymore, it still wasn't a good idea to piss off the guys who maintained an entire nuclear arsenal they could aim at you if they wanted. The Russians might have destroyed a lot of weapons under the various treaties in place since the Berlin Wall fell, but that didn't mean they had nothing left.

They had plenty, and everyone in this organization knew it.

"If we get caught interfering in a Russian operation," Richie Rich growled over his comm link, "there will be diplomatic hell to pay."

"We won't get caught." It was Hawk who'd spoken that time. "Dex and I can disable the helicopter, and then we'll fire on the armored car. They'll think they're under attack from outside, and they'll shift focus. If we can get them to move, Brandy'll know what to do."

"Do it," Richie said.

"Copy."

Garrett waited in an alley with Sam "Knight Rider" McKnight. Their eyes met in the darkness and they nodded. Garrett gripped his assault rifle tighter, ready to go on the attack if it was necessary.

They'd been tasked with getting into position and helping Brandy escape if it became necessary. Echo Squad was also working the scene, preventing anyone from leaving the consulate grounds without being searched. Since there were NATO troops deployed to Ras al-Dura to help the Qu'rimi government maintain the peace, Echo Squad was acting in that capacity, blending into the background and acting as peacekeepers would. They were tasked with not allowing the virus to get out of the consulate. It wasn't an easy job, and Garrett hoped like hell they succeeded.

If they were lucky, Chernovsky hadn't had the virus with him in the first place. But there was no way of knowing that for certain.

The helicopter hovering over the traffic seemed to have targeted one car in particular, but then the spotlight moved on and the voice over the loudspeaker kept issuing orders to the street in general. The Russians were searching for something, but they didn't quite know what. Still, as quickly as they'd mobilized, it wasn't a good sign they were planning to give up the search anytime soon.

Suddenly there was a metallic pop and twang—and the whine of the helo's rotors grew high-pitched as smoke poured from the tail. The pilot only had seconds to act before the fuel caught fire. The craft suddenly banked to the left, and the helo went down on the massive grounds of the consulate. Men poured from the interior before the vehicle caught fire, and Garrett turned his attention toward the intersection where the armored car still blocked the street.

The night air exploded with the sound of rapid gunfire. Hawk and Double Dee were firing on the car—and the occupants were firing back. A good sign, he hoped.

The armored car roared forward and then back again—and then it turned, facing the direction of the gunfire. Garrett hoped it was just the opening Brandy needed to get free.

"Come on, Brandy, step on the fucking gas," Garrett muttered. A second later, a Land Rover bounced up onto the sidewalk and shot alongside the traffic. Gunfire blazed from the passenger side as it careened into the intersection on two wheels. The armored car couldn't turn fast enough to stop the Land Rover from shooting into the gap.

Metal scraped against metal as the vehicle forced its way between cars that were sitting too close for it to pass smoothly. Tires squealed and engines whined as the intersection turned into a bumper-car derby—but then Brandy sped out the other side and gunned the engine. Horns blared and drivers yelled, but the Land Rover disappeared behind some buildings.

"Fuck, that was close," Sam said.

"Amen, brother. Keep going, Brandy. Drive the fuck out of that bitch and get away safe."

"We have no choice, Nick," Victoria said as they sped through the city streets. "We have to use Ian's contacts as planned."

Nick gripped the wheel hard. "He's fucking dirty, Victoria. How do we know he won't turn us over now that he has what he wants? Jesus, that helicopter arrived damn fast considering it was mere minutes since we'd fired. How did the Russians mobilize so quickly?"

She'd been asking herself the same thing. But why would Ian tell the Russians they were there when it would reveal he had knowledge about the situation?

"You may be right. But how else are we getting across the desert without his help? Unless your guys have set up an escape route for us?"

Nick growled. "This mission is under the radar, so no."

"Under the radar? You didn't tell me that before."

He threw a hard glance at her. "No."

Frustration was a solid lump in her throat. If this was under the radar, then maybe they'd promised her the moon without ever intending to deliver.

No. She wasn't going to think like that. Not yet.

"And you still aren't going to tell me a damn thing, I take it?"

"I can't. Just trust me."

"I do trust you." It was true. And not just because he'd been inside her, making love to her so sweetly she'd cried with the joy of it. She trusted him because he was too damn decent not to. "But that doesn't mean I don't want to know the details anyway."

"I can't tell you."

"I think you fucking can. We're running for our lives, and I've risked everything by getting you into Ian's organization. The least you can do is be straight with me in return."

"Jesus, you never give up."

"No."

He shot her a look. "This could mean my ass, you realize." Then he sighed. "There's nothing much to tell. This isn't a sanctioned op, and we're all taking a risk trying to expose Black. But he's getting his information from somewhere, quite possibly the CIA, and Mendez wants to know where the leak is. There's more to it, including an operation that nearly cost one of our teammates his life, and that of his wife and son too. We almost didn't get there in time. And we still don't know who suppressed the information, but there could be a link to Black. Expose him, find the bastard."

Goose bumps rose on her skin at the thought. "Your teammate and his family are fine?"

"They are. He's the one who just shot us out of there, by the way."

"Then I'll have to thank him some day. Assuming we make it."

He reached over and took her hand, dragging it to his lips. When they touched her skin, her entire body quivered with heat and need.

"I won't let anything happen to you, baby."

Warmth filled her. "I won't let anything happen to you either. But consider that if it was Ian who turned us in, there won't be anyone waiting to help us."

He squeezed her hand before letting it go. "We'll try it your way, then. If we get to the checkpoint and no one is there, we'll know, right?

"That's what I think. If he meant to betray us back there, he'd have no reason to set up an escape route."

Nick sighed. "So where's this mysterious checkpoint we need to hit?"

She took her phone out and called up the plan Ian had sent earlier. She knew it could be a dummy plan, but she had to try. He always sent an escape plan when the environment was urban, so if he hadn't sent one this time, she'd have been suspicious. Maybe this plan was simply meant to make her believe all was normal. But maybe it was real.

It was a chance they had to take.

"The old quarter. The gray building on Sultan bin Mohammed Street, behind the McDonald's and across from the vegetable market."

"God, I hate Qu'rimi addresses. Why can't they number anything?"

"They're working on it."

"Not fast enough for us."

"We'll get there, Nick."

After that crazy escape from the blocked street and the intersection, when the helicopter had suddenly banked and crashed and Nick had pointed their car between other cars set too close together and just blasted his way through, she had to believe they would make it.

The streets were normal here as they rolled through the city. Not deserted, but not packed either. It was late, and many of the residents were at home. The drama at the consulate did not translate to the city as a whole. She knew their car bore obvious damage, but it wasn't the kind of thing most Qu'rimis would pay attention to. The streets here were usually jammed with any combination of rusted-out vehicles, donkey carts, motor scooters, and pedestrians. A scraped-up SUV was nothing in a city that constantly worried if it would have enough to eat this week or if the opposition forces would cut off the supplies to the city.

But the sooner they got another car, the better she'd feel.

Nick's phone rang and he slid the bar before putting it to his ear. "Brandon. … What? Seriously? … You guys fucking rock, you know that? … Yeah, love you too." He laughed and she realized it was the first time she'd heard him laugh without any kind of restraint. "See you in Baq. … Fuck yeah, you can count on it."

He dropped the phone into the cup holder. "Echo Squad has Ian Black in custody. They'll question him closely, relieve him of the virus if he has it, and let him go. But not before we can get back and search that server room."

Victoria blinked. "Wow, they have Ian? I didn't think he'd get caught."

"He's surrounded by the best of the best. How could he not get caught?"

"He won't tell them anything, you know."

"No, but if he has the vials, they'll at least be safe."

Victoria leaned her head against the seat and watched the city lights slide by overhead. She was more tired than she thought she'd be. The adrenaline rush from earlier was seeping away and leaving her boneless. She'd barely slept at all last night, and while she'd snatched naps today, it hadn't been quite enough. She'd been far more keyed up before an op than usual.

But that was because of Emily.

She'd kept thinking about Emily sounding so frantic on the phone, which had messed with her ability to rest. She'd had to shove all that emotional turmoil down deep to get the job done, but now it was out again and swirling inside her belly and brain. She was tired, but terrified for Emily.

It wasn't a good combination.

They eventually found the building they needed. Victoria dialed the number Ian had given her. If no one came, they'd know the entire mission had been a setup. But if someone did…?

It didn't mean Ian wasn't dirty, but it at least would help her feel less heartsick.

When a Qu'rimi man met them, she was still wary. Nick looked ready to shoot the man if he so much as looked at them cross-eyed, but the guy didn't show any signs of deception. He brought them a different car, wished them well and Godspeed, and took the one they had. He also gave them a key, but he told them he didn't know what the key went to.

Victoria dialed the next number in the plan, her heart thumping as she waited for everything to go to hell. But the next contact gave them the landmarks they needed and yet another contact gave them the street and building description. When they finally reached the safe haven for the night, she was beginning to believe it was real. The house was small and nondescript and had gates that opened and let them drive into a courtyard.

No one came out to greet them as they pushed open

the doors to the Jeep the first man had given them and stepped out into the silent night. This house was on the edge of the city in a quiet quarter, and nothing stirred other than the occasional cat on the prowl.

"I think we're alone," she said.

"I'll search the house."

He took the key and disappeared into the night. She let him go, leaning against the side of the Jeep and yawning. He returned a few minutes later, materializing out of the darkness and nearly scaring her silly.

"It's empty. I need to turn the Jeep, in case we need to leave fast, but take your pack and go inside. I'll be there in a minute."

She did as he said, too tired to argue as she trudged toward the darkened house. When she stepped inside, she realized he'd turned on a small battery-powered lantern for her. The house probably had electricity, but it wasn't a good idea to use it and become a beacon.

Victoria yawned again as she dropped her pack on a table. The house was small and made of mud brick, but its interior was cool and bare.

There was a bed in the main room and a crude shower with what turned out to be cold water. Victoria turned the tap off and dried her hand before returning to the bed and sinking down on it.

Nick came into the room and dropped his burden in the corner. The room grew smaller with him in it. The air thickened until breathing was almost impossible. She couldn't think of a single thing to say.

Nick came over and lifted her to her feet, dragging the burka over her head. She'd forgotten she was wearing it until that moment. She was cooler suddenly, lighter. She took a deep breath and let it out again.

Nick's hand ghosted over her cheek. "You're exhausted. You need to sleep."

"It's been a long day."

"A long few days."

"That too."

He tugged her T-shirt from her pants and lifted it over her head. She didn't protest as the cool air slid across her heated skin. Next he pushed her pants down, bending to untie her boots and slip them from her feet. When she was standing there in her underwear, he dragged the covers back and urged her into the bed.

"Where will you be?"

"I'll be watching for a while. If it stays quiet, I'll get some sleep too."

"Sleep with me."

It was a command and not a request. He chuckled softly.

"Nowhere else I'd rather be, sunshine."

Victoria turned onto her side as he pulled the covers back up. He bent and kissed her on the cheek. "Sleep, sweetheart. I'll keep you safe."

Nick prowled the small house and grounds for the first hour, listening for signs of anyone coming for them. But it was quiet and still, nothing but a dog barking here and there and a couple of cats yowling as they fought over territory. He cradled his MK 16 and patrolled the perimeter for another hour, checking and rechecking entry points and listening for traffic.

After the third hour, he decided they were safe for the night. Whatever Ian Black's reasons for being at the consulate tonight, he'd intended them to finish this job and get out safely. Nick went inside and propped the gun near the bed before stripping out of his T-shirt and lying down beside Victoria.

As much as he wanted to be naked with her, it was best if he keep his boots and pants on, just in case. He stayed on top of the covers, his dick hardening painfully as he listened to her breathing.

He dozed a bit, always waking every few minutes and listening to the night sounds. When Victoria turned in her sleep and threw a leg over him, his heart beat harder at the realization she'd pushed the covers down and her body was now bared to him. Her hand came to rest on his naked chest and she snuggled in closer. He put an arm around her and lay there with his cock throbbing and his blood humming.

"Nick," she sighed… and then her mouth opened over his skin, her tongue swirling along the ridge of his pectoral. When she found his nipple and tongued it, need arrowed through him, centering in his cock and making it impossibly hard.

"Victoria… honey, don't do that. Jesus, don't do that."

Her hand snaked down his body, beneath the waistband of his pants, and cupped the hard length of him.

Nick groaned. "Fuck."

"Yes," she said, though he'd meant it as a curse and not a suggestion.

Though it was a hell of a suggestion. He was wound tight after the events of the day, and coming would be the perfect way to relieve some of the tension. Apparently, she felt the same way.

With a growl, he pushed her onto her back, ripping the covers out of the way and snapping her bra open in quick succession. He lifted it off her arms and dropped it. Then he proceeded to attack her breasts, licking and sucking her nipples while she fisted her hands in his hair and moaned.

He slid down her torso, licking a path to the sweetness he craved. He could smell her desire, feel her heat as he pushed her panties down her legs and stripped them off.

"That's not what I was asking for," she gasped as he pushed her legs wide. "I wanted to please you."

He took that moment to slide his tongue into her wetness and lick his way up to her clitoris in one long swipe. "This does please me," he said as she moaned.

He pushed her folds open and fastened his mouth on her clitoris, licking, sucking, nibbling softly as her hips writhed and her body jerked. She arched her back, the peaks of her nipples the highest point on her body as her head rolled on the pillow.

"Nick, God... I want to come..."

He lifted her to him as if she were a buffet, eating her pussy like a man starved. She turned her head into the pillow and screamed as she came, and a wave of satisfaction rolled through him.

He got to his knees and started unbuckling his belt. He took his time freeing his cock, because she was still panting and gasping for breath. Then she looked right at him, her eyes gleaming in the meager light coming in from outside. He could see the hunger building again as she let her gaze sweep over him.

"Do you want more, Victoria?"

"Yes. Hell, yes."

He wrapped a fist around his aching cock and stroked it. Victoria scrambled up and pushed his pants down his hips. Then she bent and took him in her mouth, her sweet tongue curling and stroking the sensitive skin as she sucked him.

He was tempted to let her do it, let her finish him this way. But he wanted to be inside her. Needed to be.

As if she sensed his need, she lifted her head and looked up at him. Their eyes locked for a long while, and then he reached down and cupped the back of her head, lifting her to him and crushing her mouth to his.

They knelt together on the bed, arms wrapped around each other, mouths fused and hungrily demanding more, bodies slick with sweat and need.

His blood pounded in his veins, urging him to impale her and thrust hard, but last night was her first time and she wasn't quite ready for that. He had to take it easy with her. Treat her as delicately as she deserved.

What he hadn't counted on was her pushing him down to the bed, straddling him. She reached for his cock and guided it to her entrance. And then she sank down on him with a hiss and soft moan.

"You don't have to if it hurts," he whispered in her ear.

She pushed herself upright, sinking lower on his cock. "It hurts not to, Nick."

TWENTY

VICTORIA SAT VERY STILL, NOT moving. She was full, so full, her body stretched wide by his invasion. Yes, she was still sore, but she actually relished it. It wasn't bad, but all day long she'd been reminded of what she'd been doing to create that delicious ache between her thighs.

Skin against skin, breaths mingling, bodies joined deeply, the world slipping away for a few hours as they lost themselves in each other.

She wanted that again and again.

The night was quiet, the air charged as he lay beneath her, his hands on her hips, holding her still. She felt safe with him. Protected. A wave of warmth flowed through her, over her. She shuddered with everything she was feeling. His fingers tightened, digging into her skin.

"It's amazing being with you," she said, the darkness giving her courage.

His fingers tightened again, but he didn't say anything. A tiny shard of sadness pricked her, but she refused to let it take hold. Instead, she lifted herself slowly, deliberately, his cock sliding to her entrance, before sinking down again, taking him all in.

He let out an explosive breath when she did it again.

"You like that?" she asked, emboldened.

"Like it? That's a pretty mild word for how good it feels."

Victoria bent and kissed him, and he lifted his head to capture her mouth with a growl. As she grew accustomed to the feel of him, she moved faster, her body rising and sinking, taking him deeper, her clit grinding against his pubic bone whenever she lowered herself.

The pressure inside her built until she was moving frantically, trying to reach that peak once more. Nick held her hips hard, thrusting up inside her again and again. Her pussy tightened, the walls growing slicker than before, the tension spiraling to almost painful heights.

Victoria wrenched her mouth from his and lifted herself, throwing her head back as she rode him. He followed her up, his mouth fastening on one of her nipples, sucking hard. His fingers slipped between them, worked her deliberately, pushing her toward the edge.

This time when she came, there was no pillow to stuff in her mouth to mute the sound. She exploded with a sharp cry, her body milking his as tender walls clamped down and wrung every last ounce of pleasure from him that she could take.

"Fuck, you're tight," he groaned—and then he flipped her over while she was still shuddering and pounded into her, his cock taking her higher once more when she would have thought it was impossible.

She came again, even though she wasn't finished with her last orgasm. The power of this one caught her by surprise as it rippled over her, joining the first and expanding it beyond anything she'd yet experienced.

Victoria saw spots. Her vision blackened and her lungs refused to work for long seconds. Later, she would swear she passed out for those few seconds. When she came back to herself, Nick stiffened, his body jerking as he poured himself into her with a harsh groan.

When he was finished coming, he propped himself on his elbows, taking her mouth in a hot, thorough kiss that still managed to leave her panting in spite of everything they'd just done.

"I'll be your spotter for the rest of my career if every mission can end like this," he said with a soft laugh.

His voice warmed her. She was never quite certain how to act when they finished—what... fucking? Making love? Having sex?—but he made her feel at ease. Special. Beautiful.

She lifted her legs, sliding her knees along his sides before he caught them and pushed her open wider. His cock was still hard, and a shiver ran over her.

"Let's just skip the missions and do this," she said, shocked at the sensual purr in her voice.

"Sold," he whispered. "Let's get out of this one alive and then find an island somewhere. I'll make you come as often as you want. I'll be your sex slave to command."

She laughed. "Do you think you can make me come again, slave?"

He shifted his hips, his cock swelling inside her tender sex. "I *know* I can, sweetheart."

He wasn't lying.

They were on the desert highway early the next morning. Getting out of Ras al-Dura hadn't been difficult since the NATO peacekeepers controlled access. An assassination at the Russian consulate wasn't as important as keeping things running smoothly in the city and keeping the Qu'rimi opposition from invading.

Victoria was quiet as she stared straight ahead. She kept checking her phone, and Nick knew she was hoping for a message from Emily. But since that call early yesterday, there'd been nothing.

There'd been nothing from Mendez, either. He didn't question it too closely. The colonel had told him he was on his own from the moment he'd sent him on this mission.

Nick had known what he was getting himself into. What he hadn't known was how much he'd start to worry about Victoria and what happened to her while they played the part of mercenaries for Ian Black.

Or how much her quest for her sister would affect him. He didn't begin to know where to look for Zaran bin Yusuf, but for all he knew HOT was already doing so on this trip to Ras al-Dura.

He hoped like hell they were because he wanted Victoria to be happy. He wanted it with a strength that surprised him, in fact. More than that, he wanted her. Naked and leaning over him, her face contorted with pleasure as he stroked hard into her. God, he loved the way she looked when he took her.

Like she'd found heaven on earth. Like she was continually surprised at what her body could do when he made love to her.

She laid her head back on the seat and rolled her gaze toward him. When he looked at her, she smiled, and his heart gave a hard thump in his chest.

What the fuck was that?

"Whatever happens now, I want you to know how perfect you made my first time. And my second, third, fourth…" She laughed. "All my times, really. What a stud you are, Nick Brandon."

He laughed, though he was still trying to puzzle out what this sharpness in his chest was. "Yeah, if only you'd realized it back in sniper training."

"Yep, you could have tortured me with pleasure instead of harassing me with words. What a beautiful way to go that would have been."

He rubbed the back of his neck. Now that he knew her better, he knew she'd taken his trash-talking more seriously than she should have.

"I'm sorry for that. I told you why I did it."

She leaned over and kissed his cheek. "I know. Competition, blah blah blah. Over and done."

She sat back again. Her brows drew down as she watched the scenery pass them by.

"Leaving is the right thing to do," he told her, knowing what she was thinking. "Mendez will find Emily."

"I feel like she's there, waking up in Ras al-Dura right now, and I'm doing nothing but putting miles between us. It feels wrong, Nick."

He gripped the wheel harder. "It's not wrong. HOT will find her."

Victoria's head whipped around. "Did you just say

HOT? My God, I thought that was a myth. A shadowy special-ops team more secretive than Delta Force—and with more money and less restrictions on how they operate."

He almost groaned. Shit, she was affecting his ability to compartmentalize the job. Not a good thing.

"I can neither confirm nor deny," he said, and even he knew it sounded like a load of bullshit when he said it. *Busted.*

She whistled softly. "I'm impressed. It was always a rumor, but no one ever had proof. If you're a sniper for them... wow. I'd have loved to get recruited for HOT." She frowned. "Do they even take women?"

He thought of Lucky MacDonald. "It's beginning to happen, yeah."

"Awesome."

She didn't say anything for a couple of miles, and he wondered if he should ask what she was thinking.

"One of the things I hated about the Army," she said, "was how hard it was to get to do what I was good at. On the one hand, the Army is awesome for making changes and being blind once they've done so—gays in the service, for instance—but let a woman into a Special Forces group? Hell, no."

"Change takes time."

"Ian didn't give a fuck that I didn't have a dick. To him, the ability was all that mattered."

Nick ground his teeth together. Sometimes he hated the way she said that man's name. "I don't think Ian Black had the leisure to be picky."

Wrong thing to say, dude.

He could feel Victoria bristling like a porcupine.

"So if he *could* be picky, then he wouldn't choose a mere woman like me to do the job, is that it?"

"That's not what I meant."

She huffed out a breath. "Believe it or not, I know. But it still pisses me off. If you were a woman, you'd know exactly what I'm talking about."

"If I were a woman, you wouldn't have screamed my name six times last night."

She was silent for a long moment. And then she laughed. "Touché, asshole."

Warmth spread through his bones, his blood. Goddamn, he really liked this woman. She never backed down. She gave as good as she got, but she had that aura of sweetness and vulnerability to her that he couldn't help but be drawn to. She brought out his protective instincts, even though he was pretty certain she was more than capable of taking care of herself.

He liked her. Really liked her.

But once this mission was over, he'd probably never see her again. They'd go their separate ways. Him to HOT, her back to the States and her sister if everything went as she hoped.

This time together, this mission, was all they had. For some reason, that bothered him more than it should.

After sharing driving duties, they reached the last checkpoint at nine o'clock that night. It had been a long day filled with tension and urgency, but at last it was time to pull over and get a few hours' rest before continuing. The desert was dark and cold, a change from the blazing heat of the day. Several cars were clustered on the side of the road, the occupants resting before continuing toward their destinations across the vast emptiness of Qu'rim.

Victoria checked her phone for messages. She'd shut it off while they were driving, but periodically she would turn it on and check. There'd been nothing for hours. Now, however, there was a text from Ian.

Good job at the consulate. I wasn't certain you'd do it.

Her fingers flew over the keypad even while her heart throbbed with anger. *Why were you there?*

"Who is it?" Nick asked, glancing over at her.

"Ian."

"Fuck, he must be out of custody."

She waited for an answer to her question, but there wasn't one. "Your people didn't hold him for long." She didn't know why she felt a twinge of relief, but she did. "He didn't have the virus on him, obviously."

Nick found a spot and pulled the parking brake. "What the fuck did he do with it?"

"Maybe he never had it. Maybe Chernovsky didn't bring it."

"It's possible. But Ian was there for a reason. You saw him drop something, Victoria. Chernovsky picked it up and followed him, which indicated he'd been waiting for that meeting."

"That's also what gave us a clear shot." She closed her eyes. "I hate everything about this. I hate that you and your colonel bribed me into working for your organization, I hate that Ian showed up in Ras al-Dura and made you both seem rational, I hate that I doubt him and second-guess everything he tells me now. I hate that I keep looking for a connection to the Freedom Force and that I'm afraid he kept me from Emily on purpose in order to make me do his bidding."

He reached for her, unclipping her seat belt and dragging her into his arms. She stiffened at first, but then she went willingly. A wave of emotion engulfed her as he held her close, as if she were something precious to him. Why did she feel such passion and belonging when he held her?

It was needy, and she wasn't accustomed to being needy. That was Emily's modus operandi, not hers. She didn't need a man. The only thing she needed was to protect her sister, and she would sacrifice a lot to do that.

He laid his cheek against her head. "I'm sorry I ever told the colonel it was you who ruined the mission. If I hadn't done that, you wouldn't be here."

She smoothed her hand over his chest, his arm. It was such a sweet thing for him to say because she knew how pissed he'd been that day. "I'm not sorry. Who would have shot those men in Akhira if you hadn't been under orders to find me?"

"Fuck," he breathed, squeezing her close. "If I'd lost you that day…"

Her heart jumped, pounding suddenly in her chest. If he'd lost her? She wrapped her arms around his neck and held him tight. Maybe he was as overwhelmed by this thing between them as she was.

"Nick," she said, because she couldn't say anything else.

His mouth sought hers and found it, his tongue stroking hers so expertly that she could have cried. Oh God, how she loved his tongue. Loved his body.

Loved him.

No. The minute she thought it, she immediately told herself it wasn't true. She didn't love Nick Brandon. She didn't *know* Nick Brandon.

He was a man she was attracted to, a man she'd given her virginity to, but that didn't have a goddamn thing to do with love. She wasn't Emily, searching for love and desperately clinging to the first man who made her feel wanted and alive. She wouldn't make Emily's mistakes, defining herself by a man, losing herself to a man.

God, no. *Hell, no.*

She stiffened in his embrace and he sensed it immediately, easing his hold on her until she could push herself away and retreat to her own space.

She could feel his eyes on her, questioning her. But he didn't say anything. The silence grew thick, hard.

She glanced at him, but she couldn't keep her eyes on his.

"We should sleep," she said, her voice rusty. "It's a long drive tomorrow."

"Yeah." He cleared his throat. "We'll take shifts."

"You sleep first."

He was looking straight ahead. "No, you go. I can't sleep right now."

Her heart hurt. She wanted to reach for him. Tell him she was sorry for pushing him away but that the things swirling inside her were too strong, too frightening, and she wasn't sure how to deal with them just yet.

"Wake me in a couple of hours."

It was dark, but she could see the hard set of his jaw. It made her ache.

"I'll wake you. Now go."

She crawled over the seats and into the back. They'd put the seat down before they'd started this journey, arranging the packs closest to the front and leaving the space behind empty. It wasn't as roomy as the Land Rover, but it was enough for her to curl into. She lay on her side, her heart aching with regret and anger.

She wanted his body wrapped around hers like it had been last night, his warmth cocooning her, his presence making her feel safe and loved.

Loved? She blinked back hot tears.

There was no love here. Only heat and passion—and a need that would burn out given time. Except they were running out of time. Once they reached Baq and his people got what they wanted from Ian, this was over.

TWENTY-ONE

IAN BLACK WAS FUCKING PISSED. He hadn't intended to go to Ras al-Dura, but when Victoria had threatened to quit, he hadn't trusted that she'd go through with the job. And the job was much too important to leave it to chance.

Hell, right up until the minute she'd fired, he still hadn't been sure. It's why he'd had to be there. If she hadn't killed Chernovsky, then he would have. Maybe he should have just done the job himself in the first place, but he had too many irons in the fire and not enough time to be everywhere he needed to be.

This is why he hired people, goddammit.

Victoria had been reliable for two years. She was a professional who did the work and left emotion out of the equation. God knows he'd admired that about her. He'd thought they were alike. He'd thought there was quite possibly something there between them that would still be there when things were different.

He'd been wrong.

He didn't have to ask himself what had changed to

know why she'd suddenly turned confrontational with him.

Nick Brandon was what had changed. Since the moment that cocky asshole had swaggered into the cafe, Ian had known he was trouble.

Ian stuffed his tie in his pocket and undid the buttons on his tuxedo shirt. The soldier across from him didn't look happy. And he wouldn't be, since he'd just had to hand Ian back his phone and wallet. Ian had promptly texted Victoria, partly as a "fuck you" to this guy and also because he wanted to know if she'd made it out. Relief had flooded him at the evidence she had.

It was all he needed to know.

The man across from him watched with interest. He wanted to know what Ian was doing here, no doubt about it, but there were reasons Ian was able to operate the way he did.

Powerful reasons.

It had taken these guys a few more hours than Ian would have liked to learn they'd have to let him go, but now he was free. He stood and gave the soldier a look. He knew the man was special operations. He could always spot a highly trained and disciplined warrior when he saw one—perhaps because he was one too.

Except that he operated alone. Even with a team around him, he was alone. Victoria was certainly proof of that since she'd abandoned him too. Or worse.

It was most interesting that a spec-ops team had descended on the consulate after the hit. He didn't think it was a coincidence they'd been waiting. And they'd been looking for him, which most definitely wasn't a coincidence. Since no one had known he would be in Ras al-

Dura until the last possible minute, he was intrigued that they'd seemed to expect him.

Ian got to his feet slowly and stretched as if he had all the leisure in the world. The other man stood too.

"Thanks for the hospitality," he said. And then he headed for the door.

Another soldier opened it for him and Ian walked through, whistling as he went.

He kept whistling until he reached the darkened street. And then he took his phone out and sent another text. Within moments, his phone would be wiped remotely. Another few minutes, and it would all be restored but without whatever extra software his captors had installed. He knew they hadn't opened the phone because it would have destructed had they done so.

Amateurs, he thought, strolling down the sidewalk. When he reached an open cafe, he ducked inside and waited. Once his phone was restored, he made two calls—one to the airport and the plane he had waiting, and another to Washington.

"This had better be good, Black," a voice growled on the other end.

"Trust me, Congressman, it is."

Victoria was jolted awake by shouting. She shot upright, reaching for her guns. Nick was already cranking the motor into life.

"What's happening?"

"The opposition seems to have cut off the road."

Victoria climbed into the front seat, her heart pounding as she cradled her assault rifle in her lap. The lights of many cars started snapping on, and people scrambled to get moving before they were caught in the opposition army's trap.

Nick didn't bother following the pack. Instead, he took the Jeep wide, driving into the desert and away from the road. Suddenly they were rolling down a sharp incline, and Victoria snapped a hand up to press against the roof while propping her foot on the dash.

They'd gone over a dune, which wasn't necessarily a problem if you knew to expect it, but she wasn't sure that Nick had known. Still, he rolled the wheel back and forth, keeping the Jeep as straight as possible as they rocketed down the side of the massive ridge.

When they hit the bottom, the Jeep bounced hard. Victoria thought her teeth would come out of her head as her jaws cracked together.

Nick whipped the wheel left and pressed the accelerator. They bounced along, parallel to the dune, the lights shining on nothing but sand and more sand up ahead.

Victoria gripped the rifle tighter, ready to blast anyone who got in their way.

"How did you know it was the opposition?" she asked.

"Lucky MacDonald."

"What?"

"A teammate who's fluent in several dialects. She taught me some useful words and phrases. Not to mention the way everyone panicked—that was a dead giveaway we shouldn't stick around."

"Do you have any idea where we're going?" The desert was rolling by fast, but there were no landmarks, no indication they were even going the right way.

"North. If we outflank the opposition army, we can rejoin the highway a few miles up the road. If we're lucky."

She wasn't sure they would be, but she'd have done the same thing in his place. It was best to get away from the crowd and not get funneled into a trap somewhere they couldn't escape because of all the traffic. "We need a backup plan."

He shot her a glance. "I'm listening."

"I'm thinking."

They seemed to be the only ones taking this route. For all they knew, this trench between dunes was taking them east or west, not north—but it was a chance they had to take.

Victoria gripped the dash and prayed they'd get out of this alive. Something flashed in the distance. She fixed her gaze on the spot and tried to determine if there was something out there or if it was her imagination.

But then it flashed again and she knew it wasn't her imagination.

Nick had seen it too because he turned the Jeep and started toward the opposite dune. They were nearly there when gunfire sounded—and the Jeep careened out of control before coming to a bone-jarring stop in the sand.

"Nick!" She unclipped her seat belt and scrambled toward him, afraid he'd been hit. He turned his head, his gleaming eyes meeting hers.

There was a trickle of blood running down his cheek.

"Are you hit? Talk to me!"

"Shoulder," he said.

She turned him as much as she could. The blood on his cheek was spatter. The blood oozing from his shoulder was much worse.

Victoria turned and scrambled for the packs. They had first aid, and she found it quickly. She couldn't search the wound for the bullet now. All she could do was staunch the flow. She ripped open the field dressing.

"Go," he said. "Run."

"Fuck no," she growled, applying the field dressing to the wound and securing it. She didn't have time to inspect it or rip his T-shirt first. This would have to do until they could get somewhere safe.

"Victoria, get the fuck out."

"Only if you come with me."

He studied her in silence.

"Nick, for fuck's sake, let's go."

"Copy," he said.

She reached over and opened his door. Then she opened hers and ran around to help him out of the Jeep. He had one foot on the sand when she got there.

In the distance, she could hear the roar of an engine and voices shouting in Arabic. But she didn't see anything yet. They'd hit the dune face-first, burying the front of the Jeep into it. The battery had been disconnected in the impact, most likely, because there were no lights to illuminate the interior. Thank God for modern safety features.

Nick climbed the rest of the way out and stood there tall and strong. "We have to take as much of this as we can."

"I know."

She got busy shoving the seat forward and throwing

the packs onto the sand. Nick grabbed two and put them on his right shoulder. His left would be out of commission, of course.

Victoria lifted everything she could and slung it over her shoulders.

"Leave the rifle," Nick said when she hefted it.

She shook her head. "If we get a chance, we can use it to pick them off. No way am I leaving it here."

"We won't get that far, Vic. They're coming too quickly."

"Just go! Let me worry about the damn gun."

"Jesus H. Christ," he muttered. But he turned and started trudging up the side of the dune, tracking away from the Jeep and the rapidly approaching enemy forces.

Sweat streamed down her face as she climbed the sand behind him. Her heart felt like it would burst from her chest as her lungs dragged in air and her muscles burned. If she felt like this, what must he be feeling with a gunshot wound added to the burden?

He reached the top of the dune—and stopped so quickly she plowed into him from behind.

"Get down," he ordered as he dropped and dragged her down with him.

Victoria lay against the sand, panting, her eyes stinging with sweat. "What is it?"

"A patrol."

"On the other side of the dune?"

"Yeah. Not leaving anything to chance, I guess."

"Shit."

"Exactly."

She reached for the rifle case and started to unzip it.

"Assemble it but don't fire. It's possible they may not

spot us up here."

"For God's sake, I know that as well as you do. Stop giving me orders."

She put the rifle together quickly and aimed the night-vision scope. She had to belly crawl up the dune a little ways to do it, but what she saw made her pulse kick up. Three big trucks, filled with fighters, rolling south. Maybe they were headed to Ras al-Dura. Maybe they were just trying to cut off the road and stop the flow of supplies into the southern quadrant.

Or maybe they were after the uranium mine. It was well guarded, but it was certainly a target in this war.

The trucks were going slow, but they didn't show any signs of stopping. Victoria's blood pounded in her ears, her throat.

They might just make it. If they lay here quiet and still and waited, they might be okay.

She turned to say something to that effect to Nick. But before she could get the words out, a spotlight shined on their position, illuminating them for the soldiers below.

TWENTY-TWO

VICTORIA TRIED TO TURN AND aim the rifle, but it was too late. The men fired in the air and someone shouted something in Arabic.

"He said get up," Nick told her. "And drop the gun."

"I'd rather shoot him."

"I know, baby. But even if we could see them, I'm no help right now."

She knew what he meant. Without the two of them firing, the chances they'd be killed were even greater if she started to shoot. Though she hated to do so, Victoria flung the gun away and stood slowly. She was still armed—Nick was armed too—but she put her hands in the air and waited for the men to approach. A glance at Nick told her he was feeling the effects of his wound pretty badly. He grimaced as he tried to hold his left arm up.

A surge of emotion flowed through her. She wanted to stand in front of him and fire on all these bastards, but the light was too bright and she couldn't see them approaching. She had no idea how many there were or where they were. Firing would be suicide. Nick knew it as well as she did.

So they stood and waited while the men approached.

"Drop your weapons," a heavily accented voice said.

Victoria glanced at Nick. The light was still in their faces and she could tell they had no chance. She was squinting as she reached behind her back and pulled out her pistol. Nick removed two pistols and dropped them.

"And the legs," the man said.

Victoria bent and slipped her weapon from her leg holster. Beside her, Nick was fumbling for his. But he got it and dropped it.

"Kick them away."

They both did as told, then the light dropped and someone ran forward to collect the weapons. Other men strode forward and grabbed the two of them. Victoria winced as her arms were jerked behind her back and tied with cord. If they were treating her so roughly, she feared for how Nick was handling this with his wound.

She managed a glance at him. His face was agony, sweat pouring down and soaking his T-shirt. Or maybe that was blood. Victoria shuddered.

The man holding her thrust her forward. She would have fallen if he hadn't jerked her back. He rushed her down the dune, then picked her up and tossed her into the back of a truck.

Before she could get up and look for Nick, he clambered into the truck and sank down beside her. Her heart hammered and her mouth felt gritty and dry. Swallowing hurt.

"Are you okay?" she asked as several men climbed in the back of the truck with them.

A door slammed and the vehicle lurched into gear.

The men seemed uninterested in them now that they had them captured and tied. One of them took out a pack of cigarettes and passed it around.

"Yeah," Nick said, his voice hoarse.

She couldn't really see his face in the darkness, but she could tell by his voice that he was in a lot of pain. She couldn't reach for him to find out if his shirt was soaked with blood or sweat, and worry tightened her chest.

Victoria couldn't reach for his hand, but she managed to shift herself until she could press her thigh against his. She shivered and he moved his leg just slightly in what she thought was meant to be a caress.

She closed her eyes and leaned her head back against the truck's panels. "We had a good time, didn't we, PB?"

"The best, honey."

"It's not over," she said on a fierce whisper. "I refuse to let it be over."

"What time did the SOS come in?" Mendez demanded over the speakerphone.

Billy Blake answered. "Midnight, sir."

Everyone looked at each other, their expressions grim. They'd just spent one long-ass night and an even longer day in this shit-hole of a place, holding Ian Black and getting fucking nowhere while they waited for permission to haul him back to base. Echo Squad had carefully checked everyone leaving the consulate grounds. There'd been no vials of smallpox on any of them, including Ian

Black.

Either Chernovsky hadn't brought it with him, or it was still inside the consulate. One diplomatic phone call to the Russians, and it was their responsibility now. Not that Garrett had much faith in their ability to secure it after they'd let it get out of a top-security lab in the first place.

He was on edge and fucking ready to punch something or kill something, he didn't much care which.

They were at the airport, ready to climb on their transport, when Brandy's locater signal popped up on the secure link. They'd quickly gotten on board but delayed taking off while Billy Blake did his magic with the trace and Richie called Mendez.

"Fucking hell," Mendez breathed. "Where is he?"

"Two hours north by air, sir. And moving south."

Moving this way *if* Brandy was still in possession of his equipment. Or dead somewhere and someone else was moving this way. They all knew what the possibilities were, though none of them would say it.

"Find him, boys. Bring him and Miss Royal back."

Richie shot a look toward the cockpit of the C-130. "This pilot has a hard-on to return to Baq. We'll need you to run interference, sir, if we're changing the plan."

"Goddamn Air Force," Mendez grumbled. "Don't worry, I'll fix it."

The line went dead. Richie looked determined as he studied their faces. "You heard the man. Let's figure out where our teammate is and bring him home."

Victoria didn't know how many hours they were in the truck or how far they traveled, but they eventually came to a halt near a cluster of mud-brick buildings. They'd reached a road a while back, for which she was thankful since it meant Nick wouldn't be jostled so much.

At one point he'd stopped answering her questions when she spoke to him, and she'd nearly panicked. But then he'd snored, and relief melted through her that he wasn't dead. Now the tailgate of the truck fell open and men jumped down, talking loudly. It sounded like a reunion out there.

Nick stirred, and she leaned into him carefully so he'd know she was still with him.

"We've stopped." He sounded groggy.

"A village of some sort. I think…"

One of the men still in the truck jabbed her with a rifle. She took it as a sign to stand. Her legs were numb after so much sitting and the vibrations of the truck, but she managed to get to her feet with only a little swaying.

Nick had to be jerked to his feet, and her heart hammered at the rough way their captors treated him. Soon they were both on the ground and being hustled into one of the mud-brick buildings.

They passed through the front rooms of the building and got shoved into a smaller room before a door slammed and a lock twisted. It was completely dark in the room. There was a window set high up in the wall, but it was very small and didn't let in much light.

Victoria tested the strength of the cords tying her wrists. They were tight, but if she worked her way down into a crouch, she could get her hands in front of her by sliding them under her butt and stepping through her arms.

It wasn't easy, but she was flexible and she'd done it before. It was a good skill to have in her line of work.

"Are you okay?" she asked Nick as she carefully worked her way down, stretching her arms to go beneath her.

"Been better."

Her arms ached with the effort, and the cords cut into her skin—but then her butt popped into the circle of her arms and she was able to slide them down until she could step through.

"I've got my hands in front of me," she said.

He made a noise that might have been a laugh or a snort. "Don't need to think about how flexible you are right now, Vic."

"I don't know, babe, maybe you do." She walked over to where he'd leaned against the wall and groped for the knots at his wrists. "It'll take your mind off things."

She felt the knots. Carefully, she followed the ends of the cords, traced the knots, and tried to figure out how they were tied.

These men weren't Boy Scouts, thankfully, and she eventually worked it out. Nooses secured by slipknots and secured again by simple overhand knots. It took a bit of tugging, but she worked them free and the tension in Nick's arms eased.

"Goddamn," he swore when the cords slid free. "That fucking hurts."

"I know. I'm sorry." It had been about four hours since he'd been shot, she reckoned. Fear tasted bitter in her throat as she prayed the wound wouldn't get infected before they could get help.

Before they could get help, not *if*. She wasn't thinking

in terms of ifs.

"Can you get me free?"

"Yeah."

She stood in front of him while he worked the knots on her wrists. It took him longer, and he fumbled and cursed a bit, but she knew that every movement of his arm had to be agony.

Finally, the knots eased and she worked the cords open just enough to slip her wrists free. Then she reached up and touched his face. He turned his cheek into her palm, and she felt her heart clench. She had to get him out of here.

She made a circuit of the room, finding a mattress on the floor. There was nothing else, not even a chair.

"There's a mattress to sit on."

She helped him over to it, and he lowered himself. Then she knelt beside him, wrapping her arms around his head and pulling him to her chest, just relieved for the moment that they were both here and both alive.

He wrapped one arm around her and held her tight. She stroked his damp hair, twisting her fingers into it and remembering how it had felt when she'd dug her hands into it while he'd been making love to her.

God, she wanted that again. She wanted that and more. So much more. But right now she wanted to keep him talking. If he was talking, then she knew he was okay, at least for the moment.

"These men are opposition, aren't they?"

"I think so. The Qu'rimi Army isn't much more disciplined than this, but they have better structure. Usually."

He would know better than she would because his job often involved other nations' militaries. Hers didn't. "If they were going to kill us, they'd have done it. Ransom?"

She eased away from him and started to feel carefully along his shirt. The field dressing was still in place, but he needed a sling. His T-shirt was damp, but she couldn't tell if it was blood or sweat.

"Ransom is a good possibility," he said. "They always need money to fuel the cause, and taking Westerners is often profitable for them."

"That's the best-case scenario." She stood and removed her T-shirt. Then she tore it so she could fashion a sling to help support his arm.

"Stripping, Vic?"

"Just for you, sexy man."

He laughed, though it didn't sound particularly happy. "Wish I could take advantage of it. Would love to lick that sweet pussy of yours until you screamed for me."

Her body tightened at the image that put into her brain. "And you will, I promise. Just not right now."

She put the sling on him while he winced and groaned. But then it was done, and he let out a long sigh.

"Is that better?"

"Yeah, thanks."

She took his good hand and squeezed. "I know it hurts, but maybe taking the weight off will help."

He pulled her hand up to his mouth and kissed it. "It does, baby. Thanks."

His skin was hot where it touched hers, but that wasn't necessarily anything to worry about. Yet.

If he didn't get medical attention soon, however, she was afraid he'd deteriorate fast. And she didn't know what she would do when he did.

TWENTY-THREE

VICTORIA WAS DOZING WHEN A crash woke her.
Belatedly, she realized someone had flung the door open
and it had hit the wall. For a moment, her heart soared as
she hoped that somehow they'd been rescued.

But that hope was proven futile when a light shined
on her and Nick and a man laughed. She'd spent time
prowling the room, looking for anything she could use as a
weapon, but all she had were the clothes on her body and
the cords they'd been tied with. It wasn't much, but if
someone got close enough, at least she could attempt to
strangle them. She sat up and felt for the cords in her
pocket.

Suddenly, an electric lantern lit the room and she
could see three men. It was the one who was laughing that
made her blood chill.

Beside her, Nick had grown very still. He was lying
down, and while she'd felt him jerk with the crash of the
door, he wasn't moving now. His eyes were closed and her
stomach fell. But he was still breathing, and that made relief flow through her. She could see now that the darkness

on his T-shirt was blood, not sweat as she'd hoped.

She got to her feet, sick inside. Whether it was to shield Nick or confront the man laughing at them, she didn't know. Anger and terror swirled in her belly.

Zaran bin Yusuf had changed since Emily had sent smiling selfies of her and him a few years ago when they'd first started dating in New Orleans. He now sported a black beard, cropped to nearly a point, and he wore Qu'rimi dress—a thobe and keffiyeh with black cords holding the headdress in place. He also wore a curved dagger at his waist, and a gun holstered near that. He looked absolutely formidable—and pleased beyond belief.

"When they told me they'd taken an American man and woman with enough guns to start their own army, I admit I'd hoped. There's only one American woman I could think of who would be wandering the Qu'rimi desert with an arsenal at her disposal. Greetings, sister-in-law."

Victoria's skin crawled at the way his gaze raked over her bra-clad torso. Her stomach churned. She hadn't wanted to believe that Emily had married this man, but it must be true. "Where is my sister?"

"Safe. For now."

She didn't want to know what that meant—and yet she did. She had to. "I want to see her."

Zaran sat in a chair that someone had brought into the room for him. He stroked his beard as he studied her. "So you keep saying. Yet you are a bad influence on my wife. You make her remember her life before."

"I'm her family."

His expression clouded. "No, I *am*," he shouted as he leaned forward to glare at her. "I am her family. I saved her, Victoria. I got her off drugs and alcohol when you could not. When you didn't care."

Victoria shivered as guilt slid through her. She knew it wasn't her fault that Emily had spiraled into addiction, but she always wondered what she could have done differently. How she could have helped by staying instead of leaving Emily in treatment and going into the Army. She'd been trying to build a better life, but it had all imploded on her.

And led her to this moment, apparently, where she was at the mercy of a man who'd already tried to kill her once before. If only he would come closer. She thought about how she might take the gun from him if he did.

A sharp step to the instep, a blow to the kidney...

"I do care. I've always cared." She wanted to ask him why Emily was calling her and saying she wanted to go home, but she knew that wouldn't be a good idea. If he'd exploded over her saying she was Emily's family, what would he do when she suggested Emily preferred her to him?

"If you cared, you would stop trying to be a part of her life. She is confused when you speak with her. This is her life now, yet she feels nostalgia for her old life when you interfere."

She clasped her hands together and decided to try to pacify this man. If she could just get him closer. It would be a risk, but if he was off his guard, she could take the gun. She was small and agile, and she had training he couldn't imagine.

"Then I'm sorry. But you didn't have to try to kill me for it."

He snorted. "You are a hard woman to kill, it would seem. My men were never heard from again, yet here you are."

"They were probably terrified that I got away from them. I imagine they're on a beach in Thailand or something."

His eyes narrowed. "Yes, perhaps." His gaze slid to Nick and then back to her, one eyebrow arching. "And perhaps you had help escaping and disposing of the bodies."

Victoria swallowed. "I guess we'll never know." She lifted her chin. "It's good you failed, Zaran. Think how horrible it would be to have your wife's only sister's death on your hands."

"It would not have been on my hands. It still will not. I am not the one who will do it."

"But you will order it done. You can't escape culpability with semantics."

"This is a choice I can live with, Victoria. It must be done for Emily's well-being."

She couldn't fathom the sickness of his logic. And she knew she couldn't argue with him, either.

"The least you can do is allow me to see her one last time."

"The least I can do is make sure you do not suffer when the time comes."

Victoria pulled in a deep breath, though her insides were churning and her anger was so palpable she thought Zaran could probably see it pulsing in the air between them. She threw a look at Nick. He hadn't moved.

"Let him go," she said. "It's me you want. He's got nothing to do with this."

"It looks to me like the choice has already been made for him."

"Send a doctor then. Clean the wound, remove any fragments, and give him painkillers. He's worth something to you. To the Americans. They'll pay to get him back."

He cocked his head. "Not to Ian Black? Most interesting."

Her heart thumped. So he did know Ian. Of course he did. "Did Ian know you intended to kill me that day?"

"I don't have to clear my plans with Ian Black. He's a tool, the same as you are. He is useful to the Freedom Force, though not as useful as he could be."

Though she was furious with Ian for working for this asshole in the first place, she was thankful that her instincts about his involvement in the attempt on her life hadn't been wrong. It wasn't much, but it was something.

Zaran sat back and folded his arms. "You shot the Russian."

She had no idea whose agenda she'd been carrying out last night, but at this evidence that Zaran bin Yusuf knew about Chernovsky and the smallpox, her anger spiked anew.

"Isn't that what you wanted?"

"I did. Thank you."

God, she hated this man. She wished she could rewind a few weeks and take a different shot. Or that she'd been a split second too late with her shot, because Nick would have made his.

Maybe she'd had it all wrong. Maybe it would have given Emily the opening she needed to escape this man instead of endangering her.

"Be careful what you unleash into the world, Zaran. You can't control who it sickens or how far it spreads. It could be you... or Emily."

He got to his feet in a swirl of robes. "These are the chances we take in war."

Then he turned and strode from the room. The two men who'd stood silently also went with him and the door shut with a thunk.

Victoria swore. If she hadn't pissed him off so quickly, she might have gotten her chance. Though it was lucky the two men hadn't been ordered to kill her when Zaran walked out.

But the men were gone, she was alone with Nick, and they now had a chair and a battery-powered lantern.

She bent over the mattress and smoothed her hand over Nick's hair. His eyes shot open, their hazel depths angry.

"Oh my God, I thought you were leaving me," she cried before she sank down and took his head in her lap.

"Not planning on it." His voice was hoarse and she realized his skin was hotter than before.

"Good, because I'm not ready for this to end. I want more time with you. I want more *time*."

He squeezed her arm with his good hand. "Hang in there, babe. Might... work out." He sucked in a deep breath, let it out with a groan. "You did... good. Brave girl."

She decided not to tell him she'd have done better if Zaran had gotten closer. In his condition, he didn't need to worry about her more than he already was. "You heard him?"

"Yeah. Thought it... best if... didn't look lively."

"Good idea. He's demented." She lifted his hand to her lips and pressed her mouth to his skin. Definitely hotter than he should be. "We'll probably need a miracle to get out of here."

His eyes glinted. "Could happen."

She searched his gaze—and then it dawned on her that he expected his guys—the Hostile Operations Team— to rescue them. He fully expected them to ride in like knights on white stallions and extract them from the craziness that was Zaran bin Yusuf's world.

And for the first time, hope blossomed in her soul.

"How…? They took our phones."

"Backup plan. Tracking device… sewn in pants pocket."

"I think I love these guys you work for."

He gave her a grin before taking a deep breath and closing his eyes again. His breathing was even, but she still feared for him. But now she hoped too. Hoped like hell that the reputation of HOT was well deserved and not just myth. She'd do what she had to do to protect them both, but it would be so much easier if the white knights would show up.

"I'll love them forever if they pull this off," she said softly. "But I think I'll love you more."

Victoria sat on the chair where she'd pulled it over next to the mattress. She watched the door, and she watched Nick, reaching out to push his damp hair off his face when he moved. She didn't know how long she'd been sitting there before she thought she heard a woman's voice. She stood and went over to the door, listening hard, her hands on the cords. A key turned in the lock and the door pushed inward.

Victoria waited, ready to spring as soon as someone walked in. But it wasn't a man.

A woman in a full burka stepped through the entry, and Victoria took a step back. The woman turned toward her, pushing her veil aside.

"Emily!"

They rushed into each other's arms. Victoria squeezed her baby sister tight. Emily squeezed back just as hard.

"When I heard there was an American woman who'd been captured with a big rifle, I knew I had to try to see her. And it's you! I knew it would be!"

Victoria wiped her sister's tears from her face with her thumbs. "Sweetie, I've missed you."

"I've missed you, Victoria."

Victoria glanced at the door and realized a man stood there silently. Her heart dropped, but it wasn't bin Yusuf. "How did you get Zaran to let you come?"

Emily snorted. "He didn't. I lied to Ahmed. Don't worry, he doesn't understand English." She bit her lip. "I feel bad. He's a good bodyguard, and Zaran will be furious. But I *had* to see you."

Victoria hugged her again. "Oh, Emily, it's good to see you."

Emily's eyes roved over her. "What happened to your shirt? Did someone hurt you?"

"No. I needed it for my partner."

Emily hugged her again, and that's when she realized there was something hard lying against Emily's belly. Victoria started.

But Em held her tight and whispered in her ear. "I've

brought you a pistol. It's the best I could do. I know what he intends to do, and I'm not going to let him do it. Reach inside while my back is turned and take it. Ahmed won't know."

Victoria did as her sister told her, shoving the pistol into the back of her pants once she'd retrieved it. It all happened fast, and then Emily stepped away and they stood looking at each other for a long moment. Ahmed looked bored.

"Who's he?" Em said, tipping her chin at Nick.

His eyes were open this time, and he was watching them. Once again, Victoria's heart thumped at this sign he was still alive. Who was he? So much she could say to that, but she could hardly voice it. So she told the simple truth.

"His name is Nick. He's my partner. Em, he's hurt. Can you get a doctor? Or get some first-aid supplies for me—bandages, alcohol, painkillers?"

Emily frowned. "I'll try."

She turned to Ahmed and spoke in fluent Arabic. The man shook his head sharply. Emily spoke again, and Victoria recognized the wheedling tone her sister had often used with her. Ahmed's expression grew stony, and then it grew soft. Finally, he ducked his head out the door and called to someone.

A few minutes later, a man brought a first-aid kit and some water. And a button-down shirt that had probably once been white. Ahmed handed everything to Emily, who promptly handed it to Victoria. Gratefulness rushed through her as she slipped on the shirt. It was dusty and smelled a bit like a camel, but it was something. Not only was she no longer naked, but she was also able to cover the gun at the back of her waistband.

"Thank you, Em."

"It's the least I could do." She huffed in a breath. "My God, the shit you've had to put up with because of me. I'm so sorry. I should have listened to you."

"We all make mistakes, Em. I still love you, no matter what."

Victoria hurried over to Nick's side. She used the scissors in the kit to cut Nick's T-shirt open. The blood on the shirt was sticky, but it pulled away easily enough. She gave him two ibuprofens and a sip of water, then she removed the field dressing and cleaned the wound with alcohol while Nick grimaced. He was definitely feverish, but he was holding on to consciousness.

"I'm sorry, Preacher Boy," she whispered.

He nodded.

She tended the wound as tenderly as she could. He'd lost blood and she had no idea if there were fragments in the wound, but she couldn't take the risk of probing around in there right now and making him bleed anew. She had to hope his guys got here soon and could take care of him properly.

"Is he going to be all right?" Emily asked, her voice small.

"Yes," Victoria said, because she couldn't contemplate otherwise.

"Zaran should have given you these things. It was cruel of him not to."

Victoria didn't want to comment on that statement. "Are you okay, Em? Has he ever hurt you?"

"Sometimes," she said softly. "But we're going to get away from him, Victoria. You and me. Somehow."

Victoria turned to look at her. "Oh, honey. I hope we do get out of here. But I can't guarantee anything."

Ahmed said something to Emily. Her expression fell. Victoria hated that look on her sister's face. It was the look of a girl who'd been searching for something her entire life and had never yet found it. A girl who trusted too easily and fell too far when that trust was broken.

"I have to go."

Victoria stood and hugged her again. Her sister was so small and frail that it broke her heart.

"This isn't the end, Victoria. I swear it's not."

Victoria felt the solid weight of the gun at her back and hoped her sister was right.

"No, I don't think it is either." She kissed Emily's cheek, unable to contemplate that she might never see her sister again. She *refused* to contemplate that this was good-bye.

HOT was coming, and they would get out of here. She had to believe it.

Emily walked out the door and Ahmed started to swing it shut. But raised voices sounded nearby and the door swung back open. Zaran bin Yusuf strode into the room, Emily tugging his arm and pleading with him both in Arabic and English.

He stood silently and bore it while he glared at the scene—and then he backhanded her and she fell to the floor.

TWENTY-FOUR

IT WAS A HALO JUMP into nowhere and then an ass-busting hump across the desert before they crested a dune and saw the cluster of buildings down below. There were five trucks pulled up near the compound and a group of men milling around a fire. Occasionally, someone popped off a few shots on a Russian-made rifle, and laughter burst into the night.

Drinking, probably, though alcohol was forbidden in Qu'rim. Never stopped anyone before. Garrett's great-granddaddy had been a moonshine runner back in the day, and his family had proudly provided liquor to anyone with the money and guts to purchase it during Prohibition.

Not that you'd better say that to his mama, because Mary Beth Wright-Spencer made her living teaching the children of Paris, Georgia, how to be proper young gentlemen and young ladies. The suggestion that her family had ever been anything less than proper was not one she appreciated.

Garrett's comm link crackled. "Brandy's still in the third building, west corner, at the back."

It was Billy the Kid talking.

"Copy," came Big Mac's answer.

Richie spoke next. "Dex and Hawk will provide cover fire. Ice and Knight Rider, go get our boy. The rest of us will take care of business on the exterior. If Victoria Royal isn't with him, we'll do a search of the other buildings. Copy?"

"Copy."

"Let's roll. No one left behind."

"Fucking A," someone said.

They flew down the dune like an approaching storm and broke over the compound with all the firepower and fury they were capable of—which was a fucking lot.

Brandy was coming home alive.

"Don't," Nick said softly, forcing the word from his dry throat as Victoria started to reach behind her for the gun her sister had given her.

He'd been saving his strength as much as possible for the moment when HOT would arrive. But now Victoria's sister was begging for their lives, Zaran bin Yusuf was furious, and Victoria wanted to kill him for hitting Emily.

He understood it. He wanted to kill the asshole too. But they didn't have the advantage. Even if she got off a shot, there were too many men in this compound. They'd burst into this room and kill the two of them—maybe the three of them, since Nick was certain Victoria would take out bin Yusuf at the minimum and no one else would give a shit about Emily's life if that happened.

Maybe it was worth it to Victoria. It wasn't to him. Any scenario in which she didn't live was not a scenario he cared to contemplate. No, it fucking terrified him to think of her dying out here.

She stilled, facing bin Yusuf with her fists clenched at her side. Emily pushed herself up, clutching her cheek with both hands. Her eyes were filled with hatred when she looked at her husband.

"I told you to stay in our room," he bit out. "To wait for me to return."

"You tried to keep my sister from me," she cried. "How could you do that? I hate you!"

Jesus, that was not what they needed right now. A fucking domestic. Bin Yusuf looked utterly furious.

"She is a bad influence on you, *habibti.* She does not care about you the way I do."

Emily's face was red and tears streamed down her cheeks. "You lie, Zaran! You always lie. I want to go home. I want to have a normal life again."

"Normal? What is normal? Where you lie in a gutter and shoot poison into your veins? Where you drink so much you pass out and don't know your own name? Who saved you from that, Emily? Who cared enough to lift you up and make you whole again?"

The whole time he spoke, he walked toward her until he could pull her against his side and press her head to his chest. She fought, but he was stronger—and determined to win this battle. The man had a savior complex. No doubt he'd helped Emily get clean, but hitting her and manipulating her were not in the least bit loving or caring. He wanted to control Emily, nothing more. Nick recognized the signs because it was exactly the way his father behaved.

But Emily did not want to be controlled. She screamed and cried and tried to shove him away, but his grip on her tightened.

Victoria's knuckles were white as she struggled not to act.

"I will put an end to this," bin Yusuf muttered. Then he reached for his gun.

But Victoria was faster. She had her gun pointed at him before he'd finished raising his. Still, her sister was plastered to his side and she hesitated, which gave him the second he needed.

An evil smile curled bin Yusuf's lips as he slewed his own weapon toward Nick.

"Drop it or I will kill him."

"Not if I kill you first."

He pulled Emily in front of his body. "Go ahead. Will you risk your sister's life?"

Emily was sobbing and squirming, which meant she was in danger if Victoria fired. And Victoria knew it.

Still, she didn't lower the gun. A surge of emotion flowed through Nick at her determination to protect him. He should be the one protecting her, for fuck's sake, not the other way around.

But he knew she didn't need him to do so. She was a beautiful, lethal killer in her own right. She'd survived out here for two years, working for Black and methodically taking out the targets he gave her. Victoria was a force to be reckoned with.

And still he feared for her in this situation. Because her emotions were engaged, at least where her sister was involved.

"We're at a stalemate," she said, her voice cool. "I'll lower the weapon if you will."

Bin Yusuf's laugh was sudden and sharp. "You don't give me terms, woman. I'm the one in charge here, not you. And if you think—"

An explosion rocked the building and then another followed on its heels. They all jumped.

Zaran bin Yusuf was choking suddenly, and Nick wondered if he'd been hit by shrapnel. But the walls were intact and everyone else was remarkably untouched.

That's when Nick realized what was happening. Emily Royal stood beside her husband with her fist wrapped around the dagger he'd been wearing at his waist. She'd shoved it in deep, somehow missing bone and cartilage and driving it into his torso.

He staggered backward, finding enough breath to curse in Arabic. Emily let go of the dagger as he stumbled. Her face was white. Ahmed, her bodyguard, had wide eyes and seemed immobilized. But it didn't last as he began fumbling for his weapon. Bin Yusuf still had the gun he'd been holding when Emily stabbed him. As he fell against the wall, he raised it in a shaking hand, aiming for Emily.

There was no way Victoria could shoot two men at once, which is what she needed to do to save both herself and her sister. Bin Yusuf targeted Emily while Ahmed targeted Victoria. And Nick knew, without a doubt, she was going to fire on bin Yusuf and save her sister. He understood her compulsion to do so, but he couldn't lie here and let her sacrifice herself for Emily.

Because the world would be a darker place without her in it.

Time slowed until it seemed he could see the scene in

slow motion, the men aiming weapons, the women in their sights. Outside, the explosions and gunfire grew as HOT— it had to be HOT—infiltrated the compound.

But inside, all he cared about were the next few seconds and stopping Ahmed from killing Victoria. Because HOT was here, but they wouldn't reach this room soon enough to prevent Victoria's death if she was determined to save her sister first.

And she was. He could see it in her eyes.

With every last ounce of strength he had, he launched himself from the bed just as the crack of a gun sounded.

Victoria dropped to the floor with a cry. Her thigh burned as if someone had jabbed her with a hot poker. But she had no time to worry about herself. She'd fired at Zaran bin Yusuf, and Ahmed had fired at her—but not before Nick launched himself at the man. She scrambled to right herself and bring the gun up.

Zaran lay still, and she knew her shot had gone true. Right between the eyes. She'd killed him, and she'd saved Emily. If she gave herself time to think about it, she would probably start to shake with the enormity of what had happened. Not killing a man, because she'd done that before, but finally killing the one man who'd hurt her sister for so long.

Though Emily had already done that, because Zaran wouldn't have survived the stab wound. Victoria had only finished the job.

But she had no time to dwell on it because now she had to kill Ahmed. Nick had taken Ahmed down by launching himself at the other man's legs. Ahmed had shot wide, thanks to Nick, but he'd still hit her.

Victoria rolled forward, gripping the gun, and aimed for the tangle of men on the floor. But Ahmed's robes made it difficult to tell where he ended and Nick began. They moved too fast for her to get a clear shot. If she timed it wrong, she'd hit Nick when she aimed at Ahmed.

The men continued to struggle—and then Nick's arm wrapped around Ahmed's neck. Nick flipped until he was behind Ahmed, squeezing the man's windpipe with all the strength he had left.

It was a surprising amount for a man who'd been prone on the bed until just a few moments ago. Victoria struggled to her feet. Her leg nearly buckled from beneath her and she cried out in pain. But she had to get to Nick's side, had to press the gun against Ahmed's temple and make him stop struggling.

She was certain that if he fought hard enough and long enough, Nick's strength would give way. And she had to stop Ahmed before it did.

Outside, there was gunfire and an explosion, closer to the building this time. The walls shook and chunks of mud-brick dropped from the ceiling.

A quick glance told her that Emily was alive. She was leaning against the wall, her hand to her throat and her eyes averted from the scene. Her shoulders shook, and Victoria knew her sister was crying.

She wanted to comfort her, but first she had to help Nick. She hobbled toward him, each step agony. Blood seeped from her wound and stained her torn pants. For all she knew, Ahmed had hit her femoral artery and she'd be done for soon—but she didn't feel light-headed so much as sick from the agony of moving across the room.

Ahmed's legs kicked out and Nick's arm tightened. Ahmed's face was turning purple—then he went limp, sliding to the side as Nick finished the job and shoved him away. Nick looked up at her, his hazel eyes feverish in the flashes of light that made the room so much brighter than the lantern alone did. Ahmed's body was still partially covering him, but he dragged himself from beneath the dead weight of it and staggered to his feet.

Victoria didn't know how she did it, but she closed the distance and threw herself into his arms. He squeezed her tight, his head bowing to her neck. His skin was hot, and fresh fear ricocheted through her.

"You scared the hell out of me," he said.

She pushed away and cupped his face in both her hands. God, he was burning up. "You scared me too."

He was still scaring her.

"Victoria?"

It was Emily calling to her. She turned to see her sister staggering toward them, her hands outstretched, staring at the blood on them like a demented Lady Macbeth. Emily's gaze bounced to Zaran, where he lay in a pool of blood with part of his head blown away.

That's when she started to shake.

"Go to her," Nick said. "She needs you more."

For the first time in her life, Victoria was torn. Instinct told her to go to Emily, to comfort her sister and take care of her as she always had.

But a different emotion told her to stay with Nick, to never let him go. If she let him go, she had the irrational fear she would never see him again. That things would change so irrevocably she would never get back the man she'd spent the past few days with. The man she'd grown to love, as impossible as that seemed.

How did you fall for someone so quickly? How did they become the guiding star in your heavens practically overnight? It shouldn't be possible, and yet...

"Victoria," Emily cried again.

Victoria closed her eyes. If ever she needed to be reminded of what falling too quickly for a man could do to you, she only needed to look at her sister. Emily had followed that urge that told her Zaran was *her* guiding star, and look what had happened.

Victoria shuddered. And then she stepped away from Nick and held her arms open. Emily closed the distance between them and wrapped her arms around Victoria's waist just as two spec-ops warriors burst into the room.

They were big and lethal-looking, and she'd never been so glad to see anyone in her life. Once more, she'd been saved by the Army. Odd, considering the Army hadn't shown her much sympathy in the first place.

"About fucking time," Nick grumbled.

"Got here soon as we could, Brandy." The man who'd spoken was tall and broad. His greasepainted face looked menacing. "See you got yourself shot."

"Fuck you, Iceman."

The other man laughed. "You'll live. Thank God."

A second later, Nick crumpled to the floor.

TWENTY-FIVE

HOT STOLE ONE OF THE opposition's trucks in order to race to their extraction point. They'd done a lot of damage at the military outpost, killing or wounding scores of men. No one challenged them when they climbed into the truck and tore into the desert.

The one called Iceman tended to Nick, injecting him with something and inserting an IV drip. He couldn't do much in the truck other than stabilize his teammate. Another soldier tended to her. He grinned and told jokes while he worked. It didn't stop the pain, but it kept her distracted until the painkillers kicked in.

Emily stayed as close to her side as possible. She'd retreated into herself, rocking back and forth and shaking her head as if trying to shake out the memories of what had just happened.

She kept repeating "Oh God, oh God, oh God..." as if it would somehow make it better. Her hands had been cleaned, but she still had blood on her burka. There was nothing to be done about it just yet.

Victoria reached for her hand, and Emily clung to it

like a lifeline. It broke Victoria's heart. No matter what she thought of Zaran bin Yusuf, he'd once been good for Emily. That he'd changed and become controlling and abusive didn't mean that Emily would have an easy time with all that had happened tonight.

She'd stabbed the man who was her husband with his own dagger. And then she'd watched helplessly as he tried to shoot her with his dying breath. How long would it take her to make peace with all that had happened?

For all Victoria knew, she never would. Because Victoria didn't know what Zaran had done to her over the past three and a half years. He might have started out being good for her, but he certainly hadn't ended that way.

The ride across the desert was tense, but they soon were racing across a broad expanse of flatland. It took Victoria a few minutes to realize that a plane was waiting for them in the darkness, its lights turned off and engines on low.

The man who'd been tending to her picked her up and carried her onto the plane, running up the ramp as if he were carrying a child instead of a full-grown woman. He settled her on a gurney strapped to the wall, buckled her in, and disappeared. Another man deposited Emily nearby. She'd started crying again.

Victoria twisted her neck, looking for Nick. It took two guys to place him on a bed and strap him down. The plane was already taxiing into the night. Another minute and they'd lifted off the desert floor, the engines whining as they climbed into the dark sky.

She held her breath for long seconds, praying there was no opposition force out there with a rocket launcher just waiting to take down a plane. But they kept climbing, and she finally let out a shaky breath, a little more certain they were going to make it than she had been just a few moments ago.

Whatever she'd been injected with must have made her sleep, because when next she woke, the plane was on the ground and the smiling soldier who'd given her drugs was standing over her and unbuckling the straps that had held her in bed for the trip.

"Where are we?"

"Baq."

"Baq? We made it?"

"Yeah, we made it." He winked. "Told you we would, though I don't think you remember that part."

She put a hand to her head. "I don't remember much of anything. What the hell was in that shot anyway?"

"Something to make you relax. Worked, didn't it?"

She turned her head. "How's Nick?"

His smile slipped a fraction, but she didn't think she was meant to see it. "He's been better. But we'll fix him up, don't worry."

She did worry, but before she could ask more questions, she was lifted, placed on another gurney, and rolled off the plane. They put her in an ambulance and drove her the short distance to the base hospital. It wasn't a big structure, more of a field hospital really, but they were equipped to deal with gunshot wounds.

A doctor in surgical scrubs appeared, and then another joined him. She realized it was a surgical team, not just a doctor, when someone came over and spoke softly to her while someone else inserted a needle and set up an IV.

"Wait... what's happening...?"

Victoria never knew if she completed that sentence.

The next thing she knew, she woke up in a white room. She was lying in a bed, and machines beeped nearby. There was an IV and an oxygen tube.

Her leg was suspended in a sling and covered in thick white padding. She groped for a call button, finally finding it threaded through the bedside rail, and pushed it repeatedly.

An Army nurse appeared, her face both serious and warm at the same time.

"Welcome back, Miss Royal," she said briskly. "Are you in pain? Do you need anything?"

"I... Where's my sister? Where's Nick?"

The nurse fiddled with the tubes and dials on the IV. "Your sister is in the next room. We've given her something to help her sleep. She's under psychiatric care, never fear, so we'll be monitoring her closely. Sergeant Brandon is out of surgery. He hasn't awakened yet, but the doctor says he'll be fine."

Relief flooded her even as fresh anxiety took up residence in her belly over her sister's condition.

The nurse smiled. Then she picked up a tube and put it in Victoria's hand. That's when she realized there was a button on it.

"Morphine," the nurse said. "When you need it, press the button. It will only give you so much per hour, but it will help. Don't wait until it hurts too much."

Nick felt like he was fighting his way out of a forest. He kept tilting headlong into trees. His head hurt. His body hurt. He was hot, and then he was cold. He was also alone. No one was in the forest with him. He searched for faces—Shelly, his mom and dad. Victoria.

They weren't with him.

He didn't know how long he fought, how long he searched, but suddenly he broke free. Everything was white and bright…

He blinked, confused. A white ceiling. The beeping of machines. The odor of alcohol and antiseptic.

Images dripped into his head one by one. He'd been shot, and he'd been captured—

And Victoria had been captured with him. He tried to shove himself up as panic took root in his soul.

A hand smoothed over his forehead, and a voice whispered to him. He stilled, searching for the source of the voice. It kept speaking, soothing him, and he realized who it belonged to.

"Victoria?"

His own voice was a croak. She appeared in his vision then, leaning over him, her hair dropping over her shoulder and tickling his face before she pushed it behind an ear. It smelled good.

"It's me. Nice of you to decide to come back to us."

"Thirsty."

She lifted a cup and put the straw to his mouth. He took a long drink.

"How long have I been out?"

"A couple of days."

He processed that information. And then he let his gaze slip over her. She looked good, her red hair long and full, her gray eyes filled with concern. But she was sitting in a wheelchair, and that's when he remembered she'd been shot too.

"How's the leg?" he asked.

She smiled softly. "Hurts, but it's getting better. You?"

"Fuck," he said, closing his eyes for a second. "I think I got run over by a truck."

"I know the feeling."

"Where's your sister?"

Her smile slipped. "She couldn't stay in the hospital, but thanks to your colonel, she has a room at the Visiting Officers' Quarters. She's not hurt, but she's still a bit in shock, I think."

"She stabbed bin Yusuf."

Victoria's lips pressed together. "Yep, she did. I'm not sure she'll ever recover from it, quite honestly. But the psychiatrist seems to think she will."

Nick reached for her hand. Squeezed. "Takes time, Vic. You know that."

She nodded. "Yeah."

But she didn't say anything else, and he wondered what she was thinking. He remembered those few terrifying minutes with Zaran bin Yusuf, Emily, Victoria, and Ahmed. He hadn't been certain any of them would survive it.

"You were going to sacrifice yourself," he said, remembering, and her eyes widened just a fraction. But then they were solemn again.

"I couldn't let him kill her."

"And I couldn't let the bodyguard kill you."

The silence was heavy. And then she lifted his hand

to her mouth and pressed her lips to his skin.

"I don't know how you did it, but you saved me." Her laugh had an edge of hysteria. "Again, I should say. You saved me again."

"Had to."

She licked her lips. "Why, Nick? Why did you have to?"

He felt his brows drawing together. Why? He still wasn't sure how he'd found the strength to launch himself at Ahmed, or why he'd done so other than he would have done it for anyone.

"It's what I'm trained to do. No choice."

But that wasn't the whole answer and he knew it.

Her expression clouded for a second. Then she smiled. "Of course you are." She let his hand go and sat back in the chair.

He wanted to call her back, wanted to reach through the bars and take her hand in his. But she was sitting with her head bowed and not looking at him.

Then she lifted her head and folded her arms over her middle, her eyes bright and her smile firmly in place.

He didn't know what to say to her. He didn't know what the hell was going on, or why his heart thumped so hard he thought it might pound out of his chest, or why his eyes felt so gritty. She was here and he wanted to hold her tight, but that wasn't the right answer either.

He wanted her, but Emily needed her. Emily had been her entire focus for years. Now that she had her sister back, she didn't need anything distracting her from the life she wanted to have.

Except he wanted to distract her. Badly. "I'm fucking this up."

"It's fine. You don't owe me anything. We've had sex a couple of times. No big deal."

No big deal?

"Victoria."

She huffed and turned her head to look toward the door. There were people moving around out there, nurses and staff, but he wanted her to look at him. She wouldn't.

"I'm sorry," he said.

"For what?" She waved a hand. "Already told you it's no big deal."

"I care about you," he began, and she whipped her head around to look at him. *That* got her attention. He swallowed. "I care. We've had, uh, some fun... and not so fun."

When he'd thought he might lose her out there... God, it had killed him. It was better if she went home with Emily. That way she'd be safe. Always.

She shook her head, laughing. "Yes, we've had fun. Great fun. And not so fun. You, my friend, are a wizard with the words."

A body appeared in the door, blocking the light, and Nick looked over to see that it wasn't just one body, but several.

"Not interrupting anything, are we?" Richie said.

Victoria motioned them in. "You aren't interrupting a thing. Come on in."

Flash walked over and gave Victoria a peck on the cheek. "How you doing, angel?"

Nick would've asked when the two of them had managed to get so friendly, but he was too stunned to speak when Victoria gave Flash a dazzling—and real—smile. His heart felt like someone had stomped on it.

Mine. The word echoed in his brain over and over. *Mine, mine, mine.*

"Doing just great, Ryan. Thanks for taking care of me."

"Anytime, angel. Anytime."

Victoria pulled the wheels of the chair backward, rolling away from the bed. "I should go."

"No, sweetheart," someone else said. "Stick around for a while."

"You don't have to leave because of us."

"Plenty of room for all of us here."

Victoria laughed. "No, really, it's fine. We were done anyway."

He wanted to say there was no fucking way they were done, but how the hell was he going to do that with all these guys here and him as weak as a newborn kitten?

Flash rolled Victoria to the door. Then he bent and said something that made her giggle right before she disappeared around the corner.

Nick saw red as Flash came back over. The rest of the guys shuffled their feet or stared at the monitors. Someone turned on the television.

Nick sucked in a breath. If anyone said anything to him about how hot she was, Nick was going to pull himself out of this bed and clock them.

But then Iceman whistled. "What the fuck did you do to her, dude?"

Two days after Victoria left Nick's hospital room, there was a knock on her door. She'd moved to the VOQ to be near Emily since she wasn't in need of hourly monitoring anymore. Her leg hurt like a son of a bitch, but it was healing. She'd been lucky that it was a clean shot through the outer fleshy part.

The bullet hadn't hit bone or major blood vessels, so while it hurt and she had to take it easy—and use crutches now—she'd be good as new in a few weeks.

Thank God.

Her heart, however, wouldn't fare as well. Stupid her wanting to know if Nick had launched himself at Ahmed for a different reason than just because he'd been trained to do it. Stupid her for pushing him for an answer when he clearly didn't have one she'd want to hear.

"Come in," she called, figuring her visitor was Emily. Her sister was quiet and intense lately, but she was doing remarkably well considering the circumstances. There was still a lot that Emily wasn't telling her, but she thought with time it would come out.

Time and distance. She needed to get Emily away from Qu'rim for her healing to continue, but she didn't know when that was going to happen.

The door opened, but it wasn't Emily. It was Nick.

Her heart thumped at the sight of him looking so big and well. She wanted to get up and fling her arms around him, but what good would that do? It would only embarrass her further. Pitiful little virgin girl, falling for the first man to show her how good sex could be. It was like a silly romance novel or something. Since when did that happen in real life?

Nick frowned. "You didn't come back."

She told herself to stay calm. "No, I didn't."

He walked inside and shut the door. His arm was in a sling, but he didn't have to hobble the way she did. He looked remarkably fit for a man who'd seemed to be at death's door only a few days ago.

"Why not?"

"I, uh, wasn't sure I should."

He walked over and stood above her, looking formidable and irritated. "I thought we were friends, Victoria."

Oh God, could he torture her any worse? She clasped her hands in her lap and looked away. "We are friends."

He reached down and gripped her chin, forcing her to look at him. "You're pissed at me."

She worked to keep her expression blank. "Why do you say that? I'm not pissed. I'm fine."

"Fine? Yeah, you act fucking fine—why won't you talk to me? Tell me the truth?"

Anger built inside her, billowing and rolling until it had to break free. She slapped his hand away.

"You're a complete dickhead, Nick Brandon, and you don't even fucking know why!" She pushed herself upright, grabbed her crutches, fumbling with them and nearly falling in the process, then put some distance between them. Then she turned and shot him a glare.

He was looking at her like she'd grown an extra head. "Why is it I never understand what the hell is going on with you? You're the one person I can't figure out no matter how much I try."

Oh, that did it. "My God, you must be one of the densest men on the planet! And I am most certainly one of the stupidest women. You swagger into my life with your badass attitude, your"—she waved her hands around—

"ridiculously muscular body, and your complete and total decency as a human being, and then you talk and talk, and I fall for all your bullshit charm. Next thing I know, I'm all over you, wanting you like I've never wanted any man before, and you're rocking my world and making me feel amazing—"

He was looking at her with big eyes, and she suddenly felt so stupid and so defeated, like she was utterly pitiful and he was just now learning it. No, she wasn't cool. She wasn't in control, and she damn sure wasn't getting out of this with her heart intact.

She sighed and plopped down on the bed. "The problem, Preacher Boy, is that I like you. Really like you. As in I want more of you, and I want it pretty much all the time. When I thought you might die out there, I prayed that you wouldn't. I told God I'd rather he take me than you because at least I wouldn't have to know what it was like to live in a world without you in it."

She looked up, found him watching her intently. She laughed. "How fucked up is that, right?"

He looked shell-shocked. "Jesus, Victoria."

"I know. It's absolutely crazy, but I fell for you. And maybe it's good you don't feel that way about me, because look at what happened to Emily when she went chasing after a man. I can't—I won't—be that incomplete without you. I'll figure it out, so you just turn around and walk out that door and congratulate yourself on a lucky escape."

TWENTY-SIX

NICK'S HEART WAS POUNDING OUT a crazy rhythm. She was sitting there on that bed, looking so beautiful it hurt, and telling him she loved him. At least that's what he thought she was saying, because she hadn't actually said it.

He'd heard it before, usually from women he'd dated for a few weeks, or sometimes from a woman he'd just fucked. Those women were usually tipsy and a little too effusive with their praise.

Once those words were said, he was gone. It was better that way.

But now it was odd because Victoria hadn't said the words, but he wanted her to. Wanted to hear them damn bad, in fact.

"I didn't want you to die out there either."

He hadn't made any bargains with God, but he'd made them with himself. Get her out of danger, no matter the cost. Take the bullet meant for her if it came down to it. Because he had to. Because he couldn't contemplate doing any differently.

And it wasn't just the job. It was her. He wanted her

to stay with him—and he needed her to go so he could breathe again.

"That's sweet, Nick. I appreciate your saying that, but it's not quite the same, is it?" She sighed. "I wasn't very specific with God, I'm afraid. I said I'd rather not live in a world without you in it. I didn't say I wanted to live with you if you survived, and I guess I should have. God has a sense of humor."

"Go out with me," he said and then felt ridiculous for saying it. How the hell was that supposed to work? But he had this idea that she'd go back home and he'd see her in the States. Somehow, they'd work it out.

She blinked at him. And then she laughed. It felt like she'd dug a rusty knife into his heart and twisted.

"Date you? How am I supposed to do that? You're in Qu'rim at the moment, and I'm about to head back to the States with my sister. And even then, you live in DC and we'll be in New Orleans." She shook her head. "No, we can't date. It's impossible."

Sudden anger swirled in his gut. How could she just blow him off when she claimed she loved him, even if she hadn't said the words?

"What do you want me to do? Propose? Is that what it takes to get you to be with me? Goddammit, fine." He dropped to his knees while she looked at him as if he'd lost his mind. Hell, maybe he had, because what the fuck was he doing? He'd just asked her to date him and now he was fucking proposing? How insane did that make him, especially since he was trying to be noble and let her be with Emily?

"Nick—"

Someone rapped on the door, startling them both. He

got up and went over to yank it open.

"Interrupting something, soldier?" Colonel Mendez stood there with an arched eyebrow and a knowing look on his face.

"No, sir," Nick said, pulling the door open wider. His heart was pounding, and he felt like an asshole. A confused, contradictory asshole. "I was just leaving."

Mendez's eyebrow lifted a fraction higher. "Why don't you stay? You'll want to hear this too."

He strode inside, and Nick closed the door. Victoria was flushed, but she did her best to look cool and calm.

Mendez pulled out a chair and sat. Then he looked at Nick until he sat too.

"Glad I've got you both here," he said. "Thought you should know that Ian Black is gone."

Victoria gasped.

Fury rolled deep in Nick's gut. After all they'd fucking gone through?

"He abandoned his compound a few days ago. We sent a team in. There was a server room, but the server was gone. Bastard had a Faraday cage to prevent electronic eavesdropping. This wasn't just chicken wire wrapped around supports either. Not a surprise, really, but he's certainly well funded."

"Ian's gone," Victoria said numbly. Then she laughed. "I guess even if he'd tried to call me first, I wouldn't know it."

They'd both lost their phones in the desert. He'd been issued a new one, but it was a little different for her. Still, she looked like she'd been abandoned by a friend. He hated that she felt that way about Ian Black, but there was nothing he could do about it. At least he knew it had never been more than that.

"Any idea who he was working for?" Nick asked.

Mendez leaned forward. "No, but I'm not done trying to figure it out." He looked pensive for a moment. And then he shook his head. "He left something."

Mendez took his phone from his pocket and pressed a couple of buttons. Then he held it out to Nick.

Nick took it—and his jaw nearly hit the floor. Inside the abandoned Faraday cage was a table that held three vials sitting on top of a small case.

"The smallpox?" It was unbelievable. Unimaginable.

"Yes. And there was a note." Mendez took his phone back and showed Victoria the picture. Then he called up the note and read it. *"See this is disposed of, will you? Thanks, Colonel."*

"I told you he wasn't dirty," Victoria said.

Mendez's gaze slewed over to her. "Not sure I believe that, Miss Royal. But he's smart. Letting this into the world isn't wise, even for someone who only cares about profiting from others' misfortune."

But Nick was focused on something else. "How did he know about us?"

He didn't think for one minute that Victoria had told Black. Nor did the colonel, apparently.

"Good question." Mendez sat back, tucking his phone into his pocket. "And I plan to get an answer, though it may take some time." He shot an intense look at Victoria. "You want to help?"

Nick blinked. Victoria looked taken aback.

"I… What do you want me to do?"

"Work for us."

"My record…"

"Fixed."

She looked puzzled. And then she looked angry. "Is that only if I work for you? Or is it fixed now and there's no obligation?"

He huffed out a breath. "It's fixed. There's no obligation."

He stood and looked down at her like a stern father. It was the softest look Nick had ever seen him give to anyone. Even Lucky MacDonald hadn't gotten that soft of a look, and God knew she'd gone through some hell for HOT.

"You got a raw deal, Victoria. But you're a helluva shot and we could use you—and yeah, your knowledge of Ian Black. You'd be doing your nation a great service."

She lifted her chin. "I'm a traitor, or didn't you know?"

He laughed. Nick nearly fell out. He wasn't sure he'd ever heard the colonel laugh before.

"You're as much of a traitor as Brandy here." He shook his head. "No, you're a rebel, Miss Royal, not a traitor. There's a difference. I think you know what it is."

She lifted her chin. "And my sister? What's she?"

"She's a woman who's been through hell. I can't promise she's going to have it easy from here on out, but I'll do my best for her."

"And will you do that regardless of my decision?"

"Yes."

"Why?"

He barked a laugh. "You don't give up, do you? This is why I want you on my team, Victoria. You don't fucking give up."

The colonel turned to Nick. "Solve your differences

288

with this woman, Brandy. We need her."

"Sir?"

He stood and walked over to where Nick sat. "I'm fucking serious. Tell her you're sorry and beg her to stay. It's the only sensible course of action."

Nick waited until the colonel was gone. Then he looked at Victoria. "Why the fuck does everyone always blame me?"

He looked adorably confused. She wanted to laugh, but that was rather difficult when your heart was breaking. She got her crutches and stood. She could see him blinking, maybe working up to doing what his colonel had said.

But there was no way she was going to let him sit here and beg her to stay when he was only doing it because he'd been ordered to do so.

She wasn't that pitiful, for God's sake, though a part of her wanted very much to hear him ask her to stay and mean it.

"I think you should go," she said.

He got to his feet slowly, as if he ached in a thousand places. His expression was intense—confused, pissed, determined.

"The colonel's right. We need you. You could work for HOT, do what you're best at... but I don't want you to."

She closed her eyes. She could almost picture herself there, being one of the best of the best. An elite operator, working at the side of the man she loved. The man who did not love her and didn't want her there.

"Emily needs you," he said. "You should be with her."

Victoria opened her eyes, shuttering the pain in her gaze. "I know."

His jaw flexed. "I want it to be different, but there's nothing I can say that would make it worth your while to stay."

"No," she said, her throat aching, "I suppose there's nothing."

Because if it didn't come from his heart and soul, then it wasn't enough. Yes, he'd dropped to his knees earlier, and God knows what he would have said if Mendez hadn't arrived, but it hadn't been real. It was done out of anger and a need to win, not out of any true feeling. If he felt it, she would know.

He would know.

But he didn't, and that wasn't good enough for her.

"You're a good partner," he said, "a good shooter."

"Thanks."

He blew out a harsh breath. "Fuck, Victoria, at least consider seeing me when we're Stateside. I want to see you. We'll figure it out."

Her heart squeezed. She hopped over to him and steadied herself. Then she laid a hand against his cheek. She hadn't touched him since that day at the hospital when she'd held his hand. It was like touching a match to dry tinder, because her skin sparked and caught, and her nerve endings sizzled with heat and need.

His eyes dilated as if he felt the fire too.

"You're a good man, Nick. A decent man. I love that

you have such strength and passion and that you do the right thing no matter the cost to yourself. But I can't be with you anymore. It's not good for me, and it's probably not good for you either."

He caught her to him and kissed her. It was a hot, tender kiss, tongues stroking, teeth clashing, mouths feeding off each other. And it was also a good-bye kiss. She could tell that it was by the way he kept her at a distance, not melding her body to his, not melting into her.

He ended it and stepped back abruptly. "You're the most amazing woman I know, Victoria. I want you to live, and I want you to be happy. Go back to the States. Take care of Emily. Find happiness."

He backed up, his eyes on hers while she stood with her heart hammering in her throat—and then he turned and walked out the door, taking her happiness with him.

TWENTY-SEVEN

Maryland
Two months later…

VICTORIA WALKED INTO THE GUN range with her new rifle and a couple of pistols. She'd started working part-time at the range because it gave her something to do while she figured out what she was going to do with the rest of her life.

Besides, working here came with bonuses. First, she got a discount on weapons and ammo. Though she had plenty of money set aside after working for Ian for two years, it wouldn't last forever and she had to be careful. Second, she got to use the range for free when it wasn't busy, like now. It was nearly nine o'clock at night, and the only shooter was a fat man at the end who stopped and leered when she walked by.

She ignored him, same as she ignored every guy who'd tried to ask her out over the past couple of months. She wasn't ready, and that was fine with her. One day, sure. But not now.

Victoria set up her equipment in the middle stall and lifted the rifle to her shoulder. It wasn't the long-range shooting she needed, but she had to drive farther out into Maryland for that particular sort of range. The next time she had a full day to spare, she would do that.

Which would probably be soon since Emily was getting tired of her hovering.

The rifle was smooth and solid in her grip, the stock almost soft against her cheek. She sighted downrange and then squeezed the trigger on the exhale. The gunfire from the fat man stopped abruptly, as if he was suddenly interested in what she was doing. She fired again and again, making a tight grouping in the bull's-eye. She didn't have to see it to know that's what she was doing.

She lowered the rifle and huffed out a breath. It felt good to shoot something. Good to work out some anger and aggression.

"You fired wide on that last one."

Victoria gasped and spun around. Nick stood there behind her, dressed in faded jeans and a black T-shirt that showed his muscled arms. Her heart thumped and her throat felt suddenly tight.

Two months since she'd seen him. Two months since she'd spoken to him. She'd thought her stupid heart was getting better by now because she could go entire hours without thinking about him.

Without thinking about lying in bed with him, his body a part of hers, making her dissolve into a pleasure so deep she lost herself inside it for the hours they were together.

"I did not," she said, remembering his statement. She heard the door to the range close, and she knew the fat man was gone.

He shrugged. "No, probably not. I couldn't think of anything else to say."

"How about hello?"

He grinned. "Hello."

She gripped the rifle where it lay on the shelf, needing something to hold on to. "What are you doing here?"

"It's a shooting range, isn't it?"

"Yes."

"Maybe I came to shoot."

Her throat tightened. "Fine, go shoot. Leave me alone."

He didn't move. "How are you, Victoria?"

"I'm fine, thanks. You?"

"I've been better."

Fear worked its way into her belly. "Are you sick? Did something happen?"

He laughed. "Yeah, something happened. But no, I'm not sick. I'm not in imminent danger of dying, if that's what you're wondering."

"That's good."

"Yeah, I suppose so." He raked a hand through his hair. "Jesus, I suck at this."

"It's been two months, Nick. I'm not sure there's anything you can say that would make this less awkward than it already is."

"I love you."

His eyes burned hot as he stared at her, and her heart began to pound. Then angry tears sprang up, and she dashed them away before they could make a fool out of her.

"You come here two months after you pushed me

away in the desert—pushed away my feelings for you—and expect that will make it all better?"

"It's all I got. The most powerful weapon in my arsenal. And I'm not afraid to use it."

"I don't understand you."

He snorted. "And I don't understand you. But I need you. I can't live without you."

"What's changed?" Her throat was tight and the words hurt.

His eyes were intense. "Everything. Nothing."

"It took you two months to figure that out?"

"No, it took me a week. I admit I'm a dumb ass."

"A week? It's been two fucking months, Nick."

He spread his hands. "I've been on a mission. I almost called at one point, but I thought this was the kind of thing a man should say in person. I've spent two months trying to figure out how to do it." He took a step toward her, stopped as if he were unsure. "We just got back this morning or I'd have been here sooner. Had to be debriefed first. And then I had to figure out where to find you. You aren't in New Orleans."

She shook her head. Her pulse was skipping and jumping, and she wasn't sure if she was crazy or he was. Or maybe they both were.

"No. The government wants Emily in DC, so here we are. Your colonel arranged for her to get counseling and a job. He kept his word."

"He's the one who told me where to find you. How is she?"

Victoria swallowed. "Getting better. She's tougher than I thought. I still don't know what she went through with Zaran, but she's not lingering over his death. She's not blaming herself either."

"That's good. Real good."

"Yes. She's working as a barista and seems to like it. She's even talking about college."

"And what about you? How are you, Victoria?"

"You asked that already."

He moved toward her, closing the distance this time until he was right in front of her and she had to tilt her head back to meet his eyes. His heat reached out and enveloped her, made her remember what it was like when there'd been nothing between them but that heat and a passion so strong it had made her tremble and gasp and feel whole in a way she never had before.

"But I don't think you told me the truth."

Her heart thumped. "What do you want me to say? That I've been lonely and miserable without you? That I go to bed every night and wish you were there? That I've had to invest in a bigger vibrator just so I can pretend it's you?"

His eyes widened at that last, and she tilted her chin up, daring him to say anything. *Asshole. Adorable asshole.*

He reached out and put a hand on her cheek. Her body sang in instant recognition. Her brain said she was letting him off too easily, but her body told her brain to fuck off.

"Oh honey, the naughty images in my head right now. I'm getting hard just thinking of it. And jealous. Fucking jealous that anything besides me is getting you off."

She tried not to respond, but of course that was impossible. Her pussy grew wet, the tissues swelling and aching for his touch.

She pushed away from him, putting distance between

them. He dropped his hand and looked at her sadly.

"This is crazy. You show up out of nowhere and say you love me. And you just expect me to believe it." She folded her arms over her middle as if to protect herself. But there was no protecting herself from him. "You had your chance in Qu'rim, Nick. But you sent me away. You told me to take care of Emily. And that's what I'm doing."

"I thought that's what you wanted. Hell, I wanted it for you. But I'm selfish, and I need you too—maybe more than she does, because without you I'm not whole. I'm not me anymore without you."

She bowed her head. It was everything she wanted, and yet it terrified her too.

"I know why you're scared, Victoria. Hell, I'm scared too. I think we're both used to the people we love leaving us or disappointing us. But we don't have to do that to each other. We don't have to watch over our shoulders and constantly wait for something bad to happen."

She wanted to believe him. So much. For the first time in her life, with him, she'd felt like she had someone she could trust to be there for her no matter what. But then he hadn't been. He'd walked away.

She lifted her head and fixed him with a glare. Or she hoped it was a glare, anyway.

"You still haven't told me what made you realize you love me. Loneliness and longing aren't love, Nick. And if all you've missed is fucking, then that's not nearly enough, is it?"

His eyes widened. And then he looked angry. "Fucking? You think that's all I care about? Pussy is pussy, sweetheart. If that's all I needed, I know where to get it. But it's the whole package I want—the gorgeous woman with the heart and guts to do whatever needs done, the woman with the sweetness to care about people like Ian Black even when all evidence says she'd be better off not caring at all, the woman who fights for those she loves and never gives up, the woman who had the balls to tell my colonel—the scariest man I know, by the way—to fuck off, and who somehow got him to give her everything she wanted and more. I want that woman, and yeah, I definitely want to make love to her as often as possible—but that's not all it is. Not by a long shot."

Victoria blinked. She was… stunned. That was the word. *Stunned.*

But he wasn't finished.

"When did I realize it? That's what you asked, right? I think I knew when I walked out of your room that day in Baq, but I thought I was doing the right thing by sending you home where you'd be safe. But no, I didn't admit it to myself then. I…" Here his voice choked off, and she was stunned to see that he had to get control of himself. Of his emotions.

"I got a picture from Shelly. An ultrasound. I've never felt so proud or so alone in my life as I did that day. And the one person I wanted to share it with wasn't there. *You* weren't there, Victoria. That's when I knew how stupid I'd been. I should have been happy, but I was alone and miserable. I love you, and I've been an asshole, and I'm sorry. I let you go, and I let you think it was because I didn't love you. There's nothing I regret more than that."

She didn't realize she was actually crying until he moved toward her and lifted his hands to her cheeks. She felt the moisture when he rubbed it dry with his thumbs.

"Please don't cry, honey. I hate it when you cry. And

I hate that I'm the one who made you do it."

She bowed her head, and he pulled her forward until she touched his chest. She could feel his heart beating hard and fast, and her own leapt in response.

Slowly, she put her arms around his waist. When she did, he shuddered and hugged her tight. Joy unfurled in her soul then. She believed him. She really believed him.

She tilted her head back to gaze up at him with shining eyes. "You're a dickhead, Nick Brandon, but I love you anyway."

"Thank God," he said.

And then he kissed her.

"Hey, Brandy, did you know you've got a goofy look on your face?" It was Iceman who'd sidled up to him at the outdoor bar.

"Yep."

Nick took a sip of his beer and continued to watch Victoria laughing with Hawk's wife, Gina; Richie Rich's fiancée, Evie; and Lucky MacDonald. Knight Rider's Georgie and Billy Blake's Olivia were playing a game of cards with Emily, who looked happy and healthy these days.

Flash took her a drink and she looked up at him with a smile. He lingered for a minute, but then Dex and Chase "Fiddler" Daniels came over and dragged him away.

"So you fell to cupid's arrow. Damn shame." Iceman took a swig of his own beer. "Thought you'd hold out longer."

"Shut up, Ice. And hey, you could be next, so don't gloat too much."

Ice snorted. "Me? Fuck no. Not happening. Not a woman alive has a pussy golden enough I need to keep going back to the same one."

Nick laughed. "That's what we all said. And then you find out pussy hasn't got a damn thing to do with it."

Ice looked as if Nick were speaking a foreign language. "Dude, that's insane talk."

"Yeah, whatever." He started to stand up and go over to Victoria, yank her away from the ladies, and see if she wanted to go join him in their room for a few minutes.

Hawk and Gina had a house on the Eastern Shore, and they liked to have everyone over to share it with them. The house was big enough so they all had their own rooms if they wanted to stay for the weekend, and everyone had a good time. It was a place to decompress and just be with a bunch of people who understood you better than anyone else.

He was halfway to Victoria when someone new arrived. Colonel Mendez always looked a touch strange in jeans and a button-down instead of a uniform, but the colonel still managed to wear civvies with as much authority as if he had his birds on his shoulder boards instead.

The men all snapped to something resembling attention. Even Lucky perked up.

"For fuck's sake, as you were," the colonel grumbled.

Everyone relaxed. He went over to Gina and gave her a hug and a peck on the cheek, then he shook Jack's hand. After that, he grabbed a beer and went to sit on his own at one of the tables. Victoria ambled over and sat down with him. Nick thought about joining them, but the colonel looked serious and Victoria was nodding.

He wanted to protect her, but she didn't need protecting. And she wouldn't appreciate it if he tried. She'd tell him what it was about when she got a chance.

She swiveled her head until their gazes met. That was his signal. He walked over and put his hand on her shoulder. Mendez's eyes were filled with good humor.

"You too, eh, Brandy? Fucking knew it the second you walked into my office in Baq with this girl."

Nick wanted to protest that *he* hadn't known it then, so how could the colonel, but what was the point?

"Yes, sir, me too." He squeezed Victoria's shoulder. "Best decision of my life."

"Good deal, son. Good deal."

Victoria looked up at him and his heart hitched. He still wasn't used to that sensation, but he liked it even while it scared the shit out of him. He was so deep in love he'd never find his way out again. Nor did he want to.

"The colonel repeated his offer for me to join HOT. What do you think?"

What did he think? He thought he didn't want her in the line of fire ever again. But then he thought that there was no better partner on earth in a firefight than her.

"I think you should do what your gut tells you to do."

She smiled and his world lit up. "You are one smart man."

"When I'm not being a dickhead, right?"

She laughed. "Right." Then she looked at Mendez again. "I accept your offer, Colonel. I think my sister is ready to have me out of her hair, and I'm ready to get back to doing the work I know best."

Mendez's grin reminded Nick of a wolf just before it ate you. "Excellent news, Miss Royal. I'll start the wheels in motion. You'll be onboard within days. Now, if you'll excuse me, I should mingle."

Mendez got up and went over to talk to some of the other guys. Nick pulled Victoria to her feet. She looked a little worried and a little excited at the same time.

"You sure about this?" he said.

"Yes. Very sure."

"Then that's all I need to know." He lifted an eyebrow. "Want to take a stroll with me? Maybe check out the firmness of our mattress?"

She laughed. "Didn't we just do that this morning?"

"And your point?"

"Yeah, you're right, I don't have one."

Nick pulled her toward the house. Within minutes, he had her naked and pinned beneath him. He tasted her while she shuddered and begged him for more, his tongue sliding around her swollen clit, into her wet pussy, then back up again and again.

"Love doing this to you," he said against her wet flesh, and her thighs trembled.

"You'll pay for this, Preacher Boy. Just as soon as I… ah… oh God…"

He licked her ferociously then, taking her mercilessly over the edge. When she was still quivering, he flipped her over and pulled her up until she got on her knees. She gripped the headboard when he entered her, and he bent over and bit her shoulder as he slid all the way home.

"Love you," he growled. "So much."

"I love you too. Now shut up and fuck me."

He pulled out and rocked into her, watching as his

cock disappeared into her slick passage. He did it again and again, watching, holding himself back while she writhed and moaned.

He loved the sheen of her skin, the dip of her back, the way her hair slid against her skin as he slammed into her. He loved the way she gripped the headboard and pushed herself back against him. He loved the sounds she made—her moans, her keening cries—and the sounds they made together, as well as the wet slide of his dick into her pussy, the slap of flesh against flesh.

He loved it all, and he was so grateful he'd found the courage to tell her how he felt. He told her every day now. Every way he could think of. Victoria would always know, so long as he lived, that he loved her.

"More," she said, and he pulled out of her. She looked over her shoulder at him.

"You on top," he told her, and she climbed on and slid down his cock, her eyes closing in ecstasy.

He loved the view from the rear, but this view was even better. Because he could see what he did to her, see the love and pleasure on her face as she came.

They rocked together, faster and faster, her breasts bouncing, her hips thrusting. His orgasm hit him like a freight train, bowing his back and making him gasp her name as he lost himself inside her.

She came with him, shuddering, her mouth opening in a scream. They collapsed together, sweating and breathing hard.

He was boneless and broken, but as soon as he could move, he reached over to where she'd rolled onto her back and traced a lazy finger around her nipple. He hadn't sucked those beauties this time, but he would soon.

"Luckiest day of my life was when you walked into it. Too bad it took more than three years to figure that out."

She rolled back on top of him, clearly possessed of more energy than he had at the moment. "What you lack in brightness, you more than make up for in beauty and brawn."

He snorted a laugh. "Trash talk, babe?"

"I learned from the best."

He pushed her hair behind her ears and cupped her beautiful face. Yeah, he said this a lot, but he couldn't stop. He didn't want to stop. "I love you so much, Victoria."

"I love you too. More than anything."

He pulled her down and wrapped his arms around her. She lay against his heart and he sighed happily.

Sex was terrific, but this was better on so many levels. It was belonging, friendship, and perfection, all wrapped up in one person. There was nothing like it on earth.

Yeah, he'd fallen. And it was a damn good place to be.

ACKNOWLEDGMENTS

THANKS AS ALWAYS TO MY fabulous team! Mike, Gretchen, Anne—along with everyone at Victory Editing—and Frauke at CrocoDesigns. You help make my books the best they can be and I thank you all!

I say this every time, but the Hostile Operations Team is a completely made-up team of Special Ops guys. I make the rules in this world, so if you're concerned a real Spec Ops team might not be able to do some of what my guys do—you might be right. But that's why it's so much fun!

And many thanks to all of you, the wonderful readers, who keep asking for more HOT. If you're wondering about Ian Black, you may see more of him in the future. And don't worry, I think Mendez may just get his own happy ending eventually, too. ;)

ABOUT THE AUTHOR

USA Today bestselling author Lynn Raye Harris lives in Alabama with her handsome former-military husband and two crazy cats. Lynn has written nearly twenty novels for Harlequin and been nominated for several awards, including the Romance Writers of America's Golden Heart award and the National Readers Choice award. Lynn loves hearing from her readers.

Connect with me online:
Facebook: https://www.facebook.com/AuthorLynnRayeHarris
Twitter: https://twitter.com/LynnRayeHarris
Website: http://www.LynnRayeHarris.com
Email: lynn@lynnrayeharris.com

Join my Hostile Operations Team Readers and Fans Group on Facebook:
https://www.facebook.com/groups/HOTReadersAndFans/